THE
POISON
GARDEN

MARY OLDHAM

Print: ISBN: 9798865258230
Kindle: ISBN: 979-8-9878547-4-7
Ebook: ISBN: 979-8-9878547-6-1

Any references to historical events, real people, or real places are used
fictitiously. Names, characters, and places are products of the author's
imagination.

Story Editor: Sue Grimshaw, Edits by Sue
Grammatical Editor: Arleigh Rodgers
Cover Design: Lynn Andreozzi
Interior Book Design: Teri Barnett/Indie Book Designer
Author Photo: Tanith Yates

Printed in United States of America
By-Creek-Ity Publishing
Portland, Oregon

www.maryoldham.com

For my mother, Caroline Snook Oldham, who wouldn't let me eat the Yew berries and gave me many stiff warnings when I was a little kid. Thank you for saving my life.

CONTENTS

CHAPTER ONE

Jane aka Amber

The woman who would be Jane Miller for less than three more hours added the boiling water to her French press coffee pot. It held exactly seven tablespoons of the very strong Peet's Coffee Major Dickason's Blend waiting at the bottom of the pot because she felt like a badass — and with good reason. Her cellphone, which had been quietly resting on the black slab granite of the drainboard, began to bark, the ringtone reserved for several of her gossipy Ashland Drive, Colorado neighbors. One glance at the caller ID had her smiling. Took her long enough to call. Jeez, she had thought the call would happen a good half hour earlier than it had. Needless to say, she liked the bark.

Maybe next season she would use a song like the theme from Midnight in the Garden of Good and Evil. Or just plain old Dracula. The thought made her smile. She might have even said she chuckled.

"Never, ever lose your ability to laugh," she said aloud. She needed to remember that. She was tired, it had been a very long season.

The screen that flashed Felicity's name seemed to grow brighter in anticipation. She was Jane's best informant on the street. You always needed one of those, and thankfully someone always volunteered for the job. Felicity had stepped up as if she'd been born to do it. Her life's work culminated to this one task. Too bad Jane could never congratulate her.

"Hello," Jane answered as if they were good friends, which one of them thought they were. And that one was not Jane.

Felicity's voice was excited. "Do you see the ambulance and police outside of Jon and Paula's? It is still there and has been there for over an hour. I finally went over there and found out what was going on."

"Tell me, is everyone alright? I'm just having breakfast," Jane said with a smile. Really, the homemade marionberry jam from next door neighbor Karen was divine. She was taking it with her, maybe the stainless steel French press too. She casually glanced into her living room and through the large picture window saw the flashing strobe lights in red and blue from down the street. Well, that is done, and now she was done with Ashland Drive. This was a relatively easy season. That's what she called them. *Seasons.* Jane liked it when they were easy. She would miss none of these people, especially Felicity, who reminded her of a basset hound, no offense to basset hounds. Although, truth be told, Jane loved dogs.

"Oh, my gawd, Jane. It is Jon," Felicity sounded both breathless and excited to be delivering such important news. *Interesting.* This adrenaline crash that would probably hit in the next hour after she'd finished sharing this news with the rest of the hood would be epic. Felicity would get a headache or need to take a little nap for the rest of the day…

Maybe Jane should suggest a shot or six of Bailey's in the coffee to calm her down. Felicity would listen. She wanted to be liked by Jane. She was nice and impressionable. If Jane had been a nun, Felicity would have thrown away her worldly goods purchased at the plus size area of Kohl's and Kmart to join the cause. It was a little scary actually what influence Jane had on the other woman. Eh, power was power. You either had it or you wanted it. At the end of the day, it was sexy.

She liked this season's persona as a financial planner. She felt powerful in a different way than usual.

"You were saying something about Jon?"

"I don't know how to say this."

"Just say it." *Spit it out girl. Don't be a weak sperm.* Felicity was scared of her own shadow which got on the nerves.

"He's dead. I talked to a cop who seemed bored. I don't think he meant to tell me, but I kept after him until he did. Like he deals with death every day."

I just bet you did. Poor cop.

"Jon? No way," Jane said as she slowly pushed down the plunger of her coffee pot having returned to the kitchen. She hoped the ground up beans had absorbed the boiling water and done their job to get soft enough to release the coffee. If she pushed it too quickly, coffee and bean parts would spray out of the spout and onto her granite in a spew of heat and beans. One, big, hot mess. Then she'd have to clean the filter or end up with a coffee cup of grounds. She hated that. It was all about patience, and Jane was very patient. But damn it, she wanted her coffee. Yesterday had been a long, hard day. Thankfully, it was successful!

"He's dead," Felicia cried.

"Jon? No, he can't be," Jane said adding a little doubt to her tone. "Are you sure?"

"Yes, Jon is dead. He died last night in his sleep. If fact, Paula said he didn't talk to her when she got home after being out with us. She thinks he might have already been dead when she crawled into bed. She slept with him next to her, a dead man. I hope she didn't try to touch him or kiss him goodnight. That has got to mess a person up. Think of the therapy she will need."

Jane doubted he'd been dead when Paula crawled into bed. Dead bodies let go of things like their bladder and their bowels. You'd know if you were crawling into a bed of that.

On the whole, dead people weren't all that scary. They were just quiet and, well, dead.

Forget Paula, she'd be fine. Too bad about Jon. Jane had hoped he'd be awake when he died.

Cyanide had such interesting effects on the flesh. Something told her that you just knew you were dying when your stomach acid reacted with different chemicals to produce cyanide and the effects kicked in. The taste of almonds in the mouth. It was too late to save you by then. The cramping and anxiety as your organs failed, specifically your kidneys, started to break down, and liquify would prove that. What an experience! And Jon had slept through the whole thing or been in a coma. Damn it! He deserved to know what was happening to him.

Jane flashed back to harvesting the cherry pits. That hadn't been easy. It was tedious. Well, boring as it had been to harvest all those pits, it had worked. Damn, she loved stone fruit.

"But he was a young man. What happened?" Jane asked as she bit her lip to keep from smiling. Not waiting for a response, she added, "Did he have some underlying medical condition? I didn't like his color at the BBQ last week. He looked kind of gray." Plant that seed of concern, why don't you? The barbecue. He'd looked fine for someone dipping his pen in company ink and being caustic to his wife. Hell, he was glowing with the guilt and secrecy of it all. He was diddling someone who was not his wife, and not for the first time. His secretary this time, to be exact. Tossing away his wife and marriage as if they were nothing, the tool.

"I...I don't know."

"If the police are there, they must suspect foul play." If they didn't, they needed to go back to the police academy. Wait for it: *He's been poisoned.*

She'd been a little reckless because by the time the police started looking around, Jane would be gone. Like a puff of air. Vanished.

"Oh gawd, poor Paula," Felicity said. "What if they think she did something to him?"

Jane felt like adding: *The abusive son of a bitch got exterminated like he deserved...*

"Paula will be fine," Jane said. After all, Paula was drinking with the ladies of Ashland Drive just last night. It established an alibi. Jon died alone. Hadn't Jane gone to a lot of trouble to make sure Paula wouldn't be suspected? Like it was her first rodeo! She wasn't an amateur! This was her fifth season. She had several notches on her lipstick case, although she could admit there had been a lot to do on Ashland Drive.

"I can't believe this. First Lars, then Grant, now Jon."

Yeah, it had been a very busy season. Her busiest to date. Never had she ever killed three men in such a short period of time! Hopefully, it wasn't a trend because it was exhausting. Felicity would talk about this year in the Ashland Drive neighborhood history for the rest of her life. She lived through something amazing. What she didn't understand was that she was friends with the person responsible. The murderer.

"Now Felicity, you need to calm down. Lars was an old man with terminal cancer. Grant had a drug and alcohol problem. All situations were different. Maybe you should brew some coffee and add a few shots of Bailey's." The dead neighbors really only had Jane in common. And she had drawn some easy conclusions that led them to her close, personal acquaintance.

Grant was also a serial cheater and didn't care if his wife knew. Besides, he was burning through their savings by snorting it up his nose. And when Vicki asked him to stop, he hurt her. As in Grant was a physically abusive jerk. He thought she could just deal with his indiscretions; boys could be boys. And how dare she get between him and his fun?

Vicki was better off without him and whatever foreign lipstick she'd have to clean off his shirts or underwear. He was so narcissistic that he didn't care how much his wife knew. He wanted her to see it. After all, he deserved to be happy. Besides, he worked hard for his money. She was a user, taking all his money. She didn't respect him. She deserved to suffer. Now, Vicki could move forward and have a good life, same with Paula, whose husband was no better.

As for Lars's Marguerite well, that was a bit more complicated. She just didn't want him to suffer. And he had suffered. Mercy was mercy. His illness was taking a toll on her and their dwindling bank account. She couldn't afford nursing care. She was doing it all on her own. And it wasn't like Lars wasn't going to die soon, hell, he was terminal. The yew berries mixed with a bit of liquid oxycodone that winter just sped it along. Gave it a little painless kick in the right direction. Caring euthanasia.

Now, Marguerite could travel, going on cruises that Lars didn't want to go on. She could live, spending the rest of her life as she wanted, not tending to a man that was half dead. Jane felt good about that. She had saved Marguerite's life. Heck, maybe Marguerite could marry again once she got over the trauma of loving and losing Lars. It had been a few months, so maybe she'd transition soon. A new man would be good for her. Get a little of the "hide the sausage" action. She needed it. Marguerite was in her late sixties. There was life yet to live..

Jane said all the right things to Felicity, the voice of reason, a port in this unknown storm for the worrying woman who could benefit from a life herself. Eventually, Jane feigned a need to get off the call for a pending Zoom appointment involving an investment client. There was no client, but she had said it enough in the last year she was starting to believe she did have clients. She drank her coffee with a heavy dollop of half and half, which she savored, and a perfectly toasted English muffin with butter and lots of the neighbor's jam. When she was done, she put the marionberry jam in a small cooler with ice and wiped down the few items in her fridge including the fridge itself. She had started wiping everything down yesterday after drinking with the Ashland Drive ladies, only she still had the kitchen, bedroom, and her bath to do. Would it really matter? On Saturday, her house would be overrun with people and their finger-prints. Perfect. She loved it when a plan came together so perfectly. She needed it after this season. She was so tired!

The estate sellers, whom the grieving Jane had hired, would be there tomorrow to prepare for the large sale they'd have this weekend. She'd left them a key under the ceramic garden gnome in the backyard. They completely understood her desire not to watch her Aunt Betsy's possessions get organized and sold to strangers. She and Betsy had been so close. Betsy was more of a mother to her after her mother died. She was perfect. She was also imaginary.

Jane's mother was in Las Vegas. Married for the seventh time, or was it the eighth? It didn't matter, she increased her personal wealth with each additional husband she added to the list of former husbands. But it hadn't been an easy road for good old Jennifer Deluca. She'd earned every dollar and botoxed wrinkle she had. The woman calling herself Jane would have to visit her "Mom" and check in, someday. She could always hope that one day when she'd call the number would be discon-nected. Then she'd know the person who made her childhood a living nightmare was dead.

Heck, Old Jen knew her daughter had something going on as an adult, she just didn't know what. After Jane left home as Kelly, the name Old Jen had given her at birth, Old Jen didn't ask questions, but she did seem a little upset that her best meal ticket was going away. You see, they had run the same game again and again. Her mother had hidden cameras in the house. They would record the stepdaddy or boyfriend of the moment trying something with little Kelly when her mother was off at "work," which probably equated to being a hostess or high-end prostitute for one of the "classier" casinos.

Her mother did this purposefully, spending time away from their house with only Kelly and the stepdaddy of the moment left to entertain themselves. Old Jen would leave to see if one of the rats would take the bait. Unfortunately for Kelly, she was the cheese in the trap in this little scenario. Every stepfather or boyfriend of the moment tried something with little Kelly because her mother had a gift when it came to picking the worst of the worst. Sometimes it was just wanting to show her what he had, *"Look at my big dick,"* or sometimes, he wanted her to play adult games with him when her mother was out. *"Come here and sit on daddy's lap."* Well, she played along until she didn't.

When she was almost eighteen and the last stepdaddy tried that *"lets us have some fun,"* Kelly had hit him with a ceramic lamp so hard it had broken. Bixby, her stepfather, wasn't doing too well either. Old Jen was upset over the mess she came home to an hour later. She didn't let Kelly forget that it was all her fault. But Kelly wasn't sure if her mother was more upset over the loss of the lamp or all the blood. Bixby, well, there wasn't much to say about him except her mother had to pay some friends to make him disappear.

Kelly was more upset over the fact her stepfather, whom she had liked at one point, had tried to rape her. Well, he hadn't taken no for an answer, and she had a few bruises to show, but no one cared enough to look at them.

The bottom line was this, the house was no longer big enough for an opportunistic mother and her daughter who no longer wanted to be the cheese in a rat trap. She left on fairly good terms with Old Jen before she was asked to go. Besides, when she had turned eighteen a few months later, she wouldn't be worth much to Old Jen. Hell, she'd be legal or consensual, as it were...

Efficient Jane had packed two small bags earlier that morning, her last morning on Ashland Drive. One contained clothing, one contained detritus she couldn't do without including her lucky $10 silver coin from the Flamingo that she'd won after one of her mother's weddings. Her black makeup bag that contained the tools of her trade lived in the trunk of her car. The rest of her accumulated props, including the wonderful wardrobe she'd acquired as Jane Miller, financial wizard, would be dropped off at the local battered women's shelter. She didn't need the estate salespeople curious as to why she was leaving designer duds. This was supposed to be about Aunt Betsy and Jane's constructed heritage. The stainless-steel French press, which she meticulously cleaned and dried, went in one of the suitcases.

She'd miss the clothes. This Jane persona had good clothing and cosmetics. The red lipstick alone was stunning. She made a striking blonde. But at least she knew a lot of women could use the stuff she was donating to the shelter.

She'd already dealt with the money she'd need to relax and lay low until the next season. Blackmail didn't pay what it used to. But murder paid nothing, and a girl has to eat. And now, the woman known as Jane was second guessing her life choices. This had been a common thread of rebellion since her vacation last January in Saint Barts. Damn, Saint Barts! It had messed her up. Well, he...he had messed her up. Jack Daniels. The mere memory of his smile sent shockwaves through her body. Enough said.

There hadn't been a new piglet this year. In the past, every year or so, she let one of the little piglets of her blackmail plan live. She had to finance this lifestyle someway! First, of course, she'd have sex with them and have a hidden camera take compromising photos, just like Old Jen had taught her. Then, right when they thought it might be true love and they should leave their wife, she'd end it. Then she blackmailed the shit out of him. What the guy never understood, she was never going to completely be out of his life. He was like an old sow. He was a breeder. You didn't kill your breeder until you got every last litter you could out of the dried-up old Bacon-in-Process, or every last cent, in this case. She'd even learned to develop her own photos, and they were not suitable for anyone's Christmas card. But not this season, not after Saint Barts.

For that week of vacation she had shared with him, she'd almost forgotten who she was, falling for Jack like a smitten kitten. Returning to reality hadn't been easy.

She had a post office box in Kansas with a staffer who didn't mind forwarding packages as instructed was essential to keep the money coming in. She had several post office boxes scattered around the United States, but Kansas was special. The Bacon-in-Process either paid regularly or she would visit them and their wives. Just the threat of a visit was enough to make the Bacon-in-Process do whatever she needed. It wasn't just the photos that got them handing over the money. No, she'd explain the facts of life. The facts of *her* life. That snapped them in line. It was almost time to collect another round of payments. She hoped none of them disappointed her.

But really, she wasn't going to do this forever. There were too many neighborhoods with too many men behaving badly. She needed to help free her sisters, the other women who were suffering. Life was short. Don't waste it. But she was only one woman after all. And the manipulative sex no longer satisfied a need, it kind of bored her. Damn Saint Barts!

At ten a.m., she went out to her car, a five-year-old silver Lexus she had grown accustomed to. It was so simple to leave, it blew her mind every time. She opened the garage door and drove away, closing it once again as if she was just running to the market for some plain yogurt or a pint of chocolate peanut butter Haagen Dazs.

Officials were still at Jon and Paula's, so it was a good time to be on her way. Her work on Ashland Drive was done. She'd never see her neighbors or this street again. She'd never see Colorado again. Time for her to move on to the next chapter, or season as she liked to call them of her life. She'd miss the Lexus, but she'd have another one someday. Heck, maybe that would be the one thing she would keep, with a new license plate after all...At least it was silver. She liked herself in a silver car, well, anything silver really. It had started with her lucky silver coin in Las Vegas when she was fourteen. Now at thirty-four, though she could still pass for thirty-one or two, she considered anything silver to be a good omen. Unless it was a bad man with silver hair. Well, there was an exception to every rule.

CHAPTER TWO

Gingie

Gingie Conners, licensed real estate broker, had lived in Oregon all of her life. She looked at the photos of her neighbor's house on Pioneer Pike in Eugene, she cringed with concern. It had three failed sales, all due to bad inspection reports. Three failed sales on one property was definitely her record. Okay, the seller had finally admitted that the roof, bathrooms, and the backyard all needed help. So there was a leaking, buried oil tank in the backyard that needed to be decommissioned... it happened.

And now the seller thought the property was tainted by the bad inspections and needed to be taken off the market for a few months while they gave the house a facelift and then put it back on the market. At least the seller hadn't talked about replacing Gingie. Well, the seller was distracted. At seventy, she had a new boyfriend and a gorgeous condo that had let her feel like a forty-year-old again. She said she was ready to embrace the next phase of her life. She didn't want to participate in the neighborhood parties or the community garden, and she was done with all the work associated with being a good neighbor in the neighborhood.

Fine.

Realtors, despite not being the sharpest knives in the butcher's block at times, had long memories. An old friend or high school buddy uses a different realtor to sell their house, kiss that relationship goodbye. The Gibson house needed more than a month or two off the market. It needed a good year. Thankfully, Gingie had come up with a solution, which tight, old Mrs. Gibson had loved. Gingie would rent the property to help offset the cost of the repairs. The only problem was that no one wanted to live in that ode to the 1980s. She lowered the original rent by $500 a month when there were no takers the first month and waited.

Gingie had worked so hard for this commission. It had been a bad experience up to now. Watching good offers come and go after the inspection. And Mrs. Gibson refused to budge on repairs when they had an interested buyer. The fact that she'd once lived here, made all the monthly neighborhood parties, in this unusually social neighborhood, so much more fun. Not really. It was tense, awkward. Neighbors wanted to know what had caused *Old Lady* Gibson's house not to sell. They wanted to know why *Old Lady* Gibson no longer wanted to participate in the neighborhood. They asked questions Gingie couldn't answer. She wanted to answer them, but by law she couldn't. Didn't stop the neighbors from trying.

Gingie hung her real estate license at Emerald City Realty. She was thirty-two, twice divorced, happy to be single again and liked to think her real life would begin somewhere else and someday soon. Until then, she was in this medium-sized town, wondering what the rest of the world was doing. Eugene, Oregon, wasn't exactly the center of the universe, but it didn't have the traffic of the big city. It was green. There was a university. People smoked a lot of pot and didn't wear much deodorant. She liked to fly to San Francisco a few times a year to buy clothes—that was her guilty pleasure, well, when she was making money.

At least she knew her exes were in Portland, trying to get as much tail as possible. She'd been their tail once and each one had decided to "bet the farm" that a calm, peaceful life, which would please their mothers and societal norms, existed by marrying her. They had been wrong, and so had she. Tail chasers didn't make good husbands. They didn't even make average husbands. If a dog caught the car he was chasing, then what? Like the car was impressed? No, the car would just run over the dog and be on its way.

She'd let herself be caught twice, and to what benefit? She had two hocked engagement rings, two wedding albums she didn't like looking at, and a life waiting to begin. Would she have children, a husband, a dog, to populate her house someday? Well, she could get a dog. And she could pick the breed she really wanted if she stayed unmarried. Something sleek and cool, something exactly opposite to her growing waistline. The dog might be the only child she would have.

So, she sat at her desk on Monday, woolgathering. Thinking of what kind of dog, she might want. A sweet dog who would bond with her, not a standoffish dog. What was a standoffish dog? One that didn't want to sit in her lap. But she wanted a medium sized dog, something that she could walk with at night. Something that other people might fear—like a Doberman.

"Excuse me." Gingie heard. "I don't mean to bother you."

Gingie looked up to find a petite red head with a hesitant smile framed by glossy lips that spoke of Chapstick, not lipstick. This woman was no doubt scared of her own shadow. She was dressed in the Earth Muffin fashion style of maxi dress, hippy sandals, and if Gingie wasn't mistaken, a little patchouli scent was coming off of her. Gingie wore Chanel.

"I'm sorry, I didn't hear you come in," Gingie said, smiling at the woman on the other side of her desk.

"I'm sorry, I didn't make much noise. I've been accused of being stealth. I'm Amber Jennings."

Well, at least her name wasn't Sunshine or Apple.

Gingie stood and extended her hand, "Hi, I'm Gingie Conners, and I was woolgathering. I'm sorry. Please, make yourself comfortable. Have a seat. Would you like something to drink? Water? Coffee? Tea?"

"I'm fine, really," Amber answered.

"Well, there must be something I can do for you?"

Amber sat, taking a minute to arrange her voluminous skirt of the floral minidress. It was a pattern of lavender, which fit all Gingie's judgy conclusions.

"I noticed the rental listing just a mile away on Pioneer Pike. I'm writing a book and need someplace for about nine months, maybe a year where I can work quietly. Did I see the rent was seventeen hundred a month and it is furnished?"

"Yes, but if you sign a year lease, I might be able to throw in electric, sewer, and garbage. In the winter, electric bills can be a lot each month."

"Why is it so reasonable? I mean it is a three bedroom, three bath house, right?"

"We'll need you to let in the occasional handy person to fix this or that. Maybe five different vendors all together. At some point we will be redoing the roof and cleaning out the backyard along with an oil tank. In fact, I would need you to stay out of the backyard for a bit. We have a bit of a poison oak issue. And the lawn maintenance for the front yard is included."

"Great. That's fine, I can stay out of the backyard."

"Good, great! In a year or so, the owner wants to sell. You are keeping it lived in. Do you think the occasional noise would bother you being a writer? You did say you were a writer? Right?"

"Yes, I did. Okay, that is why it is so cheap, the noise," the woman said in conclusion. Gingie wondered if she'd lost interest. "I like to write at night when everyone is asleep. That is just the way it is. So, as long as I got my alone time sometime during the day, I'll be fine."

"What are you writing?"

"A book on natural cosmetics. I've always wanted to use the knowledge I've picked up a lot in my years living with my aunt in Montana and then in the Peace Corps in Africa. You see, my aunt died not long ago, so I decided to make the most of the wealth she gave me."

"That is very cool."

"I'm excited for the opportunity."

"Would you like to see the house?"

"Yes, but the workman, will I know when they are coming? I mean will there be constant noise?"

"Only the roof. Everything else is a day, two at most. The backyard is just a mess. What isn't poison oak is blackberries. We are taking care of that, but you don't have to interact with the people outside. Just let the people inside as the projects come up."

"Well, the price is amazing, so I'd like to see it."

Normally, Gingie photocopied the person's driver's license, but she didn't have any odd feelings about this down to earth woman, so she didn't ask. Besides, men were the ones they were all weary of, they tended to be the serial killers, not some cute hippy girl.

Gingie left her office in the Oakway Mall and followed Amber over to the Gibson house on Pioneer Pike. Amber knew the way, as she'd already seen the outside of the house or at least cruised the neighborhood. Gingie let Amber walk ahead of her toward the ranch style house as they talked about Amber's car.

"Being in real estate, I'm always looking for a car that can transport people. I'll need something new in the next year or two. Do you like your Volvo?"

"Not as much as the Lexus I had before this, but it is a luxury car. Test drive a Lexus before you buy the Volvo." Amber replied.

This woman had a Lexus before? What the hey? What a surprise. Maybe it was the aunt's car. She wanted to ask her about her employment history, but she couldn't. The rental application would fill in that mystery. But really, Peace Corps worker driving a Lexus? Wow.

"Good advice, thank you," Gingie said as they made their way up the front walk to the little white cottage with the very bad roof.

"The owner moved to a modern condo, but this comes furnished. Basically, everything Mrs. Gibson didn't take to her new home. It is clean and well-cared for. It has been just Mrs. Gibson for several years after her husband died. I know it will look a little dated to you, but it really is good quality."

What Gingie didn't say was that it was furnished in a style that had been very popular in the 1980s. Wallpaper was on every wall. Even the drapes and some of the furniture were in fabric that exactly matched the wallpaper. It was a 1980s-time capsule. There was a lot of Laura Ashley décor in the bedrooms, baths, and kitchens. If you liked Laura Ashley, you were in luck. If you hated sweet peas and floral prints, too damn bad. All in all, it was a fantastic price.

"I like the idea of recycling the furniture. It so much less wasteful."

"I have to tell you, the powder room off the kitchen needs to be fixed," Gingie warned.

"Fixed?" Amber asked.

"Well, it doesn't have a toilet at the moment. We will fix that. That is one of the vendors I was talking about."

"How about the other two baths?"

"Fully operational. In fact, the master has a Jacuzzi tub. However, it is baby blue to match the wallpaper."

"I like Jacuzzi tubs," Amber said. "I can close my eyes, add some scented Epsom salts, lavender or ginger, relax, and let all my stresses fall away."

"Good idea. Who doesn't like a Jacuzzi tub?" Gingie asked rhetorically.

They toured the house, and Gingie had to remind herself to

stop talking. This was a good deal. Amber was the first person to look at the house in two weeks. Gingie would make any other concession needed because she was getting 40% of the rent and needed the money. It had been a bad September, and usually September was one of her best months. Damn interest rates. Damn low inventory. Damn multiple offers. Damn seller's market for everyone but Mrs. Gibson.

This renter could help her pay her mortgage through the winter. She needed this to happen.

Amber walked the space and said, "Okay, it will work. I like the light and the space. When can I move in?"

They had some paperwork, but it wasn't as labor-intensive as apartment complexes that had background checks. No, this was much less detailed. Mrs. Gibson was more about the money. Not that she needed it, but she thought it was a better indicator of a person's intentions. The shrewd old lady that she was, she'd have been a great "no questions asked" money launderer for the mob or some other nefarious operation.

Fine, Gingie could live with that. It wasn't any of her business if Mrs. Gibson wanted to bend a few rules. She explained the financial responsibility, and Amber nodded in the appropriate places. Then she explained the necessary paperwork. First and last months' rent. More nodding. Agreement nodding, the best kind.

"Once all that is done, and you pay your deposits, I can give you the keys. If we go back to the office, we can get it done, then, if everything checks out, you can move in."

"I have cash. How about tomorrow?"

Amber

Amber looked at her reflection in the mirror at the Motel 6 by the Denny's just outside of Eugene along I-5. She hated the hotel, but she didn't want a lot of attention. She liked her new

19

red hair. The Jane blonde had been hard to maintain even though she had loved it. She couldn't bleach it to a soft ash blonde without a professional hairstylist to help her. Unfortunately, Ashland Drive and her made-up executive position demanded professional pampering if she wanted to fit in. She had also gotten acrylic nails, monthly pedicures, and massages. Jeez, so much maintenance was tiring.

When she had tried to do her hair herself, it bleached to the color of Doritos. The red was different. She could do it herself with a bottle of Ms. Breck and a few towels she was ready to say goodbye to. And the bonus was that it looked good with her coloring. If she were part of society and didn't need to keep her identity stealth, she might consider making the red permanent because it was so easy. But that wasn't going to happen. She was living her best life. Fulfilling her destiny. Helping women that were in need so that they wouldn't have to go through what she went through as a young woman.

Fifteen miles north of Eugene was the small town of Coburg. Filled with antique stores, it offered a lot of what Amber needed. From Mrs. Dotson of Dotson's Antiques, she bought a few pieces of sterling silver jewelry that were reasonably priced with cash. In fact, she had given herself a budget for today's little adventure of $3,000, which she had in assorted bills tucked in her purse. No paper trail for her. And she wouldn't be memorable for using $100 bills. Nope. In fact, she had some anonymous, pre-purchased visa gift cards, the kind parents might give students going to school.

Next door, at Grandmother Rose's Antiques, she purchased a quilt and a few do-dads including three silver picture frames that had just the right amount of patina. Later, she'd fill them with people she'd found on the internet. People who'd been dead for two or three hundred years.

Her next stop was Goodwill. Nothing like a few lived in pieces to round out the wardrobe. Besides, her persona this season was hippy girl. She wanted a jean jacket, maybe a Kimono to act as a bathrobe. When left to her own devices, between seasons, she wore tight jeans, black patent cargo boots by AGL—which cost almost $800 a pair but were a little clunky and trendy—and a crisp black t-shirt. If she was dressing up, she'd add a Burberry Jacket, handbag, and scarf. Nothing said "casual, yet expensive" like Burberry. She had three silk scarves she had procured in her travels. One was covered with sweet deer in caramel and cream that she had found at a resale shop in Texas. One in pink with sketches of jewelry she'd bought for her last birthday, and lastly, she'd bought a Queen Elizabeth Diamond Jubilee scarf, the most expensive of the lot, and had it shipped from Harrods, which was stupid and foolish, but divine. She couldn't help it, she loved Burberry. It was one of her vices. Keeping the scarves broke all the rules, but she had never been accused of playing by the rules. And nothing dressed up an outfit like a good scarf. She'd hide them this season.

At Goodwill, she also found a straw hat, another couple of maxi dresses and a pair of Doc Martin boots that were lived in. Everything was looking good, and she was proud of herself for pulling together this new persona so quickly.

Next, she went to Rainbow Optical and explained she needed to look more serious at work. She picked out some round tortoiseshell frames and they put translucent glass lenses in them for her.

Finally, she went to the University of Oregon bookstore and purchased a cheap laptop, pens and paper, and finally some U of O duck gear with the prepaid credit cards. This was a college town, and you were immediately accepted into a group if you wore their gang colors. At the University of Oregon, they happened to be an odd dark green and bright yellow. Putting on the jersey, she thought she looked like a red trumpet daffodil with her bright hair. Maybe the hippy persona had no alliance to the local sports team. Well, she'd add a U of O bumper sticker to the Volvo just to be on the safe side.

With all of her purchases secured in the backseat of her car, she drove to Pioneer Pike to move into her new home for the next nine to twelve months. She hoped it was okay. She had never lived in a neighborhood where the landlord was essentially a neighbor, but this would offer her wonderful entrée into their world. She'd already been invited to some pool party next Saturday. She'd bring a berry pie or something sentimental from her past yet to be determined or created. And some natural lotion samples for the ladies so they would start to trust her and immediately like her because she brought them "pressies."

Gingie had mentioned the community tennis courts and discussed the community garden when Amber asked if there was one. In fact, Gingie had mentioned she could have the designated lot that used to belong to Mrs. Gibson. How nice. How convenient to her plans…She never knew which city she would end up in. Sometimes it was a game of dropping something on a map of the United States. She only had a couple of rules. It needed to be at least five hundred miles from her last location, and it had to be one of the more medium sized towns in the state.

One thing she always liked was a private garage without windows. Thankfully, she had that with her new temporary home.

She used the opener Gingie had given her and pulled into the garage, shutting the door behind her. With her first load in hand, two of her suitcases from the trunk, she stepped inside and took a deep breath. She didn't think she'd ever get used to the blue and white squiggly wallpaper in the kitchen done in 1980s Laura Ashley. It made her want to rock out and dance to Culture Club, Robert Palmer, and Madonna, only to be fair, she hadn't been born in the 1980s. Hell, the fashion from the 1980s still made her cringe. Her mother, good old Jennifer, probably was a Madonna lookalike, wearing her metal spiked bra with a jean jacket.

No wonder Old Jen wasn't quite sure who her real father was. Back then, Amber, (She had to remember she was Amber now, not Jane, or any of her other aliases for the next season, she was Amber) had been known as little Jennifer's baby, Kelly. She hated the name Kelly. In fact, she had yet to meet a Kelly she actually liked. But she liked herself. She had changed her name from Kelly to Kelan in college, which she could live with, but she hadn't lived with it for long because life got in the way. Maybe she should extinguish a few Kellys. That would probably make her feel better. She laughed. What a crazy rabbit hole her thoughts had traveled down today!

The stainless-steel French press she brought with her looked out of place next to all the old white appliances. Well, at the moment, it might be the only piece of equipment she knew how to use. She found one of her new black spice/coffee bean grinders and put it on the drainboard. It wouldn't be grinding any coffee, but it was important to buy it early like her other supplies. In nine or ten months from now, any trail of this purchase would be cold. If the police started sniffing around a purchase made so many months ago would be hard to find. Who was she kidding? She laughed a little. The police were not likely to figure out the supplies she'd used. But it was always smart to err on the side of caution.

The rest of her supplies went in cupboards behind ordinary stuff so the nosey neighbors wouldn't be likely to find anything.

As for her plants, they went on the windowsill amongst the benign plants like basil.

Nightshade didn't mind hanging out with basil. The English Yew would need to be purchased at a nursery closer to spring because it was her personal favorite and more of a shrub. Not that she really needed it this season. She had dehydrated a lot of the berries that were currently in the black bag in the trunk of the Volvo, in several Ziplock bags more for their protection than hers. It was overkill, but she thought that you could never be too cautious. She liked the fresh berries better, but it was good to have options. Sometimes she thought she was a human squirrel for her ability to hoard and plan for an uncertain future.

Aside from the dried yew berries, she had some dried rhubarb leaves and rhododendron blossoms. If a neighbor had rhododendron blossoms, she could encourage the neighbor to float them in the neighborhood party punch bowl. That would show a pattern in the neighborhood of reckless disregard when it came to dangerous plants. With any luck, everyone who had the punch would have gastric distress a few hours later, but the toxin shouldn't kill anyone. And so, the planning was already starting.

She grabbed a bag of potatoes and put them near the sliding glass door to the backyard where the poison oak lurked, in a ray of warm sun. She may or may not use them. If left to their own devices, in a few weeks, the potatoes would have a lovely green ring by their skin when they were cut into. She'd harvest the skin, dry it, grind it, and add it to her special tea sometime in the future. She might put in the leaves of dried rhubarb as well. She'd also add hibiscus and orange rind to make the tea very palatable. To make it look "herby" she'd add the leaves and blossoms of meadowsweet. Completely harmless, but fun to add. Normally, she might add the herb marshmallow, but it healed the digestive tract medicinally, and, well, she didn't want that!

The foxglove and lily of the valley would have to wait until spring. Well, they would be especially useful if one of her targets already had heart issues. Digitalis in its natural form. Just that when you ingested foxglove, it was pure, but the dosage was questionable. It could be right, that was random intervention at its best. Luck. Karma. She couldn't control that kind of development when it happened. She might have some dried flowers left over from two seasons ago. That would be safer because it couldn't be tracked back to her.

She made the bed in the master and added the old quilt she'd purchased and her silver fox plushy. The quilt smelled like old people. A mix of dust, a hint of moth balls, and White Shoulders perfume. Hmmm, she thought, what would she name the aunt who was so important in her life? Jane? Could she really do that? Easy to remember. Why not? None of these *rubes* would guess anything she did. Nope. It felt wrong and a little too close to her last season. She thought again and decided on Betty. Everyone of a certain age had an Aunt Betty.

Neighbors always gave new neighbors the benefit of the doubt. Well, until you drove too fast or walked your snippy dogs in the middle of the night with black velvet gloves on and then didn't pick up their poo. Truth be told, he wasn't doing that anymore because Tom in Ohio had an unfortunate accident three seasons ago. When the police went to break the news to his wife, they found her tied to the bed because that was what Tom did to her every night. Because Tom was one sick motherfucker. Tom's wife needed a lot of therapy, but she got her life back. Tom's wife got her freedom. Amber felt good about that one.

The point was, you couldn't dislike a neighbor on sight, especially if she fit in and brought *Aunt Betty's* famous chocolate cake with mounds of frosting to the first neighborhood event the first Saturday she lived in the neighborhood. And that also made her known for cake and not pie, a vehicle she might use for her dried yew berries.

Amber googled, "Best chocolate cake ever made." She printed out the recipe, made a note to buy enough supplies to test the recipe a couple of times before she actually presented the cake. She would cover the cake in rainbow sprinkles. If the little colored confetti didn't say friendly, she didn't know what did. Children and adults alike enjoyed sprinkles. If that didn't have the desired result, she'd hang a unicorn flag off the flagpole holder she'd noticed over the garage and say she was heavy into "corn." Hippies liked unicorns. She didn't mind being underestimated and perceived to be a bit of an Earth muffin. She knew herself and didn't need to prove her worth. How many of these *rubes* had double digit kills to their names and five men who were Bacon-in-Process?

CHAPTER THREE

Gingie

Minnesota transplant Officer Kent Logan stepped into Emerald City Realty in the Oakway Mall to "check on things." For a couple of months he'd been doing this, and Gingie did what she always did, smiled and batted her big blue eyes at the tall, handsome Norwegian policeman.

He looked like he had just enough edge to handle her. She liked that he was a cop. Some women could not handle that. Maybe the gun scared them. The ones that really liked the gun were too odd to date. Gingie got off on the authority, not the gun.

They were now at a point where he could get himself a cup of coffee and sit in front of her desk for a little chat without an invitation, which she thought was progress. Also, she had uncovered that he was divorced, lived in an apartment having lost his house in his divorce, wanted to travel and might just be a tad lonely, which mirrored her perfectly.

After two months of this she was beginning to wonder if he would ever ask her out. Maybe one of these days soon she'd suggest they take their chats out to a restaurant to share a meal. And if she was any judge of character, which she thought she was, he liked her a little bit too.

She was wearing a little white halter dress with cherries on it and a matching red jacket today, probably the last time this season for that dress. It showed a little cleavage. She hoped he noticed.

"Hey Gingie," he said as he stepped inside.

Her smile lit up as she said, "Officer Kent, I thought this was your day to say hello. I just brewed a fresh pot of coffee. Pour yourself a cup, and then come over and let's chat."

He did as he was told and they caught up with the usual pleasantries, then she told him about her week.

"Finally, thank you Jesus or Goddess above, I got a renter for Mrs. Gibson's house on Pioneer Pike."

"I didn't know you handled rentals," he said. "Is that new?"

"Well kind of. I don't usually handle rentals, but I'm doing it as a favor with the hopes she will want to continue to list this house with me. Pioneer Pike is a sought-after neighborhood, but her house has got some issues. The kind of issues that banks do not overlook when you are a new buyer trying to get a loan."

"Are they really that big of a deal?"

"Well, it is a seller's market, so buyers have to overlook a lot, but this house, there is just too much for what Mrs. Gibson is asking. Floral Laura Ashley prints and wallpaper kind of define the interior. There is a roof that is failing and covered in moss, poison oak in the backyard, and blackberries, so many blackberries you can't even see the grass if there is or ever was grass. I considered picking them for a pie, but I didn't think it would be popular to offer something that was grown in poison oak."

"Probably not! You know, eventually, I'll want a house, and I will come to you for help, but that one sounds like a mess."

"I'd be happy to help you. But that house is a mess. I really shouldn't be telling you this, but I rented it yesterday to a nice lady who wants to write a book this year. She taught English in Africa for the Peace Corps and then her aunt died and left her money. She quit the Peace Corps so she could fulfill her dream, writing a book about making her own cosmetics. Isn't that cool?"

"It is very Eugene," he said.

"Very Eugene. I'm taking the net rental income and using it

to do the roof and clean up the backyard. The other issues will be tricky because I have a small budget, but I'll make it work."

"I'm surprised you found anyone who'd want to rent it."

"Me too, but the price is right, the neighborhood is nice."

"Don't you live in that neighborhood?" Kent asked. How did he know that? Had he been checking up on her?

"I have for four years since my divorce. Nice neighbors."

"Didn't you tell me about monthly parties?"

"Yes, several houses have revolving parties. Mine was in May and I had a Cinco de Mayo style gathering. It was wonderful. I got a band made up of other realtors from our Valley River office and we had lots of food and dancing. I was lucky. It was the first nice weather of the year so we were in my backyard for most of the night. Everyone drank a ton of margaritas, but don't worry, we were all walking. I have this cool machine that makes slurpees, so I made slurpee margaritas."

"I think I like your neighborhood. Sometime can I go with you? To one of the parties?"

Oh yeah. She had to tell herself not to smile so broadly.

"Sure, in fact there is one this weekend," she said. "A potluck and pool party. Probably the last party that is outdoors until next summer. It is a beautiful space. Would you like to go with me?"

"Yes," he answered without hesitation, "What can I bring?"

"Your bathing suit. I'm making a Greek salad or something like it."

"It's a date. Shall I meet you at your house?"

"2pm. Here is the address," she said holding out a post-it note. "This will be so fun. It is a great group of people."

Gingie was on cloud nine for the rest of the day. She had a date, well, sort of, with Kent. If he was seeing someone it was highly unlikely that he'd have agreed to the pool party.

She tried to bolster her confidence. He'd called it a date, and that was something. Jeez. She had been wondering if he was gay.

He was hot, which is why she thought he might be gay. She liked gay men, and they liked her. She would have been able to set him up with one of her friends in the real estate world if he was single, but she had liked Kent enough that she hoped he liked women and she hoped he wasn't dating anyone. She knew he was single, but that didn't mean anything.

But she was having an especially lucky week. First, Amber rented the Gibson place and now Kent. Damn! Maybe she should buy a lottery ticket!

And the best part was, she hadn't met him online but in real life. She knew who he was. Their relationship had developed over time. This was the perfect situation! She hoped…but what if he was one of those guys who dated a lot of women?

He was so tall and solid-looking, like he was the human form of a Doberman. He had dark hair with sun-streaked highlights, sweet blue eyes, and tan skin, which spoke to many summer days spent outside. But he told her he was Norwegian, which added to his allure. He was exactly the kind of man she had always wanted to date. He was someone solid enough to climb like a ladder or an oak tree.

Her two ex-husbands had been short, 5'6, 5'7 in their dreams. She hadn't thought they had short man's syndrome, but then each of them had exhibited less-than-ideal characteristics. Quick to anger at the littlest things. Then it was quick to anger at her. There was no coming back from that.

The first one, Seth, thought she was always displaying too much cleavage. Too flirtatious. She was the root of every one of his problems. The second one, Michael, just decided she was a conquest. At first, she thought his controlling ways were funny, then they weren't. He'd cheated before their first anniversary. Both losers. And here she thought it was good that she hadn't gone for the chiseled, good-looking guy. She'd gone with average and what had it done for her? Not a damn thing. Well, Kent was different. She thought she might be more attracted to him than she was to any other man on the planet. That was a good start. She liked his body, the way he looked in uniform. In her darker moments, late at night, she wondered what he looked like out of that uniform.

Now, he was coming to her house, he was going to be her date for Mr. and Mrs. Glass's pool party. The neighbors would talk, they would speculate. Well, it had been a long time since she'd brought anyone to anything to do with the neighborhood. Their tongues could wag. They could talk about her. In fact, she was giving them something to talk about, besides the new neighbor Amber, who would be there. Did she have to worry that Kent would think Amber was pleasantly good looking? Now she was being paranoid, but she was a woman after all, sizing up another woman. It was stupid because she liked Amber. And if Kent was so easily swayed by another woman, it was best to know before she got too involved. Because she had known what it felt like to be cheated on and she'd prefer not to have to deal with that drama ever again in this lifetime.

Her mind traveled to more exciting elements of the party. Which swimsuit to wear? Well, she wasn't a gym rat, but she did walk with the neighbor ladies three times a week. It kept her legs toned, but what about her arms? Did she have the right to bare her arms? Well, if she was very lucky, Kent would see them eventually, so it didn't matter.

She had this new bathing suit she'd gotten with this party in mind. It was kinda retro in that it was black with white polka dots. It was a halter but showed her cleavage. The legs were French cut, giving her five foot three inches a nice line. She hadn't worn a two piece since she was in high school. But this suit did what it needed to. She also had a sheer black cover up and big black hat. She had Ray Ban sunglasses with white frames. She would wear strappy black sandals that would define her calf muscles. And, of course, she would wear her brightest red lipstick. Heck, she might resemble a 1950s pinup girl. Okay, that was a stretch, but she was excited to see the end result.

She was bringing a Greek salad. Hmmm... might have to re-think that choice. She wanted to show Kent that she was a good cook. Did the Greek salad say that? Maybe she should go with jalapeño poppers or her famous guacamole and tropical salsa.

CHAPTER FOUR

If she wasn't who she was, Amber would still find the humor in what she was doing, being domestic as she sprinkled rainbows on her chocolate cake. Had there been a birthday when she'd been growing up that Aunt Betty hadn't made the cake for her? She didn't think so. This cake was her family in a round, nine-inch confection. The lie rolled off her easily. Good.

For this season's story Amber thought that her family didn't see each other that much because they were free spirits like her and spread out all over the United States. Yes, that sounds right, but when they did get together or even when they were apart, they made this cake and life was better because it reminded them all of home and being together.

Amber kept repeating the story in her mind until she could recite it easily. Storytelling was almost as important as the story content itself. If you wanted it to have the emotional draw, tell it with the emotion it deserved.

She had made some observations over the years as she had been living in neighborhoods and 'improving' women's lives. (Yes, that's how she liked to think of it.)

The kitchen was the hub for women. They liked to come in and nest. *How many electrical outlets do you have? The crock pot needs to be plugged in. Where was the garbage? Maybe it should be out for the party. Is there room in the fridge?* The women might not have anything to go in the fridge, but it is important to at least check it out. You get to see what someone eats but also their habits toward cleanliness. A package of pig snouts from the local Asian market is a great conversation starter. Look at their brand of coffee. A lot can be said about coffee. Politics can be determined by coffee. *Whoa, she has Folgers and Starbucks? What does that say about her? How can she be conservative and liberal? Which is she going to serve with dessert tonight? Who does she think we are?*

Men liked to gather in the family room to watch sporting events. Turn on a game, any game, and they acted half hypnotized. You, the homeowner, will be forever known as cool. In fact, add a cooler to a common area like the fireplace hearth and fill it with some sort of IPA like Heineken and/or something trendy like Stella Artois. For a little whipped cream on the sundae, add a stack of mini solo cups and a few bottles of whiskey. Get a bottle of something nice like Crown Royal and something local like Pendleton, if you live in the Pacific Northwest. These men will think of your house as the cool one in the neighborhood after this. Like little boys gathering around a foosball table and eating double-stuff Oreos when it was the cool thing to do in junior high.

Amber smiled at the memory of the tree that fell during her first season in Montana. She had opened her garage and set up a bar for the neighbors. Word soon spread, and they came in droves to commiserate about the tree and pour a little something something in their glass or their coffee beverage in a thermos. Three months later one of the men got sick and just couldn't recover. When he died, the widow spoke of how fabulous the impromptu garage party was, not of her controlling pig-dog spouse, who humped anyone ready, willing, and able.

Amber wanted to be remembered at the neighborhood pool party but for the right reasons. Amber had a plain black suit with some sort of orangey flower on it with green leaves that sort of resembled a hibiscus from the Jantzen company that she had washed a lot and rubbed with a pumice stone so that the newness was gone. There was a little pilling, just as she wanted. She had a cheap yet nice black wrap and the blonde straw hat from Goodwill. Normally, she'd go with a black straw hat, but she didn't want to be too matchy-matchy in front of the neighborhood women. Let them feel a little sorry for her. *The poor hippy girl is trying to make a good impression. She has no fashion sense, how sad...*

She had returned to Mrs. Dotson's to pick up an old milk glass cake stand and dome cover in light lime green to complete her presentation.

"The cake pan was my beloved Aunt Betty's. Out of all the nieces, she gave it to me. It still makes our every other year family reunions a little tense. You'd think they'd be mad about the family jewelry even if it is only silver, or that I was Aunt Betty's favorite, but no it is the cake pan. The reunion is next year and I'm already nervous about it. Maybe I shouldn't go," she said to the mirror as she looked at herself in the new, slightly distressed bathing suit and then smiled. The yoga and Pilates she had done last season had paid off. She looked damn good.

Truth was, she couldn't wait to meet all the neighbors and find out their stories. Would there ever be a time she'd go to one of these events, step away and think, "These are nice people. They don't need me." Well, this was essentially her sixth season, sixth neighborhood, so what were the odds? She'd been needed five out of five times; would it be the same here? What did she want the answer to be? She liked her life's work. She was an architect or demolition expert, depending on how you looked at it, although few people had ever seen her work or knew she was responsible. It wasn't like a painting where you could sign your art to get publicity. Nope, she wanted to be stealth.

She had tried on six names, a new one with each season and she still didn't know which one fit her best. She was a woman without a real name. Amanda, Celeste, Rhonda, Beverly, Jane and now, Amber. Plus, she had a bunch of passports in other names. Would anyone ever figure it out? Would they try to stop it? Stop her? She didn't think so because she had been very careful, but she hadn't looked back. She hadn't visited the news stories for any of the towns she'd lived in. When she was done, she was done. No paper trails. No witnesses who had photos or true stories. No drama. She just disappeared. And they hadn't figured it out yet.

She smiled a little to the reflection in the mirror. Did she want to branch out from her favorite, yew berries, maybe switch it up. A career challenge might be to have a season without yew berries. Maybe only work with foxglove or oleander…Don't forget nightshade. And she had a soft spot for daffodils. She always liked to challenge herself.

After she finished getting ready, she found a basket she'd purchased at the Dollar Store. She'd painted it with different shades of pink and light green watered down acrylic paint to make it look a bit old and rustic. Inside, she put in bars of soap she had just made with essential oils like lemon and lavender from a huge vegan soap bar she'd ordered on Amazon and melted down. She used decorative ice cube trays to form the little soap bars into flowers and added lavender seeds or lemon peel, depending on the soap. They looked cute, if she did say so herself. She put them in yellow or lavender chiffon bags with little bows.

She had done something similar with the hand lotion. Well, she bought a few unscented bottles of Jergens lotion, poured them into a bowl, added a little cocoa butter and some essential oils of rose and mixed them with a hand mixer until they were smooth. She poured them into little containers and added pretty floral labels with the brand, "Amber's Natural Rose Lotion." She thought the neighbor ladies would appreciate the little treat. She knew from past experience that the mixture wouldn't separate, but she always suggested to the ladies that they give it a shake to let all the ingredients get re-acquainted. It added the home to homemade.

If someone asked, what kind of book was she writing? She was ready for this, had practiced on the realtor, Gingie. A bit of a how-to book. How to make lotions and cosmetics at home. Not the special concoctions that were her favorite, but the non-fatal soaps, teas, lotions etc. This was flying a little too close to the sun, but that was okay. By the time the neighbors started talking and put it all together, she'd be long gone. And the book, well, it would never be written. It gave her the little thrill that was missing in her life. The truth is out there. It is right before your eyes if you choose to see it. No, they chose to see soccer matches and dogs pooing on lawns. They'd never think a murderess was selecting her next targets from among them. *Rubes.*

The pool party was three houses down and to the right. The cake pan was heavy, but she could do it. So with cake pan in one hand and basket in the other, she made her way to the Glass house on probably what was the last great day of the summer. It was a warm day, but the fall crispness was in the air. The sun already was setting a little lower. Heck, a month from now it will be getting dark at six. Two months from now, four-thirty.

As she turned into the driveway, a smiling woman in her mid-forties stood by a tall gate

"Hello! Welcome! You must be our new neighbor!" she said in greeting. She was the kind of woman you might say 'had some work done.' Okay, lots of work. As in so much work that Amber wondered what was still real. Julia Glass was a human Barbie—well, Barbie's mother who liked to party at the dream house. Lucky damn plastic surgeon. He or she probably went to Europe each summer on Julia's yearly maintenance.

Amber dropped her head a little as if she was shy, "Hi, yes, I'm Amber."

"Welcome, I'm Julia Glass. It is so nice to meet you! Gingie has said wonderful things about you. She also told us you were an author. Show me where to rope off the streets to handle your fans!"

"I wish," Amber said. "This will be my first book, and it's just about how to make your own cosmetics and lotions. I love working with plants. I brought some samples as a way to say hello to the neighbors, I hope you don't mind." She held up her basket for the other woman's scrutiny.

"Mind? Oh hell, I love it when people try their little home-made things on the neighbors. Well, my cosmetic dermatology consultant only lets me use his approved products, which only come from Royal Jelly made by European Honeybees, but the other women of the neighborhood aren't as discerning. They love free stuff. Come in, come in," she said stepping back so Amber could enter the pretty backyard with the kidney shaped pool. Julia yelled to her husband, "Dan, I'm sending through the new neighbor, Aubry. She is the one writing the little book. Get her a drink, will you?"

She thought about correcting Julia Glass and then decided to shut up. Being quiet fits better with her 'new' shy personality.

Dan Glass, a perfect twin to his wife. He was what Barbie's Ken might look like as a grandfather and if he were modeled after a pudgy George Hamilton. He was keeping what was left of his sandy now white hair and not looking like he should partake in too much sun. She'd bet money that he had hair transplants or just plugs. Doll hair. It fit the look. He offered her a margarita, which she took gladly, while she started handing out lotions and hand creams to the neighbor ladies and introducing herself. She was right, they were the perfect icebreakers.

"Welcome Aubry," he said, staring at her cleavage.

She smiled and whispered, "It is actually Amber."

"Oh well, whatever, how about pretty lady, or damn," he

said, checking her out, "Sexy lady? You've got that hot librarian look. Will you stamp my overdue book sometime?"

Amber smiled her false smile and decided she wasn't sure she liked either Mr. or Mrs. Glass. Actually no, she was sure. She didn't like either one of them, which was a very bad first impression. She almost told Dan that he reminded her of her dad (although she didn't know her real dad) to make him aware of the inappropriateness of their age difference and his flirtation, but she would hold that in reserve. He either liked to flirt or was a hound. Time would tell, but he made her short watchlist.

She met Shelby and Clint, Dick and Libby, Valerie and Jim. They all looked happy, 40ish, but Dick of Dick and Libby stared at her for too long with very cold blue eyes. She just knew that he didn't like women. She recognized the type. The smile was more of a sneer. It shot up her personal antenna. He was a younger version of Dan Glass. Maybe they had a club. But she had no doubt, he was a predator. It took one to know one and she just knew. He made her list too.

"That is the most gorgeous bathing suit," Dan said. It wasn't, but it was tight in the right places. She was fishing and might have gotten her first wide mouthed bass. Damn, he was ugly! He looked like an angry, disgruntled IRS agent and bottom feeder fish had a baby, and it was Dan. Her earlier fish comment wasn't far off. Amber shook her head.

"Thank you," she said, uncomfortably. The way his eyes looked at each inch of her suit, well, it made her feel uncomfortable, like shivers of ice were being thrown at her. It reminded her too much of her childhood and the creeps her mother brought home. Yes, this guy needed to be watched closely...he might be the first target of the season.

She then completely ignored him, focusing all she had on his wife, Libby, who was wearing a full length coverup. Dan looked like a dejected dog. If she could guess, and her guesses were good, he had been a high school athlete. Amber bet he got injured and he couldn't get in as many women's panties as he once had, so he asked Libby to marry him. Maybe she'd been the long-suffering girlfriend who wondered if her boy would ever commit. Well, she'd gotten the ring, a half carat diamond on her left hand, but it hadn't taken long for the lover-boy to start looking around again because no one woman could hold his interest for long. And he was still on the prowl. *Scum.*

Libby indicated to a boy and girl in the pool, who looked like they were having fun and said, "Those are our kids, Katie and Jeffrey."

Amber made the appropriate complementary comments.

She handed out her samples. Everyone made the appropriate responses of thanks. Then Valerie said the thing that she had been waiting to hear. Sometimes it was just easy and this year it was easy.

"Well, since you love to grow things… Did you know we have a lovely little community garden just down the street? We are very proud of it."

"I've heard. It must be wonderful," Amber replied. "I've been told there is space for me. I hope that is still true. I've got daffodil bulbs coming from Holland for some lovely bouquets this spring. Of course, I'll want to grow a lot of herbs as well."

"Of course there is room! You can have Mrs. Gibson's space. I don't think she really ever used it, but her husband used to putter with gardening when he was alive. It will be nice to have the space used again. We have it all divided up by addresses. It will be lovely to see what you grow. Maybe you can give pointers to the rest of us since you work with plants."

Not bloody likely, but she could talk about a little fertilizer. Chicken manure was the best. She preferred it to mushroom compost. And conversations about dung or scat tended to end very quickly. Shit wasn't a popular topic of conversation unless you were 80 and liked to talk about your Metamucil intake.

Gingie arrived with a tall drink of water whom she introduced as Kent, the neighborhood policeman who always visited her at her office. As much as Amber had grown to like Gingie and think of her as an asset to her time on Pioneer Pike, the fact she was dating a cop put a wrinkle in the relationship Amber had hoped to have with Gingie. Or maybe she could have a little fun with this. She thought Gingie would be her informant this year. Well, she'd have to think about that. Possibly Gingie was too smart for that role.

"How long have you been dating?" she asked Kent, who suddenly got a strange look on his face.

"Not long, but I'm happy to be here with Gingie. She is wonderful."

Amber watched as Gingie blushed. Oh my. This was *new*. They were barely comfortable with each other. If she was a gambling woman and sometimes, she was, she'd bet money on the fact they hadn't had sex…yet. But it was coming.

"Well, you make a great looking couple," she said and meant it. Despite the fact that Kent was a cop, she was happy for Gingie. They were going to make it. They didn't know it yet, but Amber could see it.

Did this have to affect her relationship with Gingie? Maybe not. This season she seemed to be tossing out all of the rules. Maybe Gingie's relationship with Kent would help Amber. She wasn't sure yet, but she didn't know if she wanted to discount it yet.

She met another dozen people, but none of them interested her like Dan and Dick had. She'd have to observe everyone in their natural habitat over the next few months. These things took time and calculation. Amber needed to know their patterns and when it was best to act, making it look the most natural, leaving no questions to be asked, and most importantly, no autopsy.

In each neighborhood there was usually an old man who should die while the younger spouse (the trophy wife) needed to be given a second chance at life. A May to December that was at the end of the good times. It didn't matter when the fifty-year-old man had a relationship with the twenty-five-year-old secretary, but now he was eighty-five, starting to fail, maybe with a touch of incontinence and dementia, the wife, who was sixty with fake boobs and a lot of hot yoga to keep her toned, got a little restless. Things change. People no longer saw what attracted them to each other. Incontinence and dementia could do that.

Dan and Julia Glass were headed that way, but were not there yet. Julia was fighting it hard. She bet the woman hadn't eaten a carb in ten years or did eat them but liked to vomit, a lot. Julia didn't touch the margaritas. Instead, she was drinking superfood that was the color of spinach and came in an Odwalla bottle. Give it up lady, your husband is making margaritas.

Thinking of this season…What if some old goat had a large life insurance policy? Was there another opportunity here? Should Amber start converting her Bacon-in-Process situation to Trophy-Wife-Looking-for-the-Big-Score? This might be an interesting new revenue stream making itself known. A one-time payment from a grateful wife for taking care of a problematic husband and then it was over. And this way she didn't have to have sex with some limp-dicked dude. Seeing compromising photos of herself with Mr. Cheater Pants was losing its appeal to the point she was done with it. Well, since January, since Saint Barts, and the memories of Jack still fresh in her mind. She didn't want to have sex with any of the ugly *rubes*. Never again.

Maybe Amber had been looking at the old geezer and hot wife couples in the wrong way. For the past five seasons, she had identified individuals who, once removed, would make a more utopian society for everyone else. Not to mention a lot happier wife. She needed to think about this. With Lars as sick as he was, it was more of a mercy killing, and now she bet Marguerite was off traveling enjoying her life. Had she needed all that money? Something to think about. Lars had been 'Jane's' first kill last season, so she'd been able to watch Marguerite process it. It made her feel good to see the changes in Marguerite. She was reborn. She looked ten years younger not having the stress of watching her husband die. There wasn't a product you could buy at Neiman Marcus that would do that kind of thing for you.

As was predicted, Amber's background was inquired about an hour after she had arrived at the party.

Thankfully, it appeared that no one here was from the pretty landscape of Montana. She had given a few details but had kept a few close to the vest about her past. It was a gift actually, telling some, but not all. Hitting that sweet spot had taken years of practice.

"So, whereabouts in Montana are you from? I've hunted a lot in Montana so I'm pretty familiar with the state," Clint of Shelby and Clint asked.

Damn it.

"Are you familiar with the Kootenay River?" Amber asked, having visited the area a few summers ago when she'd had a season in Montana. It was research plain and simple.

"Yes, I've seen it!"

"Well, my Aunt Betty's ranch was halfway between the Kootenay and Missoula. After my parents died, that is where I grew up." There had to be at least five hundred ranches off that stretch of road.

"I'll be darned," he said. "Whereabouts between the two places?"

"Just one of the ranches along the way. If you get to the sapphire mine, you've gone too far." She had gone to one of the many sapphire mines. It was a letdown.

"Montana has a lot of them. Ranches I mean," he said, raising an eyebrow as he took a sip of his margarita.

Tell her something she didn't know. Why had she chosen

Montana? Duh! Lots of ranches. She'd never ridden a horse. She didn't know a steer from other kinds of cows. Well, dairy cows tended to be black and white, she thought. There were others, but she was going with the black and white kind.

"Yes, beautiful country, but I had to be homeschooled because we weren't near anything. Kind of a lonely existence."

"Where did you go to college?" Clint asked.

This could always be tricky. The truth was far more interesting, but they could never know.

"A little private college in Vermont," she said. "My grandmother was from Vermont, I wanted to see what it was like to live near a place she had lived." She could talk about the top five private colleges in Vermont, what they offered, even professors in her field, but she didn't want to go that detailed unless she had to.

"Pretty place, Vermont." Oh damn, he'd been there too. Where hadn't he been? Why had she chosen damn Vermont? She could talk about Texas or Florida in the same ways.

"Except in the winter it can get very, very cold. I was happy to do my time and then get away back to Montana, which is also cold, but familiar, and then, finally to try tempered Oregon. I also spent a few years in Africa with the Peace Corps, but that wasn't really my thing. I like plumbing and hot water. Or just clean water. I like that too."

He laughed. Good.

Please, no one mention skiing. Vermont and Montana, they had lots of snow and skiing. Not to mention Montana's close proximity to Idaho and all the skiing there. She didn't know how to ski. Dan Glass moved around the group, refilling glasses. He got too close to her, his belly bumping her side and breast. She stepped back, but she watched him as he went.

Was it her imagination or as Dan Glass was making the rounds, he was checking out every lady neighbor's backside and patting a few behinds as he went. No, it wasn't her imagination.

He swatted Valerie, who looked like she wanted to deck him. He sized up the man with Gingie and decided to move on. She revisited her earlier thoughts on Dan Glass. Maybe he looked a little like a snake. George Hamilton with less style and hair wearing a loud Hawaiian shirt, wearing a tanning-booth tan and flashing professionally whitened teeth. A fat anaconda with too-white fangs.

Well, well, well...the watch list was starting to form. *Dick and Dan. You are officially on notice.* She really hadn't interacted with Dick, but something was there. She felt it in her bones. Ironically, she didn't add anyone else to the list, but had the odd temptation to add Julia. It was only because the other woman made her feel small. Amber had never killed a woman.

She went to the buffet that had been set up and added to, dish by dish, by the neighbors and noticed a lot of fat-filled appetizers. So, that is the way they rolled. She had jalapeño poppers, bacon wrapped chestnuts, deep fried chicken strips, cheese here and cheese there. There was even a cheeseball from 1970. She ravaged the veggie tray, passed on the creamy dip. She'd have to watch it, or her weight would go up this season.

Her cake was going to do well, and it did. Although as she watched, Julia Glass passed by it with a judgy scowl, as if it were roadkill.

At least three of her neighbors wanted the recipe. Even though Aunt Betty's recipe was a closely guarded family secret, she trusted them enough to share with promises of the recipe to be delivered on a card in the next day or two. The ladies seemed delighted.

Gingie

Kent had arrived exactly on time. He said he'd be there at two and just as her clock turned to two, he was driving up in a jeep. Gingie liked punctual men. The fact he was gorgeous was just frosting on his personal cake.

She had been nervous about this date for three days. She couldn't believe he was coming to her house, and now he was here and they were going to the party at the Glass house.

He came to the door in shorts and a t-shirt that had been ironed because they had knife-like creases on the shirt and shorts. Did they really have to go to the party?

In his hands he held flowers for her and a bottle of pinot noir. She knew from a quick glance at the label that it was at least a fifty-dollar bottle of wine. And the flowers, well, they weren't the supermarket flowers she occasionally treated herself to. No, this was a professional bouquet of roses, hydrangeas, and other flowers she couldn't identify but thought were beautiful in the most gorgeous colors of light pink and lavender. They looked lacy and elegant. This was better than any of the fantasies she'd put together in her head about this date.

"Hi," she said, opening her front door and feeling a little breathless.

He smiled and said, "I hope it is okay. My swimsuit is on under my shorts."

She smiled. He looked as nervous as she felt.

"It's perfectly fine, come on in," she said and stepped back for him to enter her little house.

She watched him taking it all in. She had a nice place strictly because whenever she made a sale and had a decent commission, she would buy something for her house. A new couch, rug, drapes, etc. her home looked good, and she knew it. The only problem was the high interest rates and sellers' market. She hadn't bought anything for the house in a good six months. Her bank account was suffering, and she was a little scared about what was to come, but she had faith it would all work out.

"This place is really nice," Kent said. "I'm ashamed to ever have you see my apartment."

"Don't be," she said with a laugh, "I have contacts in every area from furniture to construction. And they usually give me a deal because I send them a lot of business. I haven't paid retail for any of it."

Still, he looked envious with an expression that concerned her. If he could look at her bank account, he'd know her reality.

"I meant to tell you, you look lovely," he said, and she felt her cheeks color.

"How kind of you! Thank you. This is kinda my retro look," she replied.

"You look good. And I like the hat," he said.

"Thanks, I do too. I'll grab the stuff, and we can go," she announced. She handed him the towels and the sunscreen, which he didn't seem to mind carrying.

When they got to the Glass' house, she was feeling a little odd about how she should introduce Kent, but he led the way, extending a hand to Julia Glass and announcing, "I'm Gingie's date."

"Well, well, isn't our Gingie lucky," Julia said, winking at Kent.

What, did she think that she was so attractive she could steal him away? Gingie wouldn't put it past Julia.

Why did Julia always have to be such a bitch?

Well, what Kent said had cleared up a few things, she thought. She smiled and felt her stomach butterfly's dance. He was her date! Yes! Also, she hoped that would keep old Julia from trying to poach him. The rumors were rampant that she was letting her pool boy, a cute Hispanic man named Julio, service a few other things around the house besides the pool.

In the lovely backyard, she noticed that new neighbor Amber had already arrived. She was doing well, handing out samples of some of the products she'd made. Gingie smiled to herself. The woman was not a threat. Gingie had to be a few years older than Amber, and she hadn't quite mastered her fashion sense. The coverup, hat, and bathing suit were a little hodge-podge and Gingie was mad at herself for noticing. She wasn't a catty woman, but these kinds of observations and concerns were stupid, as was jealousy, which was completely unbecoming. And somewhere along the walk from her house to the Glass', Kent had placed his arm around her shoulder and his physical proximity was close. She didn't want to lose whatever this was before it began.

They interacted with the neighbors, but mainly Gingie and Kent interacted with each other. Gingie felt that she and Kent were in their own little bubble. They walked through the buffet together and each selected the freshest ingredients they could.

"I'm very glad you brought this salsa. It is amazing," he whispered in her ear.

"Yeah, sometimes this crowd is heavy on carbs and fat, but watch, Julia won't eat a thing."

"Well, you can afford it, but not all of us can," he said with a wink.

She smiled her big smile at him and gave his hand a squeeze. He squeezed back and she wondered if he'd kiss her tonight. It felt right. It felt good. She liked this man.

Sleazy Dan Glass stopped to refill their margaritas and for the first time, he didn't try to tap her butt or say anything that was loaded with innuendo. That was a first. She thought she could thank Kent for that. He might bend Dan in half just to see if he could break him. She had no doubts he could.

Once they had finished eating and socializing with the rest of the neighbors they took a dunk in the inviting pool, carving out a little corner in the afternoon shade that was theirs alone.

"Are you having a good time?" she asked as they sat on steps into the pool and let the water cool them.

"I'll be honest with you, Gingie. I don't care about the party. I only came because I wanted to spend time with you outside of your office." Then he looked each way, leaned forward, and kissed her.

He had kissed her in front of all of the neighbors. What would he do when they got to her house? She smiled and said, "I like you too, Kent."

"Good," he said with a broad smile.

CHAPTER FIVE

On the Monday following the party, Amber sat at the desk in the converted bedroom that was now an office in her house. The walls were papered in sweet pea wallpaper. Even the lampshades were Laura Ashley sweet peas. It was like being locked in a twelve-year-old's dollhouse.

She found one of her small black moleskin notebooks that she'd purchased at an office supply store and took off the cellophane. Then she grabbed a pen and started making notes. Every couple in the neighborhood got a page. But Dan Glass, Julia Glass, and that Dick guy got special mention, so special, they each got their own pages.

Once finished with her observations, she used her best penmanship and put the recipe for the chocolate cake on old fashioned soft green recipe cards that had daisies in the corner. They fit in with the Laura Ashley theme. Then she attached a small jar of rainbow sprinkles to each card and made deliveries carrying her trusted basket from the dollar store. It was really coming in handy. Never underestimate the Dollar Store. When she once wanted to convince someone that Voodoo was at play three seasons ago, she'd gotten a bunch of black candles. Where? The Dollar Store of course!

The first house she stopped at was Libby and Dick's. Libby answered with a hesitant smile. She was wearing an apron with Daffy Duck dressed in U of O duck attire on it. Great. She was a U of O person. Amber wondered if she'd met Dick in college.

He was probably the big man on campus then. Well, that made sense. She hoped that Libby wouldn't be attracted to him if she met him now.

"Amber! What a lovely surprise and what perfect timing. Come in, I just pulled banana bread out of the oven. I'll make some coffee, and we can have a chat."

Libby seemed genuinely happy to see her. Good.

Amber thought this might offer her more background into Dick. And it appeared that he wasn't home so that was a benefit. She always thoroughly researched her intended. It was what she owed them if she was going to be judge and jury. This was a good first step.

"Come on back to the kitchen," Libby said as she walked down a long hallway decorated with photos from different milestones in their lives. Amber paused at the wedding photo. An outdoor wedding under a gazebo. Libby looked so much younger in a very pretty gown. Well, she still looked good, but the sparkle was definitely gone from her eyes. Was this Dick's doing? Had the last twenty years been that good or just that bad? Her guess was that there hadn't been a lot of joy in Libby's life other than her children.

Amber wasn't a large fan of bananas, but the wonderful smelling bread was just out of the oven, so there was that. Maybe it would be slathered with butter. Butter was good.

"How do you like your coffee?"

Amber liked it with cream when she'd been Jane, but Amber was an Earth Muffin, she wanted to taste every antioxidant possible in the beans. Cream had to be organic, and she didn't want to appear to be an asshole by asking Libby for organic cream or half & half. She could go with sugar as long as it wasn't the white refined stuff which was the equivalent to poison, although the cake she took to the pool party had several cups of the stuff in it. And don't get her started on the frosting with the box of confectioners' sugar. She'd told everyone the cake was made with organic ingredients. What was one little white lie? Like anyone could tell!

"I take it black, thank you," Amber said and couldn't help but notice that Libby used Starbucks. That was cool. She obviously didn't have a problem with their pro-gay agenda that some of her old friends several seasons ago in Maryland had. That was Oregon for you. She was starting to like this state. And she had started drinking Starbucks instead of Peet's at her own house because she was with the pro-gay agenda... well, Amber was. To be real, Kelly and some of her other personas didn't really understand or care. She had larger issues to deal with. She liked the flavor of the coffee, end point.

"How do you like Mrs. Gibson's house?" Libby asked as she set plates, napkins, silverware, and, thank you goddess, butter on the retro art deco kitchen table with curved metal legs and chairs to match. It was too nice for Pioneer Pike. Libby had a lot more style than Amber had given her credit for. Glimmers of the real Libby shown through.

"You mean the shrine to Laura Ashley?" Amber asked with a laugh.

Libby chuckled, "Well, at least it is very clean, and the furniture is nice if not dated."

They talked about the colors and the patterns for a bit. Then Amber asked, "How long have you lived in the neighborhood?"

"This was Dick's family home. I've been coming here since we got married almost twenty years ago. But when his mother died shortly after his father, we moved in. I'd say it has been almost four years now."

Could she be mistaken, or was there a hint of sadness in Libby's voice?

""Did you live anywhere else?" Amber asked.

"Oh, well, wherever my family...my children are, is home. We were living in San Francisco...so...it has been an adjustment to come to this city, but it is a great place to raise the children. And it really made Dick happy."

Say it again, and you just might start believing it, Libby.

"Sure," Amber said. "So, I've heard about the benefits of raising children in Eugene. Supposed to be very good for them. Since I don't have children, I'll have to take your word for it. What did you do in San Francisco?"

"I worked for an ad agency as an account executive. They had me working on car accounts. It was very fun, but so is this. I love this life. I'm a stay-at-home mom, which is very rewarding. It is something I always wanted to do. And Eugene, well, it can be expensive, but it isn't as expensive as San Francisco. We can make it on one salary as long as I'm respectful of the budget. And it isn't like I need the clothes I once did. Heck, I can't remember the last time I went shopping at Nordstrom and charged a bunch of clothes and shoes on my Nordstrom card. Don't get me started on the makeup. Housewives, according to my husband, don't need makeup."

If a woman wanted makeup and wore it while she was home alone and saw no one, that was her prerogative, Amber thought. Same thing with perfume.

"What happens if you aren't respectful?" Amber asked, looking at the banana bread and thinking it was better than she thought it would be. It smelled wonderful and tasted better. She took a bite and savored the taste of the bread. Lots of vanilla, that was the key. If she felt the domestic pull of baking, and it was banana bread,she'd add vanilla to make it edible. It was the miracle flavoring. It totally masked the slimy bananas. She'd consider putting in tonka beans, but she didn't need the hassle that could come with too much tonka.

"I stay to the budget," Libby said with a proud nod, and Amber knew the consequences of coloring outside the lines must be very bad. She bet when Libby was in San Francisco her hair didn't have gray running through it and wasn't pulled back in a ponytail like it was now. And her nails probably weren't uneven and broken. This current, downtrodden look wouldn't fly in corporate America, especially for an account executive at an ad agency in San Francisco.

It was a warm day in the middle of September and the woman across from her was wearing a faded, long-sleeved blouse with a rather high collar and long jeans that were comfortably worn. Libby kept fussing with the collar as if there was something underneath it, something she was trying to hide. She was, of course. Amber had seen the signs before. But she needed confirmation.

Amber remembered back to the pool party. Libby had been wearing a rather dramatic geometric coverup that she never took off and she didn't get in the pool. She had said her skin didn't like the sun. That may be true, but she also knew that bruises didn't like publicity. Time to stir the pot and see what the temperature might be.

"I don't mean to be forward, but just how long has this been going on?" Amber asked her hand sweeping the air toward Libby. She didn't even need to say what it was. She pointed at Libby's sleeves with her index finger and then stared intently at Libby. It caught Libby off guard, or the mask had slipped because the dam had broken, and Libby was crumpling before her. Her face was a wax mask that had gotten too close to a flame. It was hard to witness, but necessary. Libby had real problems and they couldn't go on. However, as fast as she crumpled, she pulled it together. Now came the denial, but Amber was prepared.

Amber grabbed the other woman's hand not wanting to touch her arm and inadvertently squeeze a bruise.

"What do you mean?" Libby asked blinking, like an innocent doe facing down a hunter's rifle.

"You know, Libby, and I know too. It is okay to tell me. You're covering up the abuse you suffer at Dick's hands. I recognize the signs. I know how it feels, but not from a husband. Why do you think I'm single?" If Libby was in full denial, she'd protest and throw Amber out, but Libby had been through too much. But with those last words, she was curious about just what Amber had suffered.

"I...I...He doesn't mean it. I just get in the way and get too close to him when he is angry. I need to be more sensitive to his feelings. Dick is just having a hard time at work. It is a tough time," she sighed and tried to explain the unexplainable. "Well, he hates his job because he hasn't found the right fit yet. He's frustrated, and they are taking him for granted. He has only had the job at university for a few months, he can't get fired. We can't afford for him to get fired again. You see, it was expensive moving up here, and although we owned the house free and clear, we had to take out a mortgage a couple of years ago to make ends meet..."

When Amber only nodded, she continued.

"He's already had a couple of issues at work, so this is really serious. One more visit with HR about his attitude, and he is done. Those damn students have complained about him. They are making up stories. He's a statistics professor, which is his dream job after teaching high school. He doesn't engage with his students. He certainly doesn't ogle the girls or sexually harass them. They are just out to get him because the class is hard."

"Sure. Have you talked to any of the girls, or are you just taking his word for it?"

They looked at each other for several moments. As Amber predicted, Libby filled the empty space.

"No, they are just trying to get him in trouble."

"Because women lie about being harassed all the time? Men are the victims. He's the victim, right?"

"That isn't it. He probably intimidates them because they aren't used to someone who tells them like it is."

"Or maybe he has an anger issue that manifests itself badly, and they refuse to put up with what you do."

"He doesn't touch them. As for me, it is different. I'm his wife. He is always sorry when he loses his temper with me. I need to help him through the hard times, be there for him. I need to be his chief cheerleader. When I'm not, it makes it worse. This is just one of those times, and I haven't been there for him. Like last week, I was at Kate's soccer game. It isn't like she needed me at that game. She has one almost every other day—"

"So, just so I'm clear, he punished you for going to you daughter's game?"

"I should have been here for him. I wasn't. I give a lot of myself to the kids and sometimes there isn't enough left for him. They demand so much."

"Aw, that must be so hard for him. Being an adult. Being a parent."

"He came first. The children came after," she said, but Amber knew that Libby didn't even believe her own words.

Amber placed a finger to her lips, looked to the side, noticed the calendar hanging on the end of the cupboard. All the kids' events were marked.

"Let me guess, he likes to remind you that you are his wife first and their mother second?"

Libby faltered. "Well, I did marry him five years before the children came along. I wanted them, he didn't. I got what I wanted, he didn't. Now, they really take all of our time and resources."

It just kept getting better and better.

"He resents the children?" Amber asked.

"It's just that he gets easily frustrated by them."

"What does he do when he gets frustrated by work, the children, or you?"

"It doesn't happen that often. We are lucky to have Dick."

"Let me take a guess here, he takes out all this work frustration on you. Doesn't he? He can't physically abuse the students, but you aren't going to talk."

Libby shut her eyes, sighed. "I'm his partner."

"You're his punching bag," Amber said.

"No, no, nothing like that. It is just shoves. I'm here and I say something that upsets him. Sometimes, I lose my balance and fall. I need to learn to control myself, control what I say. I need to stop making him angry. If I could just monitor myself, if the children would just be quiet,—they are my responsibility after all—he wouldn't have to correct me."

"Okay, so what do the children see? Because you know they see more than they say they do. They aren't stupid."

Libby couldn't hold her gaze.

"I worry a little bit. Sometimes he shouts and calls me names. I hope they don't hear, but I think they do. And I don't want our son to grow up thinking it is okay to talk to women the way his father talks to me. My dad never talked that way to my mom, and I want my son to model that. But it isn't 100% of the time, just occasionally."

"Like what does he call you, occasionally?" Amber asked. "What was the last nasty thing he called you."

Libby hemmed and hawed. Finally, she spoke.

"'Stupid fucking bitch' was this morning, but he had an HR meeting, so he was in a bad mood. I can forgive him for that."

"Because that is okay to say to your partner, the mother of your children?" Amber asked.

"It isn't that big of a deal. It really doesn't bother me. The thing is, he's very smart and I'm not. Like the other day he said when he married me, he didn't know I was so obtuse and pejorative. I had no idea what he was saying. I had to look pejorative up in the dictionary. You see why he is frustrated with me?"

"If he ever said that to me, do you know what I'd say?" Amber asked, narrowing her eyes.

"No," Libby said, watching her intently.

"I'd tell him that girls like me only knew words like bastard and asshole because that is what he is."

"He doesn't mean to be and most of the time I can handle it, but he is starting to correct the children, a little more than I'd like. I don't like that. I don't want his focus to shift from me to them. That is my concern, really the only concern I have. Other than that, I can handle it. But I worry a little about the children."

"Leave him," Amber said. "I'll help you pack. I'll get the boxes and packing material from U-Haul. I'm free today and this is the best thing I can think of to do, let's get going. We have to be sure about it. Dick will react and you need to be safe when he does."

Amber knew this was swift, but something in Libby's demeanor made her feel like immediate action was necessary. Then oddly enough, something shifted in Libby's expression.

Libby laughed bitterly, which was better than the tears slowly leaking out of her eyes, which they had been. Maybe she was starting to understand that there was a problem here that wasn't going to go away and would most likely get worse.

"Where would I go? I don't have any money. My parents, well, it is complicated."

"My house is big, and you could stay there. Any place away from him."

"Don't you think I've tried to leave him?" Libby asked. Amber thought they were finally getting somewhere.

"Tell me about it," Amber prodded. "Because you are still here, living in this house, accepting this abuse, which is wrong."

"My own parents don't believe me. They love him and he pretends to be this wonderful, loving man when he is around them, but that switches the moment we get away from them. My son always says he wishes we could live at Pop-pop and

Memaw's. I know why he says it, his father is nicer to him when they are with strangers or my parents."

Amber shook her head but said nothing. This was much worse than she had imagined.

Libby continued; the unburdening must have felt good to her because she started to open up. "The moment we are alone he tells me how much of a disappointment I am to him, how I make him look bad. I spoil the children. Coddle them. The thing is, I don't know what to say anymore. Everything is wrong."

"The house, all our bank accounts, they are all in his name. He gives me a weekly cash allowance, but he pays all the bills. I don't even have my name on the checks or the credit cards. When we moved here, he forced me to give him my credit cards. I thought about getting a post office box and reordering them, but how would I pay for any of it? The weekly cash budget barely covers the food. And if he found out, well, I can't think of it. Do you know how long I have to plan to have people over or Christmas dinner? It is horrible.

"You know it wasn't like this in the beginning. He swept me off my feet. We had a big, beautiful wedding. It was so perfect. Well, on our honeymoon, I ordered something that was expensive, but I didn't like it, so I didn't eat it. He told me I was stupid, but a few less calories would probably be good for me. He'd like a wife who could rock a bikini, but he was pretty sure that wasn't me. I remember I cried, but I tried to forget it, but I never could quite forget how it affected the honeymoon. Now, he weighs me once a week. I stay to a certain weight, or I go a day or two without food."

It was so much worse than Amber thought.

"And your daughter?"

"He said he wants to start weighing her next year. I don't know how I feel about that."

"Yes, you do," Amber said thinking of the too-thin daughter, Katie.

"I don't want her to feel bad about herself. I don't know how he can weigh her and have her not feel self-conscious."

Libby was so thin that Amber could see the edges of her bones sticking out on her wrists.

"Don't lose your daughter over this."

"She is very sensitive," Libby said.

"And what about your son, Jeffrey? Do you want him to treat a girlfriend or wife like this someday?"

"Of course not."

"And I don't blame Katie for being sensitive. Are you going to let him shove you until you fall and crack your head open on a table corner? Or maybe he'll start using his fists. That is what abusers do. It starts with verbal insults, leads to shoves, then punches, and then death. It's called Battered Wife's Syndrome. Of course that is my simplified explanation from conducting google searches, but it seems to fit."

"He'd never kill me. He loves me."

"But, if something happens to you, then he'd raise your kids. Do you think that anger will just go away, or will he find a way to transfer it to your children? What happens when he has to cook all the meals and do the laundry? Or will he make the children do it? Will he start calling them names, then start shoving them when the insults are no longer enough? What if your daughter hits the corner of the table and it takes out her eye? Or scars her for life? Because he might not want to kill you, but accidents happen."

"He'd better not lay a finger on my children. I don't let him discipline them, as much as I can control it. They know not to anger him."

"What are you going to do about it? If you are dead, you won't be here to protect them."

"But...but...I can't...I...What can I do?" she cried.

"I can help you. I can get him out of your life permanently, but we will need to trust each other. You need to be sure," Amber said.

A quiet calm came over Libby.

She met Amber's gaze and asked, "Permanently?"

"Yes."

"I'm listening."

CHAPTER SIX

Amber sighed. It was too early in the season for such action, but what was she to do? This was an immediate problem, and she didn't think they had until next spring. Libby might be dead by then. She'd be damned if that happened on her watch. So she was breaking the rules for Libby and her children. She didn't feel bad about it, on the contrary. She was resolved, but it was risky. Very risky, and she didn't like having a partner in crime. She was used to working alone. Libby would be a loose end, but her children needed her. There had to be trust.

Okay, was that really bothering her? Having this secret with another person? Yes. It was exposure and not the kind she liked. A partner meant that someone else knew her secret. Well, this one secret, but she'd probably figure out what was going on with any other dire happenings that would no doubt happen this season in the hood. Maybe it would only be Libby's husband this season. Libby wouldn't know the entire history of Amber's life. No one but the woman going by Amber knew the history, and it was going to stay that way.

She shook her head as she donned an apron.

And selfishly, here she was going to all this effort, and she didn't get to try any of the marmalade she was making to take care of the Dick problem. How was that fair? Oh well, at least Dick would get to try it, and wasn't that what this was really about? Taking care of Dick for Libby and the kids? Well, silencing Dick. Handling Dick…Thank goodness Libby said her children hated marmalade and that is why she always had a large supply of strawberry jam for them. Besides, they had cereal for breakfast not toast with marmalade. That was Dick's thing. Yet, Libby had promised to be careful, and Amber was happy about that promise. She was only going to put out the marmalade when the kids were away visiting their grandparents, which they were for another week before they came home and started school. She said Dick was much worse to her when the kids were away even though he had an issue with their presence in his life every day.

Last summer when the kids were at their grandparents, he had almost killed her. So the race was on; who would kill whom first? Her money was on Libby, but still she worried each evening for Libby since their conversation three days go. Amber only hoped Dick wasn't hurting her. She'd seen the bruises. She'd needed proof, and Libby had shown her after their very bare-bones, honest conversation. And the photographs, my gawd, they were horrific. Amber would have taken them to the police and Dick would be sitting in a jail cell waiting for his prison sentence to kick in, but that isn't how Libby handled it or wanted to handle it.

Amber took a moment and took stock.

They had a secret...But it was for a good reason. Libby had once confided to her mother, but the woman had accused her own daughter of overreacting. That is the interesting thing about battered wives, they rarely overreact. They often went to great measures to hide how bad it was. They wanted to keep the peace, and the occasional beating seemed like a small price to pay. Only in this case, the abuse was escalating. So, what could Amber conclude? Libby knew how to keep big secrets.

Amber got out her big, cheap pot from Walmart, a pot she would throw away after this. She had already found a dumpster behind a mini strip mall that didn't have a lock, nor were there security cameras. *Rubes.* When you offered no security, people took advantage of you. Like Amber was going to do. Live and learn, stupid Pollyannas.

She washed and rubbed five oranges until she knew they were clean and dry. She added a couple of lemons. The tartness of the marmalade was perfect for what she had in mind. It would mask another, less benevolent bitterness.

Carefully, she used her mandolin to cut the oranges and one of the lemons into perfect 1/8 of an inch slices. Then she cut them into quarters. She added the sugar, water, a dash of cinnamon, and the zest of another lemon and one of the oranges. She added the fruit to the pot and cooked it low and slow for forty minutes. This was going to be some damn good marmalade.

While it cooked, she put on plastic gloves, an N95 mask, and removed twenty bright yellow seeds from their squishy red bell-shaped berries of the yew bush that she had harvested on one of her walks in the adjacent neighborhood yesterday. It was so easy. The bush was hanging out over the sidewalk and dripping with berries. She had planned to find a yew bush, put on dark clothes and harvest the berries at night. If she couldn't find one, she'd use her dried berries, but there had been no need. The berries were in a secluded location, and it was easy to get them. Still, she wore a baseball cap and dark glasses with her U of O duck apparel which had already been donated to Goodwill last night. Once she had dried the seeds and put them in her mortar and pestle, she discarded pinkish red flesh that had surrounded them down the garbage disposal.

Two minutes later, the seeds were smashed into a fine, deadly pulp.

She pulled one of the jars aside, put a black X with a permanent marker on the bottom. She put the yew seed pulp inside the jar, added the hot marmalade with a ladle, and stirred the contents until it all blended with a wooden tongue depressor she threw away. It helped that the berries were bright yellow, blending with the cooked oranges and lemon perfectly. The grains of cinnamon and the zest of the lemon and orange helped to mask the grains of crushed yew seeds.

Then she finished the rest of the jars and placed them all in her pressure cooker and followed the directions to make the marmalade.

When everything was cooled and had been sitting at room temperature for the appointed time, she added labels to the jars. She placed all but two of the jars in her pantry.

Then, she took everything—the freshly cleaned pot, the ladle, the wooden stick, the mortar and pestle, her discarded gloves, mask—and purposefully put them all into two garbage bags to split up the evidence. Then, glancing outside to make sure no one was watching or walking by the house, she did what she had rehearsed. The bags went in the trunk of the Volvo. The day before she had googled how to disable her GPS tracker on the car with a cheap laptop she'd purchased in Corvallis, fifty miles away. Then she'd disabled the GPS and destroyed the laptop with a large hammer. Pieces of it went in the bags as well, but not all of it. She didn't want anyone who found the bags to be able to piece together any part of the computer.

By the time she finished, it was close to nine o'clock, and the sky had darkened sufficiently. This time she wore black and tied her hair up into a black baseball cap.

Leaving her cell phone on the counter so she wouldn't be tracked by a well-meaning cell tower, she left her house, and she drove to the quiet strip mall. She parked a street away. Casually, she removed the first bag, walked down the street, noticing that no one passed, and tossed the bag in the desolate dumpster as if she'd been doing it her whole life. Then, just to be on the safe side, she drove to the little town of Coburg, fifteen miles away and did the same thing with the other bag. At last, she stopped at Fred Meyer, took off her cap, fluffed her red hair, added a bright red sweater, some silver jewelry, added a dash of sweetly annoying patchouli perfume that wouldn't easily be forgotten and picked up some things she needed like tampons and ice cream. She could plead PMS if questioned, and no policeman really wanted to question a menstruating woman. But if the sweater, hair, and jewelry ended up on a security camera, so what? It created her alibi for late night cruising in the silver Volvo. When you needed tampons, you needed tampons.

The next morning, she called Libby. "Hello, it is your neighbor, Amber."

"Well, hello neighbor Amber. I'm sorry, I can't talk long, I'm running to the pharmacy. Dick isn't feeling well so I'm picking him up something for his tummy and well, his bathroom issues."

"Oh no, is he okay? Is it food poisoning or the flu?"

"We don't think so. Well, you know Valerie, she is a nurse practitioner and is pretty sure Dick has Crohn's Disease, but Dick refuses to believe Valerie or go to the doctor. So I'm treating him as best as I can."

Valerie was key to this story. Lucky for Libby and Amber, Valerie had come to the conclusion they wanted her to come to. Untreated and severe Crohn's. This is where luck came into their story. Valerie had almost come to this conclusion on her own, but they had given her all the clues to make this amateur diagnosis.

"Oh, I'm sorry. I just wanted to tell you that I made some muffins, and I'm going to leave them on your front porch. Do you think Dick can eat any?" She would also be leaving the marmalade.

"How kind of you! Dick's appetite is strong. It is just that sometimes the food doesn't agree with him."

Libby continued, "The poor guy has had stomach issues for several days. He is doing better, but he's losing a bunch of weight, and I'm getting a little tired of arguing with him about going to the doctor. He has a history of gastric issues, so this is nothing new. As I mentioned, Valerie really thinks he has Crohn's. I don't think she is wrong, but Dick refused to hear it."

Dick was having stomach issues, or what they would come to think of as an "episode" this time because Libby was putting rhubarb greens in everything she could think of to slowly make Dick mildly sick. She was backing off a bit so Dick would eat a muffin. With any luck, the marmalade would finish him off.

"I'm so sorry he is going through that. I love to bake, and muffins are the equivalent of homemade chicken soup. I hope he likes them." She was leaving muffins on several doorsteps that day, but marmalade on only one.

They had prearranged it. Libby would get two jars. She would look for the X. Serve that marmalade to her husband. When something happened, she would get rid of the jar with the X. That was one of the weaknesses in the plan.

Libby had to get rid of the tainted marmalade jar thoroughly and quickly. Libby confided to Amber, she had found her own dumpster, unwatched, far away. She would scoop out a few spoonfuls from the second jar, the untainted jar, and wash them down the garbage disposal to make it appear that Dick was getting his marmalade from that jar. Libby had been lectured thoroughly about cross contamination.

Amber told her if there was any timing issue whatsoever to let her know and she would take care of the disposal of the marmalade jar. Heck, flushing the contents down the toilet if it came to that. Amber knew from experience with her favorite toxic plant that one heavy dollop of marmalade should do it.

Gingie

Gingie smiled to herself. She was practically trembling. Tonight, she would have her fifth date with Kent. It had been a long time since she'd felt like this. What was the feeling? Giddy? Butterflies? Stupid? Crazy? She was half sick with anticipation. Food held no interest. Sleep was nearly impossible. Had she felt this way with either of her ex-husbands? No, Kent was different. He had to be the best kisser she'd ever kissed. She felt it in her toes. Hell, her whole body throbbed when he merely touched her.

But they were taking it slow. Why? Because the idiot that she was, she had suggested it. She didn't want to ruin it. She might die or implode, but she wouldn't ruin her relationship. And they were having a relationship. They had agreed they didn't want to meet anyone else. They just wanted to see each other. They were exclusive. And they weren't even having sex. What did that tell her? Either Kent was a good liar, or he really liked her too. Since she'd seen him every day since the pool party, even if he just stopped in her office to say hello, she liked to think he was a bit smitten with her too.

Now, all Gingie could think about was the sex she wasn't having and hoped to have. It had been a while. Heck, a few weeks ago, she wasn't sure she'd ever have sex again. What had she learned? Events and circumstances can change on a dime. She was imagining a life without sex, coming to terms with it. Now, it was back in the realm of possibilities. It was all she could think about. *Morning coffee*, touching caresses. She bet Kent liked to spoon after sex. He'd probably spoon her all night. He was protective like that. And she was glad she only had a queen-sized bed. If it was a king, well, she could lose him because of all the surface space.

At lunch with co-workers. They were talking about something. She didn't care. She was having fantasies about Kent in the shower. *Dinner.* Who ate dinner? Who ate at all? She had no appetite. But if Kent fed her anything, she'd eat it. Even cilantro. She'd eat cilantro for Kent, and she hated cilantro. Damn, maybe it was love.

The doorbell interrupted her thoughts. What if Kent had come to surprise her? What if he couldn't handle their relationship and needed a break? Would he just stop by? She took a deep breath. She was getting paranoid. Pretty soon she'd be a shut-in fantasizing about Kent all day instead of going to the office and trying to sell some damn houses. Thankfully, Kent liked to visit her daily at the office, two p.m. on the dot just to say hi. It wasn't a big deal, but it got her to the office each day. It also got her to make sure she didn't have any conflicts at two p.m.

Glancing through the peephole, she saw that her new neighbor, Amber, waited on the other side of the door. She liked Amber and needed a distraction badly.

Pulling the door open she smiled at the other woman and said, "Hey Amber, how are you?"

"I'm good, and I've been baking. Would you like some muffins? I made some honey butter streusel muffins early this morning. They are also called sweet muffins. They were my Aunt Betty's favorite."

"How sweet of you!"

"I've just been walking up and down the street letting the neighbors know how welcome I've been made to feel. Thank you for being so great to me."

"You make it easy. Would you like to come in for a bit? I could make some coffee and we could sample some of these."

"Oh no, thank you, but I think I've eaten three today, which I've got to tell you is my limit!" Amber said with a laugh. "Share them with that handsome man of yours."

Gingie couldn't help it, she smiled, and her cheeks felt hot all of the sudden.

"I thought so," Amber said.

"You know, who knows? It's a new thing, but I really like him."

"I think the feeling is mutual. I like the way he looks at you," Amber said.

"I do too," Gingie said with a sly smile.

"Well, enjoy with Mr. Gorgeous," Amber said with a bright smile.

"Do you just like to eat these as they are, or do you put jam on them?" Gingie asked, smelling the freshly baked muffins and deciding that maybe she had an appetite after all. "I mean what is the optimal way to enjoy them?"

"I like them with jam, berry or something. You know Libby's husband has some sort of bug, but she said he perked up when she served him a muffin."

"Poor Dick, I know he's had stomach issues in the past but won't go to the doctor. Poor Libby is frustrated beyond belief."

"I know, poor lady," Amber said. "She must feel really helpless that he won't do anything to get better."

"You know, sometimes when someone else makes a treat you don't usually have, it really can perk you up. I hope that is what your muffins did for Dick."

"Me too," Amber said.

CHAPTER SEVEN

Sunday morning had a little chill in the air that indicated to Amber that fall was on its way, and summer was being shown the door. Good. Amber didn't like the sun or the heat. Not with her fair skin. It didn't matter how much sunscreen she wore, it never worked, and she always burned—or worse, she freckled, which for a woman in her thirties wasn't cute.

When she'd been a little girl growing up in Las Vegas, freckles upset her mother, Old Jen. When she was between husbands, they were mentioned and examined on a daily basis. The girl then known as Kelly was forbidden to play outside in the sun. Ride her bike? No way. Playing Barbies on a camping adventure in the desert sun? Not going to happen.

Amber liked the change of seasons. She liked living in a community with trees that showed fall color. Heck, fall was her favorite season. When the world died and you mourned, then in spring it was reborn again, like her favorite Greek Myth, the story of Demeter and Persephone, which explained the seasons.

Her mother wasn't sure who Kelly's birth father was, but she knew he'd given their daughter freckles. Freckles would never dare touch her mother's skin. But nether region rashes that were no doubt a result of a random night of debauchery or whomever was Daddy-of-the-moment, well, they were to be expected, and cured with a simple shot of penicillin. But freckles, they were the end of your existence because they equated to no future. You couldn't be a model or a performer with freckles

73

unless you were dressed as a naughty schoolgirl with a plaid skirt and bobby socks to go with your patent leather Mary Jane's. Men liked women dressed as schoolgirls. No, in Old Jen's mind smallpox scars would have been more welcome than freckles.

Now that Amber was an adult and had tried to forget about freckles, she worried about skin cancer or just looking leathery when she was in her seventies. Thank goodness she'd gone to Zoom Care last week and gotten more Retin-A. It is important to take care of your body. And your skin, well, it is the largest organ in the body. A lovely side effect she had learned, Retin-A and a few plant secretions totally faded her freckles. Next time she visited Old Jen, which she thought she might do at the end of this season, well, she couldn't wait to show her the results. Not that Old Jen would be satisfied, but it would give her one less thing to complain about.

She wondered how much Retin-A Julia Glass used? She must go through a gallon a month.

It was almost noon, and despite the chill, Amber wore her Goodwill hat as she deadheaded three of the red rose bushes in Mrs. Gibson's front yard. You had to protect the skin of your face however you could! Besides, with the Retin-A, she had to be extra careful. She could burn faster, or worse.

She was proud of herself for being proactive. Harvesting the rose petals was a good idea. She could add them to tea, and other things. Of course, she could spray them with Roundup first or Crossbow, but a toxicology report would find that remnant quickly. Best to let them stay in their natural form. They added something to tea or potpourri, really anything Amber hoped to make because people recognized rose, and it added instant trust and credibility. Maybe she'd grind the dried petals into powder and add them to lotion. They should turn the white Jergens stuff to a lovely shade of pink. She could add some rose essence or oil. What a great idea for Valentine's Day!

She hoped the neighbor ladies would love it! Amber thought this was the most creative cover story she'd had yet. She'd been a financial planner, a celebrity chef on a yacht who needed a break and was between jobs, a manager at Starbucks who was planning to open her own coffee shop, and a newly divorced woman getting a degree from the community college in a new town away from her old life.

The muffins had gone over well yesterday. She hoped all the neighbors enjoyed them. She couldn't eat a bite and forget about the marmalade. Even the good stuff, the non-poison filled jars in her pantry, would be disposed of as quickly as possible. The very thought had her stepping away from her pantry. She'd stick to Smuckers, thank you very much. Concord jelly. Not that concord was her favorite, but it didn't have little bits of toxin floating around in it. And it was commercially produced. Yeah, better. This fear of her own products was something new. She hoped it wasn't some kind of paranoia. It wasn't like she could go to a therapist and explain she was scared to eat any item she had once poisoned for someone else. The whole doctor-client privilege would go out the window. And any window she might get from that point on might have bars on it.

This season, well, it was starting off so strangely. Something about Pioneer Pike was unforgettable. She liked the place so that wasn't it. She only hoped that Libby was now safe. This was the hard part. Waiting for news.

Maybe she should take a season off. But then what would she do? Get a cat, buy a sofa, subscribe to People magazine, and join Tinder? She wasn't meant for domesticity, baby. She had known that from a very early age that life had a special calling for her. At about the same time she decided that having her stepfather of the moment come on to her was sick and twisted. Her life had been an adventure since she took her first breath. When she'd left Vegas at just shy of eighteen, had Old Jen cared? Not really. She'd given her five hundred dollars and a small can of mace for the big, bad world. Then she gave her some unwanted advice, "If you find a rich one, fuck him, and act like you like it."

Old Jen wasn't making the finals for Mother of the Year anytime soon. But Amber had morphed that advice. She had some nice photos of the Bacons-in-Process in very compromising positions. The photos were in two safe deposit boxes in small banks—one in Winnemucca, Nevada, and one in Cincinnati, Ohio for safe keeping. Had she used sex as a weapon? A little bit, but not like her mother. A few times, she got something out of it, but really they shouldn't have been messing around with her.

And after her little vacation to Saint Barts last January during the Jane season, she didn't use men for sex anymore. Not after Jack. Yeah, she'd had sex for pleasure because she'd fallen for someone. She wasn't proud of it or her vulnerability. It had only lasted a week, but she didn't want to get any new Bacons-in-Process. Her body was off limits. It had been nine months. She should be over it. Over Jack. Yeah, sometimes her thoughts drifted to him, but that was only normal. Sadly, he wasn't for her. Not in this lifetime. Not the way she was, not who she was. If she'd told him...well, she wasn't the woman for him. But when she thought of picket fences and babies, he was the only man that could elicit such feelings.

Amber snipped the head of a black baccara rose off and placed the blossom in her basket just as the first sirens became recognizable. My goodness, they were getting louder. Were they coming to Pioneer Pike? No way. Was everyone okay?

She smiled secretly to herself. Took long enough. A moment later, the ambulance, followed by a fire engine banked around the corner and onto Pioneer Pike. She set down her basket when the vehicles came to a screeching halt in front of Libby and Dick's house.

Other neighbors came out of their houses and looked

around, congregating on the sidewalks with stunned expressions on their faces.

Amber made eye contact with Gingie across the street, and they crossed the distance to each other.

"Oh my god, it must be Dick," Gingie said, her hand going to her mouth.

"His stomach issues?" Amber said as she shook her head. "I didn't know they were that bad. I wonder if Libby decided he needed to go to the hospital?"

But then Libby stepped outside and dropped on all fours to the lawn, her face a mask of misery as she rolled onto her side, a picture of grief. Amber loved the acting. This woman had talent.

"Come on," Amber said, "She needs us."

They walked quickly to what had been Dick and Libby's house. Libby was crying so loudly, Amber would have called it screeching, but whatever worked in the moment. Her reaction was epically good, almost real but that couldn't be. Amber was the first to admit, she had underestimated the woman. Maybe she had loved the abusive piece of shit.

They stood at the edge of her lawn and watched the writhing woman. Gingie was the first to step in to help. Hell, Amber had only known Libby for a couple of weeks. Amber really didn't do emotions anyway. That wasn't her job, and it wouldn't be anytime soon. She listened as Gingie first reassured Libby and then held her, both women on the lawn, one offering comfort and the other taking it. How sweet was that? Gingie should have been a mother. Amber knew she'd never be a mother, but damn, you couldn't learn that kind of compassion. You were born with it. And then you passed it on to your kids. Her thoughts flashed to Jack. She doubted he'd want a murderess for the mother of his children.

Gingie

Libby was shaking, crying, and everywhere that Gingie tried to touch her, seemed to make her recoil as if she were burned. My god, what had happened? Something bad. Was it Dick? It had to be Dick. Hadn't she heard he was sick? Yes, but no one thought he was *this* sick.

Gingie could admit that she had never particularly warmed to the man who never saw boobs on a woman he didn't ogle with his cold icy blue eyes that seemed to glow. She had always worried about Libby and her marriage. He seemed too edgy, always a bit sarcastic. She didn't like sarcastic men, and she had wondered secretly if he was abusive to Libby. Her bet was that he had been.

Did Libby shoot him or something? She wasn't sure she could blame the woman, but she couldn't ask. Because if Libby confessed, Gingie would have to be a witness. And she couldn't say killing Dick wasn't justified.

"I promise, whatever happens, I'm here for you," Gingie said in calming, clear tones. She wanted Libby to know that she was an oasis, not judgmental in case some confession did pop out. Libby didn't have a gun, and she wasn't covered in blood. That was good, right? "Did something happen to Dick?"

"He…he's dead," Libby said through chattering teeth. "I found him a few minutes ago. He was alive this morning, but had terrible pain and wouldn't let me call for help. I went in and he was asleep I thought, but he wasn't. He was dead. It must have happened when I took a shower, but I only took twenty minutes. What happened to him? And the sheets had all this blood…"

Damn, Gingie thought. Blood. Gross. She bet there were some other bodily fluids as well.

People in uniforms started swarming in and out of Libby's house, and then they noticed the emotional puddle that was Libby.

Someone joined their little huddle. Gingie looked up and met

Kent's gaze. He was in his uniform, looking official and damn sexy. This was his beat, so it wasn't a surprise that he should show up. His presence made her feel better and warmer.

"Hey," she said and met his serious face.

He nodded and said, "Hey."

Reaching out, he touched Libby's shoulder. Then he said, "Libby, it is Kent Logan. I'm a policeman. I met you last week at the Glass's pool party. I'm so sorry for your loss. Do you feel up to talking about it? I'd like to know what happened."

Libby sobbed and then nodded. Kent helped her up and they walked back into the house, Kent giving Gingie a look that was part apology and part a lot of sympathy from over his shoulder. She nodded; she understood.

Gingie rejoined Amber on the sidewalk along with the other neighbors, Valerie and Jim, Julia and Dan, and Shelby and Clint.

"What did she say?" Valerie asked.

"She said that Dick is dead, and there was a lot of blood, but I don't know how or any of the details except that she found him that way. He'd been okay this morning. Well, I think she said he was alive this morning. I don't know if he was okay."

"You don't think she is a suspect, do you?" Amber asked. "She didn't...no..."

"Not Libby," Gingie replied. "She loved him."

"She is the sweetest person. In fact, this sounds horrible, especially now, but I never warmed up to Dick," Shelby said.

"Same," Valerie admitted. "I thought he had a rabid case of undiagnosed Crohn's. I've never met someone so stubborn, and look what it cost him? Poor Libby. And the kids. This is so awful. What will she do now?"

"There was something about him," Gingie admitted. "It doesn't surprise me that he wouldn't listen to you or go to see a doctor. He was stubborn, and if it wasn't his idea, it wasn't an idea worth having. And if it came from a woman, forget it."

"He liked the ladies to be pretty and quiet. He told me he

liked women who knew their place," Jim said. "I didn't like the way he ogled Valerie whenever she had something on that displayed cleavage. More than once, Valerie talked me out of having a word with him. Then she tried to help him while he was sick, against my better judgement. Did he listen to her? No. What a jerk!"

"Don't talk like that. He's dead," Valerie said. "Let's not get too specific about your feelings. He's dead now, and he didn't have to die. He should have gotten medical attention but chose not to. Now, those kids won't have their dad at their weddings, and every important moment of their lives. It is a waste and so, so sad for Libby."

"He hit on me one time. I told Clint, and it was all I could do to keep him from marching over to their house and flattening him," Shelby said. "Remember honey?"

"Oh, I remember."

"See there? I'm not sure it was a big loss for Libby," Jim said.

"Jim, shut the hell up," Valerie warned.

"We are all thinking it," Clint said.

"Well, I wasn't," Julia said, finally joining in on the conversation. "I thought he was a very nice man."

"That's only because you have the tightest ass of any of the women in the hood," Dan quipped, then smiled at his wife.

Dan was an ass.

Tough crowd, Gingie thought. The man was barely dead, and everyone was talking about what a jerk he was except a bigger jerk, Dan. Gingie decided not to add her personal observations, which would only confirm her neighbors' thoughts and comments.

Poor Amber was taking all of this in, seeing the worst of her new neighbors. It was embarrassing.

They stood outside for a long time. The medical examiner arrived in a black station wagon with "Medical Examiner" on the side of the car. He had walked in, and they were still there on the corner when he left and an hour later. Gingie wondered what that guy's wife was like. She saw his gold wedding ring. He cut up people all day, washed his hands, went home, and told his wife about his day. Then he crawled in bed and made love to her. Yuck. There wasn't enough Purell in the world to clean that guy's hands. She supposed that Kent's hands got dirty on occasion, and she didn't mind. But she didn't want any of the details.

A second crew of people who looked to be associated with the medical examiner wheeled in the gurney through the front door by. A few minutes later, a black shrouded body was wheeled out. So that was what a body bag looked like; Gingie had never seen one before. She hoped to never see one again.

She put an arm around Amber and said, "I'm sorry you are witnessing this. It has been a long time since any of our neighbors died. I think it had to be Mr. Gibson, and that was three years ago. He was in a hospital."

Amber smiled sadly, and said, "Death happens. I just hope Libby will be okay."

CHAPTER EIGHT

God, she hated black. It was so somber and washed her out when she already looked downtrodden. Amber looked in the mirror of her Laura Ashley bedroom. She had on a very tasteful Eileen Fisher dress with a tie in the front. That was, in fact, its only embellishment. Yeah, it looked a little stylish for her hippie persona, but she didn't want to stand out with her patchouli scent and over the top ensemble on such a somber day. She wanted to blend into the background and make sure everyone who was important agreed: Dick died of acute side effects related to Crohn's.

After all, the children had lost a father, although she hoped Libby would marry again and get them a better one. And for the occasion, Amber had purchased a black straw hat at a second-hand shop. It seemed appropriate for Dick's memorial service. It wasn't that she had to go to the service, but all the neighbors were going, and there would be supper at Libby's house afterward. She had to make an appearance. See and be seen, as it were.

Amber made her now famous Aunt Betty's chocolate cake and dropped it off the afternoon before with Aunt Betty's milk glass cake stand. For the somberness of the occasion, she left off the rainbow sparkles. She had added chocolate sprinkles. They were more serious yet still finished off the cake nicely. She concluded that they were appropriate and yet still fun. She told

Libby the kids should sample the cake to make sure it was okay. She hoped they had.

Amber was glad she'd been able to check on Libby and the kids when she dropped off the cake. She didn't know what to expect, but the kids were doing okay. They had cut short their visit to their grandparents when they found out their dad had died. Amber was able to meet Libby's clueless parents who had brought the children home. The heaviness she'd felt when she visited Libby and had banana bread wasn't there. Everyone seemed more relaxed. Maybe it was her imagination, but she didn't think so. The dragon had been slayed. Happiness rang through the kingdom. Balance had been restored.

Libby greeted her with a hug as she took the cake plate from her.

Libby confided that they were getting a black Labrador puppy in a week or two. Dick had hated dogs, actually all pets were hated with a passion. She had told Amber earlier that he thought they were filthy and belonged outside. A Siamese cat, Shakey, that Libby had gotten in college, had died mysteriously at the beginning of their marriage and Libby thought it best not to have any other animals around Dick despite how much the children wanted one. She hadn't said he was responsible, but it was implied.

The kids were excited about the prospect of getting a puppy and wanted to tell Amber all about it.

"We are getting a boy dog and naming him Larry," Katie told her proudly.

"I love the name. Congratulations," she had said. The naming conversation had supposedly happened the day before and had been a great distraction from trying to understand what the death of their father meant to them.

Amber was going to stop at Petco and buy a bunch of stuff for Larry, puppy toys and organic treats. She liked this kind of thing and thought it was a great idea. She was a softy for animals after all. Someday she wanted to have a dog. She'd get a little girl and name her Hemlock or Hemmie for short, maybe Lily.

Libby pulled her aside and told her the police and the medical examiner had determined that Dick died of natural causes, undiagnosed Crohn's based on the symptoms and the information Valerie shared. But if Libby wanted an autopsy, they would do it. Libby didn't want to think of it, cried at the very mention of it, and they had respected her wishes. She'd had Dick cremated as soon as they released the body to the mortuary.

Amber wanted to pop a bottle of champagne right then, but instead she said the appropriate, somber things, especially to Libby's naïve parents who seemed to have adored their daughter's torturer and seemed to be watching her closely.

A successful execution called for a celebration, but she had learned to delay this kind of gratification to a later date, when time had passed, and a celebration was socially acceptable. Maybe that is why people had wakes. Too bad Libby hadn't had one. Amber would buy the Moet anyway and stick it in the back of her fridge along with a box of Godiva chocolate, which she would enjoy piece by piece whenever she thought about it.

The afternoon she delivered the cake, Amber got a box from Breck's Bulbs covered in immigration stickers since it originated in Holland. This package contained daffodil, tulip, ranunculus, crocus, and lily of the valley bulbs in all shapes and sizes. She held up the daffodil bulb, thought of how they looked like baby onions, and felt a memory of pain so intense she set the bulb back down.

When she had left Las Vegas at seventeen, she bought a bus ticket and ended up in Seattle working as a barista at a corner coffee shop, a job she'd found by chance when she'd stopped in the coffee shop and inquired about the help wanted sign in the window. Helga was the manager and needed a roommate too.

Kelly told everyone she was eighteen and they believed her. It all worked out perfectly. They got along famously, and she still thought of Helga, wondering how she was doing. Back then, the girl known as Kelly had dreams of attending business classes at the local community college after she got her GED. But at the moment it was just good to be normal and to let the memories of Las Vegas, Old Jen, and the step daddies roll off her like water off a duck's back.

It was a time of ramen noodles and lots of tuna fish eaten over the kitchen sink. She purchased clothing at Goodwill. But she was more than a little happy she had the money for rent and enough food to not starve. It was a great time of her life. Within a few weeks she was part of the coffee shop gang and had a gaggle of new friends.

"Hey Kel, we are having a potluck at Paul's on Saturday. You've got to come," Helga said as Paul looked frustrated and rolled his eyes. Amber remembered the interaction as if it were yesterday.

"Hey, I just hadn't gotten around to inviting her yet," Paul interrupted, swatting Helga with a semi-clean towel they used on the frothing wand between lattes. "Please come, Kel. I was hoping you could."

"I'd love to come. What can I bring?" she asked.

"I'm making this mushroom soup that my mom always makes. I'm vegetarian, so I won't be making us all Beef Wellington or anything."

"That's cool. Can I bring bread or salad?" she asked.

"Wine, please!" he said. "I have a couple of bottles, but we will need more. Helga just wants to bring a salad," he added, as if salad were liver or snout.

"I can't buy it. I'm eighteen. I'll bring bread," she said.

That Saturday night, Kelly rode with Helga, holding her artisan bread, glancing at Helga's salad, and wondering how the night would end. She kind of liked Paul. She had a feeling that he kind of liked her too.

When they got to his apartment, a slightly dilapidated space similar to what she shared with Helga, the scent of his mushroom soup filled the air and made her mouth water. Kelly's mother didn't cook. Having anything homemade was a treat. It shouldn't be, this was what normal families did every day. Just not her family.

There were six of them, three couples as it would turn out. Two more guys, Ron and Marvin. Marvin, the one who grabbed Helga and kissed her deeply. That is what she remembered, that crazy kiss that happened so easily in front of her. Ron had a flower muffin girlfriend who wasn't just vegetarian but was vegan, which was why Paul used coconut milk to thicken the soup. It became evident quickly that Kelly was Paul's date, and that was okay.

"This is so good," she said as she tried the soup. It really was amazing.

"I picked the mushrooms this morning, so they are fresh," Paul admitted.

Amber, who was then Kelly, remembers being taken aback by the statement. "These didn't come from a store? Where did you go?"

"No way, I like to forage. There is this kinda wooded forest just about thirty miles south of Seattle. They have the most amazing mushrooms."

"I would worry. Do you ever worry that you are picking poisonous mushrooms?" If he didn't, he should, and she knew that now she was concerned. She'd eaten all of her soup.

"No, I know what I'm doing," he said with confidence he should not have felt. "I even went to my parents and got some garlic and onions from their garden. So this soup is mega organic and basically didn't cost anything. This is the way we curb hunger for the whole world. Living off the land. I've been thinking of starting a website or something."

There was a saying she had once heard credited to a wise person. *There are bold mushroom hunters and there are old mushroom hunters, but there are no old, bold mushroom hunters.*

She wasn't crazy about liberal men who wanted to curb hunger for the world, but she needed to try something different. That is why she had moved to Seattle. So she went with it.

Paul had kissed her that night, wanted her to stay. Helga begged off to stay with Marvin at his place, but Kelly, who was no virgin, didn't feel she knew Paul well enough to jump into an intimate relationship with him.

The stomach cramps started as soon as she got back to her apartment. When she started vomiting and thought her throat was closing up while her insides were fighting to stay in her body, she called 9-1-1.

Amber recognized a few of her dinner companions at the closest hospital. Paul, Helga, and Marvin were all there in various states of distress. *Fucking mushrooms. Fucking Paul.*

"So I understand you had dinner at Paul's," the ER doctor said with a sardonic smile.

"Is it the mushrooms?" she asked. "He likes to forage, the bastard. Thinks it is a way to feed the world."

"I don't think the world needs to be poisoned. And surprisingly it wasn't the mushrooms," he said. "Your friend Paul, who you I believe refer to as the bastard was trying to serve you onions from his parents' garden, he served you daffodil bulbs. Probably only one or two or you'd be much sicker. Before he feeds the world, he needs to learn what they can eat."

"Kel, I'm so sorry," Paul said from a few beds away.

"Fuck off, Paul," she said.

It had taken a week for her to feel okay. She never let Paul kiss her again. In fact, she let him forage for a new girl. Poisoning had a way of dampening the mood. But for the girl known as Kelly, a new interest raised its head. Plants could hurt you. Heck, a few of them could kill you. The passion of the flesh was replaced with another, darker passion.

Turned out, Paul's family was loaded and gave Kelly a lump sum payment not to discuss or sue the family for the unfortunate incident at his apartment. She wasn't proud. She took the money and never saw Paul or Helga again.

Las Vegas-born Kelly Deluca immediately quit her job, moved out of her apartment, changed her name legally, and although it took her a few years, she became Kelan Smith, PhD, of Biology from University of Washington. The apartment funded by Paul's parents looked down on the area of Seattle where she had once lived. Her tuition was paid for with a part time job in the chemistry lab and the rest of the settlement from Paul's parents.

Known for having an exemplary transcript, Dr. Kelan Smith had several job offers when she graduated. She decided on a big change. She went to work for a small seed producer in Iowa for a few years until she decided to poison one of her bosses when he tried to take credit for her new wheat modification. A little poison so he'd get sick but wouldn't know exactly why. Get him away from the lab. But the plan worked too well. He died, and she decided it would be best to disappear. When at last she checked, the authorities hadn't figured it out, but she had gone a different direction with her life's work.

Amber smiled as she looked at her Brecks order. She could harvest the saffron from the crocus when they blossomed in February or March and give the precious spice to her neighbors. It was so expensive, that the gesture alone should mean something even if they didn't use it in cooking. Amazing to think that a poisonous bulb could produce the most expensive spice in the world. Of course, if anyone ate too much saffron it would kill them too. So fascinating!

She'd find and give the neighbors a recipe anyways. Something middle eastern that only required a few threads of saffron. The rest of the flowers could be used for bouquets. She liked to get parrot tulips and odd daffodils that weren't like anything around the Pacific Northwest or the United States for that matter. And she liked the fact that she would soon become known for her generous bouquets and samples for the neighbors. She would ingratiate herself to them and by Christmas, they'd be amazed by her, at least that was the plan. It usually worked. One thing she had learned, never underestimate a neighborhood. Each one was different.

When she'd been Jane, always put together and wearing designer duds for her position as a financial planner, she intimidated some of the neighbor ladies. They seemed leery of her. Possibly worried that she'd try to steal their husbands. As if! They were all old, past their primes, with beer guts and jaded attitudes. Middle age had hit them hard.

The reality of her new persona, Amber, was different. She was a bit of a hot mess, and it was working for her. The women and the men, they felt a little sorry for her. Who would be the first to offer her a makeover? To bring out the beauty she was hiding? Make her a special project? Her money was on Gingie, but Valerie liked to give her hugs, so maybe Valerie would be the first to pull her aside to have a well-meaning yet completely condescending word. It would start with the hair. It always started with the hair. Julia was too self-absorbed. She wouldn't waste her time trying to fix a mess, and that was okay, unless Amber approached her, which she was not going to do.

How did you know when a disguise was good? When people totally bought it.

She called Gingie.

"How are you doing?" she asked her neighbor.

"I'm okay. I'm just worried about Libby and the kids."

They talked about Libby, and about trivial things for another few minutes and then Amber got to the point of her call.

"Listen, I know this is bad timing, but I just got a big box of bulbs. Is there any way that I could get a map of the community garden? I'd like to plant them, but I don't want to intrude on anyone else's space."

"I can show you before the service this afternoon or tomorrow, either way. The garden is amazing. I can't wait to show it to you. What are you doing right now? Do you have a few minutes?"

"Right now? Yes."

"I'll pick you up in five. Too damn hot to walk."

"That is very kind of you."

And how appropriate was it that she was in all black when she was about to meet her little plot that would forever be known as *The Poison Garden?*

Gingie

Gingie was excited to show the community garden to Amber. She needed a break from thinking of Kent. She loved thinking about Kent, but she needed to get a grip, and this was a start.

She knew Amber would be impressed with the garden space. All the participating neighbors took great pride in how it looked. They had even entered it into various contests, and their garden had won three years in a row for best community garden in the state. It was a big deal. The first prize had been a photo shoot in *Sunset* magazine and a $2,000 prize that was supposed to be split by the neighbors. Instead, they had paid for a custom wrought iron gate that looked like cut out chrysanthemums that they had ordered from Canada. Then they added a wrought iron fence around the space to make it look like an authentic English garden. That hadn't been cheap, and it had taken a couple of years, but it looked fabulous, even in the winter.

Valerie's husband Jim liked to work with his hands and had added an arch above the chrysanthemum gate that spelled out

"Pioneer Pike Community Garden" in twisted metal letters that he had hand crafted. She'd never seen any other garden like it.

"This beats walking in the heat," Gingie said as Amber got into the car and added, "I'm so excited to show you what we've done."

It was an unusually warm afternoon for September, but Gingie couldn't wait to see Amber's reaction. Most of the plants were done for the season, the summer garden had been officially cleaned out and rototilled the previous weekend, but the fall squash and pumpkins remained. The gate and fence were a conversation starter on their own.

"This little adventure is a nice distraction from the horrible thing we are doing this afternoon," Amber said.

"I know, I still can't believe Dick died. I dropped off a lasagna this morning, and I think Libby and the kids are holding up well."

"Yeah, they are probably still in shock," Amber said.

"I think, but Dick was a hard person to get to know. I always felt that Libby and the kids were a bit scared of him. I know that is an awful thing to say on this day especially."

"Well, I only met him once, but I can see it. I hope Libby has peace now," Amber said.

"That is a lovely sentiment. Peace is something for us all to strive for, but I know Libby will need all of us in the future. Right now, she has a lot of support around her. But what happens when all the guests leave, and she starts missing him?" Gingie asked. "That is when she will really need us."

"Yes, she will," Amber said. "I don't know her very well, but I'll be there however she needs me. Maybe we can take them to dinner and a movie or bowling or something, although I have to admit, I've never bowled."

"I'm in, and it has been years since I've bowled," Gingie said, momentarily shuddering at the thought of losing Kent after years together and children. It would break her, and they were just starting this relationship.

"Well, we do what we can. And thank you for showing me the garden. I can't wait to see it," Amber said. "My Brecks bulbs are trembling with anticipation."

"They will love it there! Oh, you should see this garden in its glory in the middle of summer. It is something to behold. But to be honest, it always looks pretty impressive. The gate does it."

"This way I can plant bulbs and not get touched by the poison oak in the backyard," Amber said.

"I just wonder how poison oak even got into Mrs. Gibson's yard. I hate to think of it being on Pioneer Pike. I've got a call in with a guy to get it removed."

"Good. Yeah, I don't want to get near it," Amber said. "I know it is native to Oregon, but like out in the woods or something."

"Exactly. I don't like it in suburbia. I love that dress by the way. It is very cute," Gingie said. It was black but it was the most stylish thing she'd ever seen Amber wear. She wanted to encourage this nod of style. If she got rid of those glasses, changed her hair, and wore makeup, she'd be really stunning.

"Everyone needs one nice dress. In this case I've worn it to funerals, memorials, and parties, so get used to it as it will probably make an appearance again around Christmas, but I'll add a sequined shrug or something to make it festive," Amber said as they pulled along the curb a few blocks beyond their neighborhood.

"Before I forget," Gingie said, holding up a ceramic white plumeria key chain with a key on it.

"For me?"

"Yes, you are part of the Pioneer Pike family now, you get a key to the garden."

"Wow, so the gate is always locked?" Amber asked.

"Oh yes, we like to be a little exclusive with our garden.

Even though there is nothing to steal, we like to be a bit snooty. And if I'm there alone, I keep it locked. I feel safer that way."

"Wow, I think I see why," Amber said a bit in awe. "Look at that!"

"Yeah, it is very special."

"I think you nailed it with that description. I haven't seen anything like this outside of England," Amber said getting out of the car.

"That was the goal," Gingie said proudly. "Have you been to England?"

"No, only to Heathrow on my way to Africa. Is that a boxwood hedge?"

"Yes, and it is finally tall enough that the only way into the garden is through the gate. Well, even before it was tall enough you can see the wrought iron rails of the fence the boxwood hedge is about to cover, but still, it looks elegant, I think."

"It is gorgeous. Is that a bench just beyond the gate?"

"Yes, we have several. The one you can see is a memorial bench to Mr. Gibson, Hank. Valerie's husband is a bit of an artist. When Mrs. Gibson's husband died, Jim made a memorial bench that we gave to her because Hank liked this garden so much. And the neighbors, well, we liked Hank. He was here every day. Don't be surprised if one day you come here and find a very well-dressed lady sitting on the bench and just enjoying the space. Mrs. Gibson, Martha, has spent a lot of time sitting on that bench since Hank died. But she told me last week she was glad to pass on the plot to you."

"That is very kind of her."

Gingie said, "She loves her new condo. I think Pioneer Pike holds too many memories for her. Come on, try out your key and make sure it works."

Amber stood in front of the impressive wrought iron gate and used her key. Gingie knew that Jim kept the lock well-oiled.

Amber looked impressed. A moment later, the gate swung inward, and the women stepped into the space.

"Wow, this is amazing!" Amber said, stepping onto the slate patio that acted as an entryway.

The inside was huge, two large property lots divided into different sections with brick paths that looked professional. Every few feet there was a spigot and hose. There were even statues of elegant woman, men, and small children with pets. Several plots had random bushes, one covered entirely in roses that were now at the end of their season.

"Do you use rosehips?"

"Yes," Amber said, "In tea, lotions, potpourri. I see those rose bushes. Who has that plot?"

"That was Libby's. She might let you have the rosehips when the roses stop blooming."

"Wonderful, thank you!"

Gingie smiled at the expression on Amber's face. Yes, the garden was pretty amazing.

"Look at the pumpkins!" Amber exclaimed, noticing that three plots had large pumpkins.

"They are fun, aren't they?"

"I love them!"

"We've had some very talented people lend a hand to make this space impressive. The statues have been gifted over the years. We've even had partics here because of the elegance."

"I see why," Amber said in awe.

"We are just a little neighborhood, but this is something we can all get behind."

"Who pays for all this?" Amber asked.

"Years ago, the property was gifted to us by the developers of the subdivision. It was earmarked for either a park or a garden. And the space has its own well, so you can water as much as you want. We ask that if you put a sprinkler in your garden, you only run it for no more than an hour each day, a half hour is even better. The well looks like it has unending water, but we are still careful. Mainly people water their plants with a watering can."

Gingie continued, "As for the taxes, and other monies needed for upkeep several neighbors who started this sixty or seventy years ago put money in a trust when they died to cover anything the current homeowner's association couldn't cover. Dan Glass, being a lawyer, has looked for and found every tax advantage possible. For once his slightly less-than-scrupulous ways have worked to our advantage."

"I was going to wait, but since you brought it up, was it my imagination or does he like to touch women not his wife too much?" Amber asked.

"He is a class A creeper. I was hoping he'd try something in front of Kent. I wanted to see what Kent would do. If he bothers you, feel free to punch him in the nuts. But tell me first, I'd like to watch."

They laughed.

"Okay, good to know. By the way, I think that tall drink of water you were with would have flattened him," Amber said.

"One can hope," Gingie said with a chuckle.

"What gives with the wife? Have they been married long?"

"What did you say, Aubry?"

"You heard her call me that," Amber said.

"She's a tool. I've tried and tried to be nice to her, but the bottom line, I just don't like Julia. She was stupid enough to marry him, and I felt sorry for her for that. But, after watching her for a couple of years, I have to tell you, she is almost worse than him. She has this way of insulting you, little digs that are nasty. Afterward, you say, wait, did she really just say that to me?"

"Does she till in the community garden?" Amber asked.

Gingie chuckled and said, "With those nails? Are you kidding me? I have only seen her here stealing things. That woman has no morals. And I've heard she is diddling their new pool boy. I shouldn't gossip. I'm sorry."

"You should, and don't be sorry. Does her husband know?"

"The correct question is," Gingie said, "Does her husband care? And the answer is no. He's always got a little something something on the side. He thinks he is god's gift to women. Ergo the inappropriate touching. The absolute ignorance of personal space."

"There is always one in the neighborhood," Amber said, more to herself than to Gingie.

"Yeah, he is our little creeper!"

Amber shook her head and asked, "Okay, who decides on the garden? Like what the gate will look like, etc. Do you all vote?"

"Everyone is open with ideas, and each improvement is voted on. It is amazing how we all came together. Well, the cool people. Don't include the Glasses in that."

"Wow," Amber said, "This is so impressive."

"Come on, I'll show you around. You see this area?" Gingie asked, pointing to a large plot of ground. "This is where we grow veggies for donation. We design the space each year as to what goes where. Anyone can take from this area or grow veggies in this area, but we like to donate weekly to homeless shelters and food banks, so we don't encourage random pillaging. Sometimes we have to remind certain neighbors of that. Like Julia. Everyone complies because we want to give back. We started that program the year I moved in. It has been really positive and rewarding. You see those barrels in that corner?"

"Yes," Amber answered. "Compost?"

"Organic compost. You'd be surprised by some of the stuff people had tried to put in that. It isn't a garbage can. Usually, lazy teenagers try to break the rules, but we correct them."

"Do you keep it vegetarian?" Amber asked.

"Yes, for the most part. I knew you'd get it. Geez, people

have tried to put steak trimmings in the pile and dog poo or cat litter, which smells to high heaven."

"People can be stupid," Amber said.

"Yes, they can, and it isn't just the teens. It is their parents too. We like veggie scraps and coffee grounds. We've also got an exception for eggshells. Eggshells add a lot of nutrients, so they are allowed. Neighbor Ted from down the street likes to handle that area. So, if you want compost, just talk to him. We don't allow pesticides in here. Also, about May the call will go out for anyone who wants mushroom compost in their areas. We get it delivered, and you can spread it in your plot," Gingie said as she stopped in front of a very nice, freshly rototilled area. There was a little marker that read: GIBSON.

"Wow, can I really play in all this space?" Amber asked.

"You can!" Gingie said.

"I love it, and I can't wait."

"Now, you have a home for your bulbs. I think Valerie has some peonies in her garden, I have some daffodils too, so you won't be the only one with spring flowers."

"Has there ever been a wedding in this garden?" Amber asked.

Gingie smiled and looked at the hedge.

"I see," Amber said.

"What?" Gingie asked but even at the mention of a wedding her lips were curving into a smile that she could not contain.

"You and Officer Kent must be getting along well," Amber said with a smile. "He looks like a sweet man."

Gingie didn't know where to look or what to say. "It is new, but I really like him. And yes, I think he is very handsome."

Amber smiled broadly. "There is something about you two that I see. I would not be surprised if he is your forever guy."

Gingie shook her head, "I've been married before so I'm trying not to think about it, but I really like him. I think about him all the time."

"That's a good sign," Amber said.

"It is quite the obsession," Gingie confided. "I can barely eat, sleep, and forget complex thoughts. I have butterflies. The man gives me butterflies."

"It sounds serious," Amber said with a nod.

"It sounds a little like the flu or a little case of Covid."

CHAPTER NINE

Amber gave Libby a wide berth at the memorial. So far, so good. She had taken a deep breath of relief the moment she heard that Dick had been cremated. Toxicology be damned. Good luck taking samples from ash. They just might have gotten away with it, not that she had any doubt, but it was always a good idea to keep the paranoid edge.

There was still the little matter of Libby knowing that it was her suggestion. She didn't like witnesses. For the first time, she hadn't gone solo. And since she would never take a loving mother from her children, her only choice was to disappear one day. But her work was not finished on Pioneer Pike, so she didn't want to run away and hide, tail tucked between her legs. There was additional good she could do here.

However, so far, so good. And she wasn't just thinking that it was because of the amazing community garden Gingie had shown her earlier. But, okay, she couldn't wait to get her paws in that freshly turned soil and start planting her bulbs. That was the great thing about gardens, people were distracted by the flowers, but they rarely saw the forest for the trees. Almost everything in Amber's garden would be poisonous, except for the decoy plants that were meant to distract and hide. No one would figure out which was fine with her.

Aside from the bulbs she would grow Queen Anne's lace to hide her Poison Hemlock she wanted to grow because they looked so much alike. How lucky was she to find some Poison

Hemlock when she had been visiting Coburg? The plant starts were now germinating on her back patio in a little unencumbered spot she'd found far away from the poison oak. She'd been very careful to wear gloves from harvesting to planting. She was going to plant the fox gloves in front of Queen Anne's Lace and Poison Hemlock. The foxglove really wanted to be planted in September, while it was still warm. Eventually, gladiolas would blossom in front of the foxgloves.

She saw all of the neighbors at the memorial service for Dick and then again at Libby's house. Odd to think the last time they had all been in swimsuits, drinking margaritas and quizzing her. Now, they all looked somber at a fellow neighbors' send off. This was the kind of thing that could ingratiate her into the neighborhood and the neighbors. Maybe she should always make a kill within a month of moving into a new neighborhood. Death made everyone grow closer. She'd have to ponder this idea for future seasons.

Dan Glass sidled up to her as she was at the buffet table looking at all the cold cuts and salads. Thinking of how dead Dick was, it made her lose her appetite for much more than carrots and cheese. Meat of any variety turned her stomach. This wasn't a new sensation. Death brought out the vegetarian in her.

"How are you settling in?" he asked as he almost bumped into her at the table's edge.

"Aside from this kind of tragedy, I'm doing well, thank you for asking," she said.

"Yeah, well, take my word for it, this is very unusual for Pioneer Pike," he said as he placed a meaty paw on her forearm as he winked at her. "I'm sorry this has been your welcome. You call me if it ever gets to you. I'll get you off Pioneer Pike. Give you some new scenery to look at." Then he winked.

What a jerk.

If she ignored his physical touch, which repulsed her, and only went with her gut, this guy was bad news.

"Death," she said, "It happens. I'm fine."

"Well, I'm just sorry it had to happen when you have barely moved into the neighborhood."

"I don't think the two items are related," she said, knowing that if she had never moved into the neighborhood, Dick would still be alive. However, they might be mourning Libby. One thing she knew about Libby, she was a good mother and had become a shadow of her former self trying to make Dick happy.

Did that make Amber a hero? A Robin Hood of souls?

In the moment, Amber felt good. She didn't regret what she had done. She just wondered if Dan Glass would be next. He was free with his touches and gestures. She'd kill a husband if he was this much of a flirt to other women. She doubted it stopped with a few touches. No, if she gave in to all the visual indicators, she bet she could be having sex with Dan Glass in less than a week. Hell, he'd probably steal away to a deserted bedroom or better, a bath with a locking door in this house right now for a degrading blowjob. It depressed her. She wondered if Julia wanted to kill him. It was going to be a long time to spring when she took care of business. And Dan Glass had put himself squarely in her crosshairs. Poor bastard.

Maybe this season, the wives would play a bigger role in the activities she carried out. Maybe this was the season of shared responsibility. Maybe she could have ladies' only tea at her house. She'd serve liquor, forget the tea. Maybe she could suggest they all get large life insurance policies on their husbands. She could help them collect those premiums for a small fee. Would there be any takers? She predicted there would be.

Who was she kidding? *As if...* It was a dangerous pipe dream. Someone would talk. And she did not look good in stripes, especially if they were orange. And she worked alone. This Libby complication was a one-time thing.

Then she remembered Donna Stone.

She had befriended a life insurance agent about five years ago when she was pretending to be a teacher changing career fields. The woman's name was Donna Stone. The agent's motives hadn't been pure, but Amber had helped her out when she discovered that the husband had a double life on the down low, as it were, that involved having random sex with male prostitutes. It was only a matter of time until his wife found out. The woman now known as Amber didn't have a problem with alternate lifestyles. She had a problem with lying. And hadn't what happened to the lying husband been a hoot? The insurance agent never suspected her. The woman known as Amber was simply an angel...of death. Donna's husband had a heart attack one Sunday afternoon. She was sure that Donna thought her ship had come in. Her husband had died, but so had a couple of other men in the neighborhood. It was quite the event when three men died in one neighborhood in less than a month.

Amber smiled a little at the memory of her last month in Florida. That had been a good season. Florida was always a good idea because the age of her prey fit into the older, geriatric "AARP" category. Not a lot of questions were asked when the person died at eighty-five or ninety and had pre-existing health complications.

"Well, don't forget, the offer stands. If you ever want to get together," Dan Glass said, interrupting her thoughts. "I'm here for you."

As if time with him was some sort of gift he was giving her?

"How kind of you to offer," she said flashing a fake smile. It was too bad she couldn't slip some crushed yew berries into the grainy mustard on his buffet plate. "I'll remember that."

She'd remember all right. A couple more of these conversations and that man was going down. Maybe Julia was the way she was because her husband was an ass. Maybe when she had married him, he'd been a good guy, and over time, each had changed. Maybe Julia didn't sign up for owning such an uncivilized dog. And he reeked of cigarettes. Amber noticed that he smoked at the pool party, but he had the decency to walk away from the crowd. Must have been a fluke. She hoped he didn't quit in the next few months.

Amber looked around the filled room of mourners and spotted Julia Glass who was giving her a battle-wary look.

Time to reassure the woman that she was on to her husband's little games and would not be playing.

She looked down at her buffet plate. It was only half filled. She really had no appetite. Ignoring Dan Glass's attempts to spatially pace with her as she left the buffet, she made a beeline for Julia.

"Hey there," Amber greeted. "How are you holding up?"

Julia, dressed in a smart navy-blue dress that clung to her thin skeleton, and looking older than her mid-forties, smiled bitterly, and looked down at her lowball glass that she no doubt had filled with something other than soda. "I'm holding up like I always do. Forgive me for my directness, but what did my husband just say to you? Something unbecoming of a husband I'm sure."

Amber knew she could lie, but that would not endear her to Julia. The other woman had suffered for a long time. She knew the look. She knew the sadness and it wasn't for her to sugarcoat it. Besides, she'd witnessed the interaction between Dan and all the women at the pool party. This guy was a serial cheater. On some level she bet Julia was a little jealous of Libby. Her problem was solved.

"I hate to say this, but I think he was a bit inappropriate. I didn't like it. He offered to get me out of Pioneer Pike, for what, I don't know. But I have a very good imagination. It wasn't so much what he said, but the way he said it. Nevertheless, I won't be taking him up on any offers that he might make. But if you'd like to grab lunch sometime and tell me how you came to marry the cheating pig, I'd love to listen," Amber said and then clinked her glass to Julia's.

Julia surprised her. She smiled, her latest facelift pulling hard as her lips went up. She looked like she might laugh, but this wasn't the time or place.

"Oh, little girl, you have a lot to learn about marriage," Julia said.

"Really? I just didn't like that he'd do that to you," Amber concluded.

"Grow up, honey, or the world will eat you up," Julia said. "He's just a man being a man. I only care that he is shitting where he eats. It is a bad idea to screw someone in the neighborhood."

"Excuse me?" Who was this woman to lecture Amber?

Julia lowered her voice conspiratorially, looking around, which Amber had already done but she appreciated the other woman's diligence. They were alone, in a corner, and would not be overheard by any of the other mourners.

"Tell me, what would you do about him? He is becoming more of a problem with each day that passes. Divorce isn't an option because we have a prenup in place. I wasn't his first wife. He was married to her when I showed up. When he divorced her, I thought it was because I was the love of life. I was the love of the moment. We still have a little something, but it wasn't like the illicit passion we felt at the beginning. Now, by unspoken agreement, we each do what we want."

"I'm sorry. You keep up the façade well."

"When I married him, it created a job opening. He probably started interviewing for 'young thing he could screw' while we were on our honeymoon to Hawaii."

"I would not have guessed. You were the gracious hostess at the pool party."

"I try very hard to keep up appearances. Thank you, Aubry."

"Tell you what, you can call me Amber. Do you have children?"

"No, he's the only child I'll ever have. He has a couple of daughters from his first marriage. They hate me, and I don't like them. He sees the little brats at Christmas to give them checks, and then there is the dreaded one week to Hawaii every spring break. I've bowed out the last three years, and he doesn't care. I never really cared for children, and he didn't want any when we married, so I had my tubes tied because he was too much of a baby to get a vasectomy. I wanted him more than anything else in the world, so it was never an issue."

"Interesting," Amber said and meant it. She had heard this story before, but the open talk of vasectomies at a funeral was new.

"Sometimes, I want to kill him for what he has done to me. Really, what would you do?"

"Are we talking hypothetically what would I do?" Amber asked.

"Sure."

"Take out one big ass life insurance policy and feed him lots of fatty red meat," she said with a laugh.

"I've got the life insurance, but it doesn't pay out much, because he has a heart condition. He's on digitalis for shit's sake because he hasn't met a steak, cigarette, or liquor bottle he didn't like, so I do make sure he gets a lot of his favorite things. He goes through a couple of cows a year. I also make sure he has lots of bacon. He smokes two packs of unfiltered Camels a day. He pours about a quarter cup of heavy cream in his coffee each morning. And the bourbon, he has at least three cocktails a night. And he hates to exercise. The man had liposuction for his sixtieth-fifth birthday, for God's sake."

Oh BINGO! This dude was approaching coronary city on the express train.

"He's on digitalis, smokes, and has a terrible diet? It is just a matter of time. Heck, tell him in light of what happened to Libby, you are concerned, and up his life insurance. I shouldn't talk this way. It is horrible," Amber said, wondering why she had said so much. "I'm sorry."

"I'm not. This is the kind of banter I like."

"I'm sorry. I'm going to stop talking now."

"If you were to help me, I'd be willing to help you."

Was this woman trying to pay Amber to off her husband? Amber didn't work like that.

"Thanks Julia, but talking about murdering your husband at a funeral has got to be the lowest thing I've ever done. I'm going to find the bar now."

"Don't be a stranger."

Why had she picked this neighborhood? A murder in the first month. Another woman wanting her to help murder her husband. She had better start drinking bottled water, because something was wrong with everyone, and it probably started with something innocuous like the water they all drank. Maybe it had high levels of mercury...

CHAPTER TEN

Amber silently laughed and shook her head as she walked home. Pioneer Pike was ripe with angry wives. Maybe she had not chosen it as much as it called to her because she was the entity needed to clean house. She'd barely been there for three weeks. It was like she was on an accelerated plan! Damn! If this continued, she'd be searching for a new neighborhood before Christmas, mid-season. She couldn't let that happen. The community garden was amazing.

Again, she wondered if she was pressing her luck. This was her sixth season. Maybe it was time to pay Neil, her personal hacker, for a couple more passports and get the hell out of Dodge. Then what? Where would she go? Saint Barts to relive the memories? Or some small town like in Kansas? No on any flat state in the middle of the country, including Kansas. It was too close to Iowa. No, Canada would be a smarter choice. Maybe Europe. She could pass for a woman from France, who didn't speak or understand English...maybe...*Je ne parle pas anglaise*...

Well, she still had one fresh set of IDs under the name of Judy Samuels from New York. It was the "run for your life" escape pod of identification. And it was always with her on a money belt she wore under her clothing, along with ten thousand dollars. She had another fifty thousand at the house, but if she couldn't make it back after some sort of breach, she could simply drop her purse and walk away.

Occasionally, she'd go to the public library and google search

Iowa. Dr. Kelan Smith was a "person of interest" the authorities would like to talk to. That kinda messed with your ability to put down roots. Talk about a dog with a bone! Would they ever let it go? It had been almost seven years. Bill wasn't coming back. It was an accident, but she'd done the world a service. He was an officious prick with no upper lip and no scruples, the ass. He died because he lied. She killed him because she was still learning about potencies. It was an accident for fuck's sake.

Heck, you didn't keep taxes for more than seven years! Okay, so using her real name wasn't an option. Dr. Kelan Smith died along with Dr. Bill.

She'd cruised several other libraries that same day, small, city libraries and checked on her other seasons using the computer's IP address. In two of the five neighborhoods, where she had spent time in the past, they had figured out that something was amiss. She was wanted for questioning under whatever name she'd used at the time because she had disappeared without a word. It was kinda suspicious...well, duh! Great, there was a new wrinkle that now she needed to keep dead end relationships that she had walked away from thriving. She needed to keep in touch. Or, *"Remember her? She lived in that rental for a year. I always liked her."* What, was she supposed to send a Christmas card or the occasional postcard to people like Felicity? She felt the noose tightening.

She needed to contact Neil. It had been too long, and she needed to catch up. What a character! What a sweet kid! Well, he was more of a full-fledged adult now. When she'd met him, he'd been a college kid, a cute, nerd hacker to the highest level whose boredom growing up in Iowa had led to a lot of nefarious activities with her assistance and money.

She'd met him at a bar when she was still Kelan Smith, PhD, bought him a couple of drinks as ideas formed in her mind. His false ID held up to the bartender's scrutiny, but his fresh face didn't hold up to hers. She'd pegged him at nineteen and been correct. A weary friendship was formed. Over the years it had become something more. He was the nephew she never had, the sweet boy who asked if she was taking her vitamins and understood what she was doing. Heck, he was a fan of her work. She'd helped him get rid of an abusive stepfather who liked to use his mother as a punching bag. Well, she actually hadn't done that one, only consulted, but it worked, and he was forever grateful. His mother was now with a nice, respectful man.

He might have grown up in Iowa but wanted to escape to a big city like New York. He just needed money. She gave him the money, and he helped her get her first set of IDs right after she recklessly poisoned her boss. Thankfully, because of Neil she was able to escape. He called her Aunt Kel. It was sweet, and always warmed her heart. They had even met for Thanksgiving a time or two. They were family. Last winter they spent some time in Saint Barts, only she had stayed on for an additional week because of Jack. The memory had her cringing.

Neil wasn't an artist. He didn't have to be. He hacked into the government computers. A couple weeks later, real government issued IDs were sent to one of her post office boxes. The last time she looked, the only thing he hadn't been able to get her was TSA PreCheck, Global Entry, or Nexxus card but he was close to finding a work around. Those required in person interviews. It was okay, she didn't mind having to take off her shoes before jumping on an airplane. She was just happy to have a ticket that could take her away to points unknown.

As was their practice, she opened her email and wrote a draft email, but didn't send it:

I think I want to plan a trip. I need to make sure my passport is up to date and then send it to my house in W. How does Thanksgiving look?

They had discussed the Hotel Monteleone in New Orleans.

She had a P.O. box in Winnemucca, Nevada, and it would be relatively easy to get there, a little weekend trip before snow covered the passes.

There was what she perceived to be a weakness in the U.S. Customs Department. They delivered to P.O. Boxes or wherever you wanted. *Rubes!*

Then she used Venmo to send Neil twenty-five thousand dollars. He usually only charged her twenty, but she liked to surprise him occasionally. She sent it in various denominations, $2,000, $5,500, etc., over three days from different email addresses to avoid getting the attention of IRS.

Two days later, she visited the library and looked at her email. In the draft section, her email draft had been edited and changed to read: *Happy season in advance. I like Halloween for our latest coupon. Thanksgiving is not going to work out this year, but I'm free in February for some sun. Thank you for that little something extra!!*

The passport would be arriving by Halloween. Thanksgiving wasn't meant to be, damn it.

Well-meaning neighbors would inquire about her holiday plans, and she would have to be all, "Oh I've got plans." But the savvy neighbors would know she was home alone. Maybe she should plan to leave town this year without meeting anyone. San Diego could be fun. She didn't give Las Vegas with Old Jen a second thought. It had been several years since she'd seen Old Jen, and although she felt some guilt, Old Jen didn't seem to miss her daughter.

She went back to Pioneer Pike and thought more about San Diego but decided on the beach at a little city two and a half hours away, Newport, Oregon. She rented a VRBO. Good, Thanksgiving was handled. She reserved a different VRBO across town in Eugene for Christmas. She didn't like traveling at Christmas but preferred to eat junk food and watch old movies. Well, at a VRBO owned by a professor leaving town near the University of Oregon, she could do that.

Next, she looked at how to get to Winnemucca, from Eugene. It was about an eight-hour drive each way. She could do a round trip in two days, three or four if she stopped along the way. Oregon was a beautiful state, she should explore it. Bend in Central Oregon, with Sunriver one way and come back through Burns in Eastern Oregon on the way back. She made hotel reservations in Sunriver and Burns for the first week in November.

Two days after Dick's memorial service, she collected all the tools she'd need: gloves, hoe, hand shovel, bulb planter, standing labels, hand rake, fertilizer, pesticide, watering can, bulbs, seeds, and hemlock starts. It was time to visit the community garden and start preparations putting together for her poison garden.

Okay, so the pesticides were hidden in organic neem oil spray bottle, like anyone was going to taste it! Still, she wouldn't advertise what it was. And it wasn't like she was growing vegetables. Okay, she had a little huckleberry. No one was going to mess with her huckleberries. No, she was all about the flowers and a few herbs that would almost be considered weeds. Her key fit smoothly in the lock, and she was happy to find that she was alone. After a couple of trips to cart her loot, she locked the chrysanthemum gate behind her and walked to the Gibson plot. It was so much bigger than she'd envisioned.

Some year she was going to get a private space and wall it off, maybe a greenhouse. She'd introduce bumblebees, who could withstand certain lethal nectars, and the only food source would be rhododendron. They'd have to eat it and go back to the hives to produce a small but potent amount of honey. It wouldn't kill someone, but used in combination with her special tea, it could get the ball running. That would be fun, she thought as she mapped out her garden.

She started in the back; she liked order. First went in the poison hemlock starts. Then she dug a little open trench for the Queen Anne lace. It preferred not to have dirt covering it. She had purchased some elaborate standing black wrought iron labels from Amazon that would withstand the elements and the nosy neighbors who might be curious about what she was planting. With a white grease pencil, she wrote: *Queen Anne's Lace* in careful cursive.

The next row was for the foxgloves. They were popular and underestimated. Her mind pictured Julia, and she wondered how that would play out. Did the woman know that foxgloves were the plant form of digitalis? If she were going to kill off old Dan, she could do it with foxgloves. Take some of his prescription digitalis and flush it down the toilet. Make it look like maybe he got confused.

Amber still hadn't selected Dan Glass for elimination, but that was likely to change. Actually, she was rethinking her policy about killing women that morning. *Foxgloves*, she printed elegantly.

She had been lucky to find a few small garden huckleberry bushes the size of coffee cups. She had nine that she planted in the next row. Amber made sure to spread them out. In between them, she planted a few small, black nightshade plants. Really, they should have been planted a few weeks earlier, but they were having an unusually warm fall. If half of her garden germinated, she'd be in great shape about May or June. *Huckleberry*, she printed.

Amber used her bulb planter to create a serpentine pattern next in the vast soil. Maybe she shouldn't have bought so many bulbs, but they would help to make nice bouquets. Five of the jumbo-tall tulip bulbs went in each hole. She tried to not create a row, but a nice pattern instead. Random order. *Tulips.*

To most of the bulbs she added garlic cloves to thwart the squirrels and a healthy dose of Miracle Grow was used on everything to give them a fighting chance.

She sprayed her pesticide mix on the huckleberries. Vermin liked the huckleberries. She hoped they'd try the poison hemlock.

She planted the regular tulips, daffodils, ranunculus, lily of the valley, and crocus. Little signs appeared at the end of rows. *Short Tulips, Daffodils, Ranunculus, Lily of the Valley, Crocus.*

Her work was done for the moment. In February, she'd add some bare root roses, just for the heck of it. Maybe she'd see if she could plant an English Yew or two behind the hemlock. She always wanted a healthy supply of Yew berries, but she might miss them if she left Pioneer Pike quickly. Oh well, she was being optimistic, and it wasn't like anyone would notice. This spring she would add poppy seeds for summer poppies, peppermint to keep the spiders at bay, sage, and cilantro. She hated cilantro, but so many people liked it, it would be something she could share from her garden. She made a note of which corner she wanted to plant it. She'd try to keep the pesticides away from there. But it wasn't like she was going to eat it! Really, what did she care? Well, damn it, she liked some of the cilantro-eating neighbors!

Looking at the vast space, she had an idea which was possibly motivated by all the Laura Ashley wallpaper. Sweet peas this spring. She'd pound in two, long stakes at either end of the garden plot, make a string grid and grow the heavenly flower. Maybe some sunflowers too. Ornamental, not the sunflower seed bearing. She liked them for their foliage. Lots of things could go on behind the screen of sweet peas and the sunflowers.

The thought of all these happening months from now had a profound impact on her. She had already helped one person onto the 'rainbow bridge.' And she had another one on deck. This was happening too fast. She needed to cool it. Libby would probably need to talk to her several times, the guilt and all would start coming up. She would need to unburden her soul. Happiness came with guilt.

Amber needed to be there for her, talk to her through the changing emotions, the feelings that would bubble up. It was not just for Libby. It was to protect Amber too.

Had it been reckless to kill Dick? No, it had been necessary. Dan Glass kept coming to her mind, but it was different. He wasn't beating Julia. He wasn't abusive to the children or animals they did not have. But he'd basically taken Julia's life to improve his own. But then Julia Glass was an awful person in her own right. She wasn't a victim. Who knows what she would have been like if she hadn't married Dan? Dang it! If only she had a crystal ball! Or was psychic! Now that was a gift worth having. Damn it, why was she second guessing herself? Why now? Was she getting soft? What the fuck?

Gingie

Something was on Kent's mind. Gingie hadn't even been dating him for a month, but she'd seen him every day of that month, and she could tell when something was wrong. They were at her house, and she was grilling shish kabobs on the outdoor grill. It was probably the last time she'd be grilling this season. A morning chill was announcing the change of seasons. That was okay. Fall led to fires in the fireplace and snuggles under a blanket. She could barely wait! Was it bad that she wanted him to make love to her in front of that fire? She didn't think so.

She wore a red gingham halter top that showed skin and tightly cupped her generous breasts. She wore short jean shorts, flip flops and had done her dark hair into pig tails tied with two red bows. She looked like Mary Ann from *Gilligan's Island*. Or a very naughty farmer's daughter. Either way, she thought from Kent's reaction when he saw her and looked uncomfortable that it worked.

The meat of the shish kabobs had been marinated for a day in Italian dressing as had the vegetables. Talk about delicious! It was one of her go-to recipes in the summer. Along with it, she had a watermelon & feta salad and corn on the cob. She had even made a compound butter for the corn that had finely diced jalapeño because Kent said he liked heat. They were drinking an Oregon Pinot Noir that a client had given her, which she'd been saving for a special occasion.

Kent was sitting in one of the outdoor chairs that matched the table, and she felt his eyes watching her, but he was noticeably silent. What was going on? Had she done something wrong?

She pulled the corn and the shish kabobs off the grill marveling that she had timed them just right. She would slather the corn with the butter and then plate their dinner. She had outdone herself but that might not matter if Kent was second guessing his attendance at her house. Before she lost it, she had to ask him what was going on, or she wouldn't be able to eat a bite of her dinner.

"Kent? Are you okay?" she asked, her tongs in one hand, the food on a platter in the other. "You're so quiet. It is making me nervous. Have I done something to upset you?"

He set down his wineglass and stood, crossing the distance to her. He took the platter from her hands, and then the tongs. He set them on the table. Pulling her to him, he kissed her thoroughly and then held her tightly to him. Then, at last, he said, "I'm sorry, baby. My cousin sent me an email today that really upset me. I keep going over it in my mind. I didn't mean to bring it with me."

He kissed her cheek and then her neck. Then he kissed her deeply again and said, "You are perfect. I can't think of anywhere that I'd rather be than with you." To illustrate his point, his hand slipped inside her blouse and inside her bra to cup her breast as he went in for another kiss.

She liked the feel of his hands on her bare skin. It had only happened a few times, but each time it did, she could barely breathe.

And Gingie was very relieved. They were at that delicate

place in their relationship where they either went forward having really committed or the feelings of doubt crept in. Little fears had a way of derailing a good thing. Gingie had no doubts, but Kent was used to hiding his emotions. It came with his job.

"I'm very glad you are here," she said. "If you want to talk about it, I'm a good listener, but if not, I understand. I'm just glad we are okay." If he suggested they retire to her bedroom and make love, she'd go. Damn the taking it slow. She wanted him.

"We are great," he said and kissed her again with a kiss that had her toes curling in her sandals. This man was driving her crazy.

Two minutes later, they sat down to dinner, Kent trying his food for the first time and smiling. Gingie wished her body would stop throbbing.

"Gingie, this is wonderful. You are full of the best surprises, aren't you? Thank you."

"Well, let's hope you always think that is true," she said with a laugh.

"I do, and I will. Okay, I need to tell you about this to get it off my chest, but I don't want it to ruin our night."

Leaning toward him, she touched the back of his hand with her finger and asked, "How could it? You could confess anything to me, murder, robbery, mayhem, I'm not going anywhere."

"Good…" he said and cleared his throat, trying to shift gears. "Okay. Here it is, you know that my cousin is like a brother to me. Our mothers are sisters, and we would always spend the month of August at the family lake house north of Minnesota. We learned to swim, and fish. We even learned to waterski although he was much better at it than I was. Damn, Jack is good at anything he tries…well, except this…"

"Is he okay?" she asked. She had heard about this cousin before. Jack was his name if she remembered correctly.

"Physically, yes, mentally, no."

"What happened?"

"Last January he met this woman, this Jane Miller when he was vacationing in Saint Barts. He always takes a week or two away to someplace warm to escape the Minnesota winters."

"Sounds like fun," Gingie said.

"Yeah, I've been thinking of places we might go in January or February to escape the cold here. Would you like that?"

"Yeah, I'm sure I'd like that. I'm in. Now tell me what happened."

"Good. I'll start making plans."

He was making the assumption that they'd be together in January or February, things were looking up and Gingie had to bite her lip to keep from smiling.

"Anyway, back to my cousin. He and this woman had this passionate love affair for a week, and then she disappeared. Jack thought he'd found his soulmate. But on the eighth day of his two-week vacation, he went to her room to pick her up and she'd left. In fact, she'd left the night before. Actually, she left in the middle of the night."

"What did he know about her?"

"He met her in the hotel bar on his first night. She wasn't even staying at the same hotel. They immediately hooked up, as in that night. She was everything he'd been looking for. He even called me from Saint Barts and told me about her."

"Why weren't they together the night before?" Gingie asked

"Good question. He told me she left his room after they made love, saying she left her migraine medication in her room, and she needed it because she was getting a headache. He walked her through the lobby, got her a cab, and they agreed to see each other the next day. He was supposed to go to her hotel at ten the next morning. But when he put her in the cab, that was the last time that he saw her."

"I bet she had to go home to her husband and didn't know how to tell him," Gingie surmised.

"Yeah, I thought she had someone else too. Maybe just a serious boyfriend."

"Where was she from?"

"New York City. She was a professor at the Fashion Institute of Technology, so she said. Do you know how many Jane Millers live in NYC?"

"A lot?"

"Hundreds if not thousands and who knows if she ever lived there. There were no professors named Jane at F.I.T. So it has been months and Jack just can't let it go. He hired a detective and has spent a lot of time and money. Nothing has come from it but dead ends. In fact, the hotel room in Saint Barts was rented to a Jane Miller from New York, but she paid in Euros. Cash. They wouldn't give the detective the information on the credit card used to hold the room. The airlines have no record of her, which means she was probably using a different name on her travel documents. Jack is driving himself crazy over this woman."

"She must have been something," Gingie said.

"If it were us, I'd have searched for you," he said.

"I hope so," she said with a small smile. "But then, I don't want to go anywhere that you wouldn't be."

The air seemed to change.

He set his fork down and paused, obviously thinking about what he was going to say and then he gently laid his hand on top of hers. "Gingie."

She looked at him and smiled broader.

"If I don't touch you soon, I'm going to go crazy. I can't eat, I can't sleep. I just want you to be inside of you. To kiss every inch of you. I want to taste you. I know you want to take it slow, but I don't know if I can. I don't know if I can be around you—"

She stood, freeing her hand from his, but then she extended her hand to him. "I don't know if I've shown you my bedroom. My bed is rather small, only a queen, but the sheets are eight hundred count cotton. I bought them and put them on the bed this afternoon. Shall we see if they live up to the hype?"

Placing his hand in hers, Kent stood, smiled, and said, "Yes ma'am."

Then he followed her inside and down the hall to her bedroom.

CHAPTER ELEVEN

October passed quickly but there were several developments that Amber noticed.

First, she had to smile at the activity at Gingie's house. Officer Logan's car was a frequent overnight guest of her driveway. It made her happy to think of the progression of that relationship. She hoped she was still there when they had their wedding. She really didn't want to miss it. They made a damn cute couple. And from Gingie's satisfied smile whenever she ran into her in the neighborhood, they were quite sexually compatible.

That was a gift she'd once had. Well, for the best week of her life. She just wished she'd savored it even more when it was happening. Saint Barts would always be a magical place to her.

Second, Libby seemed to blossom in her grief. The woman who had looked so downtrodden but a little over a month ago, was now glowing. She'd cut her hair, had it dyed to get out the gray, bought new clothes, bought a new car, and looked ten years younger. Puppy Larry, a handsome black Labrador, took her for a walk each morning, and she laughed openly at his antics. Amber wondered how long it had been since she had laughed when Dick was alive.

Amber had thrown away the marmalade jars in her pantry, one jar at a time in the weekly garbage. When it was all gone it felt like that dark chapter seemed to be over.

Third, the leaves were beginning to change color, the sky was getting darker earlier in the evening. They were stepping into fall. Halloween was tomorrow, and she planned to leave for her trip to Nevada on November first. She was just in time to beat the snow on the mountain passes, although seeing a little snow would be fun, as long as it didn't inconvenience her.

Fourth, she checked on her poison garden every other day. The plants had decided to move in permanently to their neighborhood, sending out roots, which pleased her to no end. The Queen's Anne Lace had germinated, although it knew that winter was coming. She could assume all the bulbs were happily underground thinking the same thing, getting cozy and taking a siesta until February. She added moth balls to the boundary of her garden. The squirrels gave it a wide birth. She didn't worry about poisoning them; she worried about them digging up her expensive daffodils, realizing they were poisonous and leaving them out of their protective earth to dry out and die. The little bastards had a way of doing that, and she was forever fighting them.

Fifth, Gingie had called her about landscapers coming to her yard to clean it up. And within an hour, they had arrived and started in on their horrible task. The poison oak as well as the blackberries had been removed. None of it had any positive uses, so Amber didn't harvest any for herself. She had harvested some raspberry leaves while out walking in her new neighborhood. A skein was just hanging over the fence, trying to grab any passersby with its thorns. Well, having fifty or so of its leaves removed seemed to even the score. And raspberry leaves made a great addition to tea. And they especially helped to mask the scent and flavor of foxglove blossoms, to name one of her little friends that could be a bit bitter.

On November first, she made the drive to Winnemucca, Nevada, to visit the postal annex where she paid for a post office box several years in advance. They knew her as a brunette. Luckily, she had a brunette wig in case the security camera footage should ever be reviewed.

She stopped in Bend the first night and took a drive around the area. It was nice, pretty, but too far away from an international airport. And the snow, she was a bad snow driver, so this was off her list, although there were a lot of nice neighborhoods that no doubt had community gardens and men behaving badly.

When she got to Winnemucca the next day, she stopped at her post office box, and true to his word, there was a manilla envelope from the Department of State. Inside she found her new passport. And what name had Neil chosen this time? It was always something interesting, usually Hitchcockian. As predicted, Neil didn't disappoint. This passport had her photo as a blonde with tortoise shell glasses and the name was Melanie Danvers. Melanie, the icy blond portrayed by Tippi Hedren from the movie *The Birds,* and Danvers for the crazy housekeeper, Mrs. Danvers in *Rebecca.* Nice, Neil. She didn't know if she shouldn't be just a little disappointed. At least Tippi was gorgeous.

She stopped by the public library and hopped on their only public computer. She opened up their shared email and typed an email that she left in draft.

Package Received. Love, Melanie.

She was tempted to stop at a Best Buy and buy him one of those Hitchcock DVD's and send it to his address in New York, but then the analytical part of her mind reminded her that such an activity was unwise. It would leave a record, the dreaded paper trail. She'd buy him the DVD and sent it to him from Amazon on her fake account. That would work, and he'd know the significance of it.

In December, after the progressive dinner at which she was requested to bring Aunt Betty's chocolate cake and received a bottle of Peppermint Vodka in the liquor-themed white elephant, (she brought absinth, of course), she called Gingie and asked a question that had been on her mind.

"Hey, after this party, which was great by the way, I was wondering, what month did Mrs. Gibson have for the rotating neighborhood party?"

Gingie had to think for a moment, then she said, "She had February, but don't feel you have to throw a party. It is a lot of work for a single person. And you're renting, unless you decide that you like us all so much that you would like to buy Mrs. Gibson's. We'd love to have you stay."

"Gingie, that is the sweetest thing I've heard in a long time. I would like to stay until August, but then I might move back to where I have some cousins in Montana."

"I'm sad that you might leave. What are you doing for Christmas?"

Amber smiled, "I'm getting together with a few of my cousins in Seattle. How about you?"

"Kent and I are going to Aspen to ski."

"Do you need a ride to the airport?"

"No, Kent has arranged everything, but thank you. You know, I'm happy for the time we have with you. And, if you decide to have a party in February, let me know and I'll do it with you if you'd like."

"Thank you, but I want to go to your Cinco de Mayo party."

"I can still help. And you'll have fun at my party. It was a blast last year."

"I was thinking of something a little different for my party, something easy like a movie night with little gift baskets. At Mrs. Gibson's I have lots of space in the family room. I think everyone would fit. Well Julia might be horrified."

"Fuck Julia, she is now sleeping with Valerie and Jim's gardener. He trims her hedge, as it were."

"The big guy with all the muscles and bad teeth, well, all the gold teeth?"

"That's the guy."

"He kisses her with that mouth?"

"He does something to her with that mouth," Gingie said with a laugh.

"Gingie!"

"Oh, you were thinking it too."

"Yeah, I kind of was. I feel a little sorry for golden kiss guy."

"I know, right? And we finally fixed your bath off the kitchen," Gingie said. "Great place for Dan to get someone drunk and pull them inside."

"Ugh, I cannot stand him."

"I actually think Julia is worse."

"She is kind of mean."

"There is no 'kind of' about it. She is mean."

"You're right. And we could watch Casablanca or something," Amber said.

"Well, these are usually dinners or potlucks so there wouldn't be lots of cooking involved, but I have a Kettle Corn recipe I'm dying to try out. And I could make wiener wraps and a veggie tray!"

"I'd like to try some skin creams out on the ladies for my book. I didn't realize it would take so long, but I'm creating each recipe."

"Oh wow! I really enjoyed the lotion you gave us at Christmas," Gingie said. "I can't wait for our next sample!"

Jergens strikes again!

"Maybe I'll make Aunt Betty's chili, and then we can have people bring fixings, like sour cream and cheese."

She would also make party favors for the ladies, of course. It was a part of her cover that could not be ignored. The neighbors loved her little gifts. Heck, at Christmas, she'd even been commissioned to make lotions and soaps for Valerie and Gingie, as well as Sharon, whom she didn't know very well. They used them as gifts for coworkers, friends, you name it. Amber made cute little baskets for each woman, and they seemed very pleased.

"That is a great idea, Amber!"

In late January, Amber drove forty miles away to Corvallis. One thing she had paid attention to were the ages of the children in the neighborhood. Pioneer Pike residents were relatively young. Most of the children were junior or high school age. If Gingie married Officer Kent, Amber predicted she would get pregnant fairly quickly and the cycle of babies in the neighborhood would start all over again. Needless to say, she wouldn't run into any kids she recognized in Corvallis, the home of Oregon State University.

Once in Corvallis, Amber went to King Street and stopped at the local megastore, Fred Meyer. It was becoming her go-to location next to Walmart. Inside, she visited the cosmetics aisle and purchased flake sea salt and unscented Epsom salts. She left Corvallis and drove another forty miles to Salem, a larger city, the state capital. There she visited a Macys' and bought several bottles of Bobbi Brown and Clinique eye creams and face creams. It was an expensive day out at the stores, but freedom had a price, and she was willing to pay it to mask any suspicion from her.

Back in Eugene, she poured all the eye cream into one bowl. Then she thinned the mixture with Witch Hazel. When in doubt, Witch Hazel to the rescue! She didn't grow it or process it because it was too much work but bought it at the store, ready to use.

She immediately discarded the boxes and jars, should a neighbor just stop by, which they had a penchant to do in this neighborhood. She stirred the eye cream and added pulverized violet blossoms. Not only would the violet add a pretty color to the eye cream, but they would also compliment and mask the scent of the manufactured stuff. Next, she grounded up some caffeine tablets in her spice grinder and added a scant teaspoon to the cream mix. This would take down any puffiness around the eyes. She added xanthan which brought texture and thickened up the mixture. For the heck of it, she added some violet essential oil to amp up the violet scent.

She put the now light violet lotion through a fine mesh to get rid of any flower or tablet parts that hadn't integrated. She loved the color, and the xanthan had done its work. The mixture was the consistency of thick, buttery frosting, which gave her another idea.

She loaded a frosting bag with a star tip at the end and piped the contents into tiny jars. It looked fantastic. She added a label which read: Amber's Violet Eye Cream with a little drawing of a violet next to it.

She had spent so much time trying to impress the women, it was time to work on the men. She poured the salt flakes and Epsom salts into two bowls, splitting the ingredients so that each had a bit of the two salts.

She added a package of pink Himalayan salt, which was more salmon in color than pink, to one of the bowls. She added powdered Kaolin Clay to the salmon salt mixture and a bottle of ground ginger. She stirred it with a wooden spoon, enjoying the scent of the ginger. To really illustrate the point, she added a few drops of coconut, almond, and ginger oil.

To the other bowl, she kept it simple adding honeysuckle oil.

She had found some little baggies from Amazon with draw sting tops. She used her half cup measurement cups to create little bags of Epsom bath salts. To these she added labels again. *Amber's Honeysuckle Epsom Bath Salts.*

The day before the gathering at her house, she visited a local soup company and purchased twenty-five portions of angus chili and twenty-five portions of corn chowder because she knew that not everyone liked chili. Was it the best chili she'd ever had? Not really, but with Old Jen they didn't eat a lot of chili unless it came from a can with the name of Hormel, and they put it over rice to stretch it.

She added several cans of black beans and a large can of mild green chilis to the soup company's chili. Then she cut up some tomatoes and pan seared them with onions that had been caramelized. She added some additional chili spices, tasted it, and called it improved. For the corn chowder, she added more corn, some grated cheddar cheese, and a heavy pour of whipping cream, and a little European salt. The result was delectable. Now, she could say they were worthy of being Aunt Betty's recipes.

For dessert, she wanted to keep up the simple food kind of vibe, and she was tired of making the damn chocolate cake, so Aunt Betty was making another appearance with her famous peach cobbler. Thanks to the food network, she found a peach cobbler recipe that had gotten top marks. To make it unique and Aunt Betty's, she added raspberries to the peaches. They gave a lovely color to the three casserole dishes she made and added another layer of flavor.

Amber started a round robin email which circulated quickly, and the neighbors picked *North by Northwest* as their movie of choice for an evening at Amber's through a voting process. It pleased her, but then all the movies on the list were her choices, from *North by Northwest* to *Vertigo* to *Casablanca*, her favorite being *Vertigo*. She could always relate to Kim Novak's character, a woman who was playing someone else.

Officer Kent arrived early to the party with extra chairs to accommodate the neighbors. She liked Officer Kent, and it was definitely the closest she had come to a policeman in her entire life. He looked around the space, helped her set up the movie.

"I like you and Gingie," she said.

"I like myself and Gingie too," he said with an easy smile.

"She said she had a good time with you in Mexico," Amber said.

"Yes, it was a blast. I've never met anyone like Gingie."

"You know what they say. When you meet the one, put a ring on it."

"Now, don't go reading my mind, Miss Amber."

Amber smiled. Good, someone was happy. Valentine's Day was next week. She hoped that Kent would close the deal and actually put a ring on it.

Within an hour all the neighbors had arrived, gotten chili or corn chowder and helpings of all the additional food that had been prepared. They started the movie, and Cary Grant was getting known for his character's moniker, ROT.

Amber went into the kitchen to check on everything right as Cary Grant was getting crop dusted and nearly killed by an airplane. Hitchcock released three tarantulas into the field before shooting just to make Cary's fear real. It worked for Amber. And when Cary looks over his shoulder, she knows it has nothing to do with acting and everything to do with fear over meeting one of "Hitchcock's friends."

She bent over to put something in the dishwasher when a warm hand cupped her butt and a bit of something even more intimate between the cheeks. He was stroking her labia, trying to push his fingertips inside her through the fabric of her dress. It was beyond just coping a feel and whoever had a body attached to that hand wasn't going to like her reaction.

Whirling around, she faced no other than Dan Glass with a shit-eating grin on his face as if to say, "We've got a little secret. Yes, we do." He was a gross man. She wondered if he'd ever been attractive. Now, he had lost most of his hair, his teeth a color that was more yellow than white. She especially noticed the pooch he'd grown over the holidays.

"What the fuck do you think you are doing?" she asked in a low tone, as she brandished one of her Henkel steak knives.

"Relax, I'm just giving you a taste. Someday I'll kiss you there with my mouth. Bet no one has ever done that to you before. I got a thing for you hippy chicks, all natural. I bet you taste good. Oral is kind of my specialty," he said, holding up his hand and inserting his tongue between two of his fingers and then waggling it in a way that made Amber wish she had some tainted orange marmalade left to finish him off.

Taste this, asshole!

"Have I given you some reason to think I'd like you to grope me? That I, in any way, find your grotesqueness or crudeness attractive?"

"Come on, baby. Unless you are one of those man hating lesbians, there is no reason to fight what is going to happen between us." Then he made the mistake of licking his lips.

Before her anger registered and he fled to save himself, she grabbed his hand and calmly ran the blade of the knife over the palm.

"Hey...ouch! What the fuck?"

"What the fuck, indeed, you pig," she whispered, then in a loud voice that sounded a bit scared and rushed, she said, "Dan, I should have warned you, the cutting board slips on this counter unless there is a wet paper towel under it. Oh god, that looks bad, you are really bleeding, I think you need stitches..."

Dan looked shocked as blood started to drip from his hand. Amber slowly crossed the kitchen, gave Dan one last warning look over her shoulder and then opened the kitchen door.

She went into the family room and said, "Julia, could you come with me? We have a problem in the kitchen. Dan had a bit of an accident."

Someone paused the movie.

Officer Kent ran into the kitchen as Julia looked irritated at her movie being interrupted.

Amber lost one of her favorite dish towels as a makeshift wrap for Dan, but at least someone else cleaned up the blood. She thought it was that kind and thoughtful Officer Kent. Julia had to go home and get the car to take her husband to the ER for stitches. She took her own, sweet time. Fifteen minutes later, they resumed the movie.

At least Dan had the good sense to stay quiet. There were moments when she wondered if he would. But then again, she'd probably scared him silent, and if he ever accused her, who would believe him? Maybe he figured out that when Amber was near, he wasn't the most dangerous person in the room.

CHAPTER TWELVE

Amber checked on her garden each day in March. The bare root roses she had planted in January were starting to have green tips. She loved their names. *Sexy Rexie, Pope John Paul, Pinkerbelle, Coco Loco,* and *Tropicana* as an ode to her Las Vegas heritage. She smiled when she thought of Sexy Rexie next to Pope John Paul. It would be good for both of them! Her other plants were sprouting, not much, but they were there. In about two months she'd have more than enough foxgloves for any project she might deem necessary in the future.

At Easter she'd plant sweet peas, poppies, and sunflowers. Her garden would be beautiful and a little deadly to the person who really examined it.

Every yard in the neighborhood, every tree, every lawn seemed to be clean and green. Her lawn never looked better. Trees were starting to have the beginnings of leaves. The lawn was getting long enough that she asked Gingie who she should talk to about yard maintenance. The other woman promised to take care of it and true to her word, the lawn was mowed each week from then on.

It always amazed Amber how the seasons appeared. First, there was a hint of them in the air, and then one day, they arrived. It proved that every plant had a life cycle, just like humans. People underestimated plants. They were living things. And they liked to survive. The poison was just a defense. She respected them.

Gingie and Officer Kent did get engaged on Valentine's Day. Gingie was now sporting a large heart-shaped diamond that had been in Kent's family for several generations. Amber was happy for her friend, who looked happier than she had ever seen her.

The previous week, Amber harvested all the crocus and used a tweezer to pull out the saffron stamens. She had delivered little Ziplock baggies to her neighbors with a recipe for middle eastern couscous with apricots and pine nuts that was very delicious according to the food network, um, Amber's mother Madeline. She had made up Madeline, because she got worried that too many recipes from Aunt Betty would raise some red flags. When asked about Madeline, she would look sad and repeat how her parents had died in a car accident when she was twelve. She only hoped she hadn't mentioned a different age at the pool party when she said she went to live with Aunt Betty in Montana. Was she losing her edge? She didn't usually make mistakes.

Today, her focus was fully on the tulips and daffodils.

She counted and wrote down notes on her favorite varieties of daffodils and tulips from her garden. She was nothing if not meticulous in every element of her life. At that moment, 96% of the bulbs had moved forward to flower. She loved the Riot daffodil and Ring of Fire, which both featured bright bold colors. Each had red trumpets which she doubted any of her neighbors had ever seen. All the butterfly daffodils were amazing in shades of peach or yellow, but experience had proved that they all didn't last more than one season although they were supposed to. They didn't have trumpets, but their color was amazing. She also had quite a few green daffodils. Green with Envy was her favorite. There were at least three dozen at last count.

The tulips were various shades of red, pink, and yellow. She had a few parrot tulips that incorporated all of those colors.

She consulted her calendar and made a decision. She cut all

the blossoming tulips and daffodils. Her daffodils were anything but the yellow daffodils with yellow trumpets that were so common. She had enough for a couple of nice bouquets, but that wasn't enough for what she had in mind.

Placing the flowers in buckets of water in the back seat footwell of the Volvo, she left the neighborhood. Twenty minutes later, she was driving on Peoria Road north of Eugene having passed through the small town of Coburg. The land around Peoria was the epitome of a small-town life full of green fields and the occasional farm. There were even several Amish communities that sold baked goods. She stopped at an unhosted roadside honor-system flower vendor, which had lots of rustic tulips and daffodils for sale. She slipped a hundred dollar bill in the lockbox and took six bundles of tulips and daffodils, adding them to her bucket.

Back home, she spread out the flower bounty on her kitchen counter and put together bouquets for each of the neighbors. There were five when she finished. She tied the stems with red ribbons and started her delivery.

The last house she visited before Gingie's was Julia Glass's. She rang the bell and waited, hoping not to see Dan.

Julia appeared, having pulled the door open as if it were a serious inconvenience, one of her ever-present Odwalla juices in her hand. Possibly Amber was interrupting lunch which Julia obviously drank.

"Well if it isn't Aubry. Are you selling flowers door to door dear?"

"No, I grew these. I've been dropping off bouquets in the neighborhood. Sharing the bounty of spring as it were."

"Well, isn't that sweet. I really would like to pay something for them considering that I know money is tight for you. I mean, look at the way you dress. Now, don't you worry, it will turn around for you," then, as if inspired, she added, "You know, we are looking for a new house cleaner. Would you be available once a week to scrub our bathrooms, wash the windows, you know, that kind of thing? I'd pay you like forty dollars."

Amber thought she probably had more ready cash than Julia would ever have, but she didn't want to have an argument.

Aw, fuck it. She did.

"Julia, I don't want to upset you or rock your perception of the world, but I do quite well. I'm slumming it here in this little slice of Americana to prove that I can still live among suburbanites as I write my book. So, you can take your pity talk and shove it up your ass while I go back to my rented hovel and plan my next first-class trip to Europe when I flee this dump in the fall when the book is finished."

Julia didn't know what to say. Her hand rushed to her mouth.

Amber stepped off the porch, turned and said, "By the way, the name is Amber. Get it right." She winked and waved, stepped away.

An hour later, she was drinking wine at Gingie's kitchen table.

"I cannot believe you grew all of these yourself. They are so unusual," Gingie said, pulling one of the daffodils close for a sniff.

She hadn't exactly grown all of them, but the neighbors didn't need to know that.

"I love unusual daffodils," Amber said. "By the way, you might hear something. I took a bouquet to Julia. She pissed me off, so I told her a story. Well, I spun a yarn. Want to hear it?"

"Um yes, oh my god! Tell me."

She did. In fact, she'd never seen Gingie laugh so hard.

"Oh my god, she is going to think you are some famous person, who is hiding out. I love you so hard right now. That rocks so hard!"

"Exactly," Amber said with a laugh. "Thanks."

· · ·

Gingie

"It is ironic that you would stop by today, I was going to call you," Gingie said, an idea forming in her mind. Amber was perfect to round out her dinner party. Since she and Kent had gotten engaged, her world was hazy and love filled. But she was forgetting small details, like calling Amber. Kent told her that morning, he didn't care what kind of wedding they had or when, he just wanted to be with her. Occasionally, she'd have to laugh. This wonderful feeling, this was hers to keep. She was getting married!

"Really? Why? What is up?" Amber asked. "Are we toilet papering the Glass's house?"

"Well," Gingie said. "Aren't you full of it tonight?"

"Julia Glass pissed me off."

"You are now, officially, a member of the Pioneer Pike Women's Club. We only have one rule. We don't like Julia."

"I can handle that," Amber said with a laugh.

"Valerie, Libby, and I formed it a couple years ago. They will be happy to know that you've come to our dark side."

Amber said, "That is the side I like. Say, is Kent coming over tonight? I don't want to interrupt your plans."

"Later. He is working until eight. Stay. I'm loving this conversation. Keep me company for a bit."

Gingie had been pouring over her cookbooks and starting to make a list for the party she was planning for Saturday night. She topped off their glasses of pinot gris and joined Amber at the table. Then she stood and held up her finger. This was turning into an impromptu party. She added some nuts and crackers in little bowls, and then pulled some cheese from the fridge that she set on a tray with a cheese knife.

"You don't have to do all this," Amber said.

"Nonsense, you are helping me calm down. I'm nervous. I need your support. And now that I know you don't like Julia, I like you even more."

"Thanks. What is going on?" Amber asked.

"Kent wants me to meet a few of his friends and his cousin who is visiting from out of town. I volunteered to do a dinner party on Saturday night because I'm stupid. We should have just met them all at a restaurant, but no, I had to make the offer thinking this was an opportunity to show my skills as a cook. I want them to be impressed and think I'm the best possible match for Kent. The problem is that my ego and my cooking ability don't necessarily match in the kitchen."

"It will be fine. I've enjoyed everything you've ever made that I've tried. You, my friend, know how to cook. You'll be great. And they will love you. What is not to love?"

"Thank you, but we don't know that for sure!"

"Why are you so worried?" Amber asked.

"Well, the cousin will no doubt report back to his mother."

"Is it a guy or a girl cousin?"

"A guy."

Amber looked at her appreciatively and said half-jokingly, "You'll be fine, especially if you show a little of the cleavage."

"No, I don't want him to like me because of the twins. I guess I really want to make a good impression on his cousin and his friends. Damn it, even though I'm in love with Kent and we are engaged, I still have to pinch myself. This feels so right. Not the way it was with my exes, but they all know I've been married before, a couple of times. How can I explain to them that it is different this time? That Kent, well, he's my guy. I don't want to mess it up."

"I'm very happy for you. I always thought you made a cute couple. It is going to be okay," Amber said. "You've got this."

"Thank you, he is very cute. I think we look good together."

"You do, you make a fabulous couple! Now, tell me about the menu."

"I've taken a lot of French cooking classes and so I've learned to make beef bourguignon. I serve it with toasted garlic bread that is really, really good. I always have some side that is good like roasted veggies to break up the heaviness of all the butter and gravy stuff. Maybe I should do garlic mashed potatoes instead of veggies or rice pilaf? I'm so indecisive. I'll have a big salad with this creamy balsamic dressing that is to die for, and I'm making your Aunt Betty's chocolate cake for dessert. I'm doing one of those charcuterie boards to start with grapes, apples, cheese, and crackers. And I'm making some caramelized onion tarts with chevre that are wonderful. But I could go Italian. I also make a mean vodka sauce with homemade meatballs, garlic bread with cheese—"

Amber held up her hand, and Gingie immediately stopped talking.

"I'm intimidated just listening to you. Beef bourguignon isn't easy. I've tried it. You are going to be great. Everything is going to taste wonderful."

"So," Gingie asked, "It sounds, okay?"

"I repeat, it sounds wonderful. I almost wish I was going to be there."

"Okay, you're reading my mind, I have a favor to ask," Gingie said. "Are you free for dinner on Saturday night?"

Amber looked shocked, then put a hand to her chest, "You want me to come to your dinner party?"

"I need another person, but not just another person, a wing woman, a friend. Since I won't know the other five who are coming, you could be my person. I should have more than just Kent at the table! And I swear, this isn't a set up. Kent's cousin is in love with some girl he met last year who broke his heart. The other four are two couples who are friends of Kent's. Kent and I didn't socialize with a lot of people early on. We pretty much just enjoyed each other, so this is a big deal. If you came, you could be my support and my friend. Then I'd have eight at my party and that would be good."

"Okay, I'd love too," Amber said. "But on one condition."

"Sure, just name it!"

"I'll make the cake to take it off of your to do list," Amber said. "Would that ease your stress?"

"You would do that for me?" Gingie asked, feeling lighter than she had since she had volunteered for this stupid dinner party.

"Yes," Amber answered. "It would be my pleasure."

"I know you are busy with your book. I hate to burden you."

Yeah, the book. She found that it was hard to lie to Gingie. She didn't want to.

"I need a break from the book, why do you think I'm delivering daffodils? Writing a book is a lot harder than I thought it would be. And I've been making this cake since I was a little girl. And if I wasn't making it, I was watching someone make it. It is fine. I can make it with my eyes closed. I'll make it and bring it Saturday night."

"You are a good friend and a lifesaver," Gingie said as she reached out, grabbed Amber's hand, and gave it a squeeze.

"No problem, now tell me what you are going to wear."

CHAPTER THIRTEEN

Amber made an effort. Not the kind of effort Jane would have made in her appearance but this was very dressed up for Amber. She didn't know why she felt compelled to do this, but she did. When she reflected on it later, she was glad she had. The cake looked great with rainbow sprinkles. They were appropriate for this evening. In fact, she'd gone online and gotten special iridescent sprinkles that included little balls and stars. It looked amazing on the milk glass stand with the dome. It was ready to go, and Amber was ready to go play the part of supportive girlfriend which she felt because she liked Gingie. They were friends. Well, Gingie was friends with the woman known as Amber, not Jane or Dr. Kellan Smith.

Amber debated long and hard about her outfit, but if she looked good, it reflected well on Gingie and if Gingie liked her better when certain events unfolded in a couple of months, she was more likely to say nice things about Amber if the authorities had any questions. She rarely fell under intense suspicion but never say never.

She wore a black pencil skirt, black tee under a multicolored silk jacket with a black background and silver thread running through it. She put mousse into her freshly dyed red hair and then used hot curlers, so it was long and curly. The silver jewelry from Dotson's was polished and set off by all the black, a necklace, earrings, and several rings on her right hand. Instead of lipstick, she wore tinted lip gloss. If she were Jane, she'd wear a tight black cocktail dress that showed off her curves, lots of perfect makeup including red lipstick, and high heels. As her Amber persona dictated, she just wore a little mascara and blush, not to mention the clear tortoise framed glasses.

Had she ever befriended a person like Gingie during a past season? She didn't think so, but Gingie made it hard not to like her. She was a sweet little thing. Amber had to watch it. Being close to anyone could potentially be fatal to them. Although Amber had never killed a good person, and she never thought she could. Amber would never be a sweet little thing. She was an evil little thing.

She arrived five minutes late. It wasn't bad, just the way she liked to do it. Slip in, slip out without a lot of fanfare. It was important not to be too memorable, though that ship had passed. But being tardy also cut down on some of the chitchat that was usually associated with the first to arrive.

Kent answered the door and warmly greeted her with a kiss to the cheek, "Amber, welcome!"

Damn, she hadn't been kissed, well, since last January.

Then Gingie appeared and hugged her, careful of the cake, which was quickly removed from her hands and placed on the sideboard in a place of honor.

"Come into the living room, I'll introduce you to the gang." Gingie was doing well, she looked calm and relaxed. She was in a cute black cocktail dress, and she was rocking it.

Amber looked at each person as she was introduced, focusing on the woman of the couple so as not to be perceived as a threat. More women should do this, but few did.

"This is Patrick and Jan, Denice and David, and here comes my cousin from Minnesota, Jack."

A tall, well-built dark-haired man whose body Amber knew as well as her own walked into the room holding a bottle of wine and several glasses. He stopped walking at first glance, and she was treated to the face that she had fallen in love with at first sight in Saint Barts.

Kent missed it. He just kept talking. "This is our fabulous neighbor, the one who is writing a book on plants and how to make them into your own cosmetics."

Amber looked at Jack only to find that he was looking at her as if she was a ghost.

Time, the world, everything stood still, and she was back in Saint Barts, and he was sitting at the bar with the view of the ocean. There was only one empty bar stool, and it was next to him. He saw her and invited her to sit down. It was the first time she'd seen that smile. Their eyes had met, and nothing had ever been the same again.

He muttered a curse under his breath as if a ghost had just touched him. Then he got control of himself. The smile that used to look at her with love now turned to confusion.

Despite her hair, the makeup, and the clothing. He knew. He looked at her as if she was Jane and they were still in the hotel bar in Saint Barts.

It was Jack. She never thought she'd see him again. And now he was standing before her and all she wanted to do was run into his arms, but that was the last thing she could do. He was the cousin from Minnesota. This was Officer Kent's cousin. The odds. What were the damn odds?

She was fucked if she didn't think fast, damn fast.

"Amber?" Jack said, not understanding, his face hiding nothing. "Jane?" he whispered, confused.

"Yes, my name is Amber, and you are Jack, nice to meet you," she said smoothly and tried not to think about how she had missed him. How confusing this was to him. Leaving him in Saint Barts was one of the hardest things, possibly the hardest thing that she'd ever done, but it was for his own good. Hers too. Now, why the hell was he standing before her again? Fate had a wicked sense of humor. He needed to get as far away from her as was humanly possible. She wasn't safe for him. Nor was he safe for her — Jack could blow this whole charade up and do it unintentionally. Why, why had she agreed to this dinner?

No this was not good at all.

"Have you two met before?" Kent asked, confused.

Amber vigorously shook her head. Then, to illustrate the point, she said, "No, but by the look on your cousin's face I must have a lookalike. Am I right?"

"I don't know what to say. You look so familiar," Jack said. "I mean, you look exactly like Jane Miller. The hair is different, you dress differently, but you could be her twin. Even your voice--"

Crap. All she could do was fake this, become ill and get the hell out of here. Maybe out of town. It might be time to use her escape passport…just when she was beginning to like this place.

Amber decided to act like he was a little off, smiled and asked, "Who do I look like? Who is this person?"

"Jane," he said, watching for her reaction.

"Pardon me? Did you say, Jane?" she asked as if he were a special kind of stupid. "I'm sorry, I don't know any Janes."

"Yeah. Well, if you aren't Jane, you have one hell of a doppelganger."

"I do? I'm an only child so you'd better tell me about her. I always wanted a sister," she said acting mildly amused. "Dad was always going off hunting, but he wasn't any good at it. We'd be excited to see what he brought home, but it was always a disappointment. Maybe he had another family," she added with a laugh.

"I spent a week with someone who could be your twin, she looks like you, sounds like you, laughs like you," he said. "We had this magical, amazing week in Saint Barts and then she just left. I have been trying to get over her for over a year. I've been trying to forget her. Nothing has helped. I've been miserable. And here you are."

Uh-oh, this was going to be hard because it was going sideways.

Amber did her best to look uncomfortable. She looked from Jack to Kent. What was she supposed to do? She wasn't this Jane person anymore. She was Gingie's neighbor Amber. She had to play this well, once again she wished she would've taken acting lessons. "I'm so sorry, that is crazy. Do you have a photo of her?"

Gingie was looking at her with such a strange expression.

"No, she was always saying she didn't look good and not to take her picture. I have a couple of side profiles or near misses, but her face doesn't show. After it was over, I was so disappointed we hadn't taken a waiter or waitress up on their offer to snap our photo together. I have nothing. It was very frustrating. Actually, it kind of broke my heart."

Not appearing in photos had not been easy, but it was purposeful. He wasn't alone in missing having a photo of her. She had wished she had one of him. She missed seeing his face too. In her life, she had missed only one person. And she was looking at him now.

"I'm sorry, maybe you can take a photo of me and say I'm her," Amber said with a laugh and smiled then thought that sounded manic. She had to be careful, or she'd give herself away.

"Change your hair, ditch your glasses, and you are her. We will have to do that tonight. Get a photo, I mean. If that would be okay."

Uh-oh, she'd been kidding. It would not be okay. Her smile faltered.

This was not the Jack she remembered. This man was haunted. He had dark circles under his eyes. He'd lost weight. The self-confidence was gone. Had she done this to him? Did he care for her that much? She was trying to save him because she loved him. He did not want to be a part of what she did. It was a sacrifice and it had hurt.

No wonder she'd spent time on her appearance. It was like she knew that he'd be here tonight.

Eventually, the conversation turned to other things, and cocktails were poured.

Cocktails were awkward because Jack couldn't stop staring at her. He tried to be discreet, but he wasn't discreet at all. He took in her every gesture, every line, every movement. She tried her best to stop any tell that would give her away, but it wasn't easy. She wanted to look at him in the same way, savor each movement of his body, give in to the passion they had once shared, but that would give it away. She lived in a bit of fear that he'd call her out on what he knew to be true.

After all, she *was* Jane.

How many times had they made love that week? Enough that if she was naked, he'd know her body as she would know his. They had a chemistry, a passion that she had never felt for another living soul.

"Okay," Gingie said thankfully, interrupting the intense scrutiny. "Dinner is almost ready."

"Here," Amber said, standing quickly, "I'll help you."

The moment they were in the kitchen, Gingie leaned close and said, "Oh my gawd, what is it between you and Kent's cousin?"

"Like I know!" Amber whispered. "He looks at me like I'm a celebrity or something. He must have had it bad for that Jane person."

"Before you arrived, he was polite and quiet, now, wow. He can't stop staring at you. I'm so sorry."

"It is okay. It is just a little creepy," Amber confided. "But he must have really loved her."

"Well, thank you so much for being here and being so gracious," Gingie said. "I can't think he'll let this go on for the whole night. If it keeps up, I'll have a word with Kent to get him to stop it."

"Shit, I hope not. I feel like I have a stalker," Amber said.

"Don't bother Kent, I'm sure it will be fine. Damn, I feel sorry for the guy. He is kind of cute."

"I'll say. He's handsome, but seriously tortured. And thank you. I'm sorry he is bothering you."

They sat down to dinner, Amber across from Jack. This was bad. She was right-handed but tonight she ate left-handed so that her mannerisms would be different. The conversation flowed around them until Denice started quizzing Amber about her homemade creams.

Amber smiled and answered confidently.

"I'm really partial to roses. Have you ever noticed how soft a petal is? They've done a lot of anti-aging studies with roses, and I've made sure to pay attention to them. I like aloe vera, but there are many different kinds and many of them can have harmful side-effects if you aren't careful."

"There are a lot of harmful things in plants if you aren't careful," Kent added.

"You're right," Amber said. "I've learned a lot making cosmetics. I want to make sure people are careful when they decide to forage for themselves. For example, I love lily of the valley, but it is so poisonous that I have to use a synthetic scent if anyone requests something that smells like lily of the valley, although I don't like using anything that is synthetic. Lavender can really mess with breathing if you aren't careful, especially if you have asthma. Lots of people are allergic, although it isn't mentioned. I do a lot with violets too."

"Wait. Lily of the valley? I had it in my wedding bouquet," Jan said defensively.

"Well, as long as you didn't eat it, it is fine," Amber said.

Patrick asked, "Okay, so what happens if you eat it?"

Amber took a sip of her wine and said, "Heart failure, I

believe." She knew. It was very painful. It started with arrhythmia, leading to raised blood pressure, and then quick heart failure. Lily of the valley was pretty deadly, actually.

"How do you make ricin?" Patrick asked. "You know that white powder that everyone was so scared of in the early 2000s?"

Amber looked at him and said, "You want to make ricin?"

"No, I'm just curious," he said with a smile. "I mean it has been in the news, and then *Breaking Bad*."

Amber smiled and said, "I saw it on *Breaking Bad*. It comes from castor beans. You've heard of castor oil? Same plant, different part."

"How do you know all this?" Patrick asked.

"In order to make good things I have to separate the good from the bad. Not too many women would want facial cleanser with poison oak oil in it. So, I study up on plants."

"I don't get it," Jan said.

Amber figured there was probably a lot Jan didn't get. Amber said, "The way I think about it is like this. The plant is vulnerable when it is growing. Look at nightshade, it has berries that go from green to red to black, but you should avoid them all, especially children. But let's say you don't know better, then let's hope you've eaten only the black berries because the green berries are the most toxic. The plant is protecting itself so that it can grow up. By the time the berries are black, they want to be eaten and carried away by birds who will take them around and distribute them so more little night shades can be born."

"It makes sense," Patrick said, and Jan gave Amber a dirty look.

"The lotion Amber brought us at her first outing with the neighbors was wonderful. It was rose-scented, and I mean it was great. I will be buying some from you as gifts for friends, maybe as thank-yous for the wedding stuff," Gingie said.

"And as a friend you will get a really good price," Amber said.

"This whole thing reminds me of the conversation we had with your friend, Celeste," Patrick said to Jan.

"She's full of it," Jan said and waved her arm dismissively. "And I don't think you should tell it."

"What was the conversation about?" David asked, participating for the first time.

Patrick started to talk, but Jan shushed him.

"Tell us," David said.

"By the way, my compliments to you, Gingie, this is wonderful," Kent introjected, and they had a toast to Gingie and the wonderful food.

Patrick started in again, "Jan has this friend who is an embalmer, you know on like dead bodies."

"Oh my god, stop talking," Jan said, tossing her cloth napkin at Patrick.

Patrick ignored her. "She won't eat crab."

"Jesus, Patrick, really appetizing when we are eating dead cow," Jan started.

Amber didn't like the direction of the conversation, but she was very glad it was no longer focused on her. Speaking of dead things while eating dead things wasn't a good idea.

"What is with the crab?" Jack asked, speaking up for the first time as he stole a look at Amber.

"Okay, okay, but let me tell it," Jan said. "It is just that they had an issue with not fully weighing down a coffin for a burial at sea. It washed up on the beach like a week later. Some idiot decided to open it to see if the body was still inside. It was and there were like several hundred Dungeness crabs eating the corpse. It was disgusting."

"I think it is an old wives' tale. They don't find us delicious. I googled it. There are other things they like to eat. We are like seventh on the list of their favorite food," Patrick said.

Amber set down her fork and looked around the table. Her doppelganger status was the second most interesting thing that had been mentioned at this dinner party

Gingie looked horrified, and Amber felt sorry for her. This isn't the kind of dinner party she wanted to have.

Gingie

Gingie wanted to cry. First the gorgeous but odd cousin was all over Amber and didn't seem to want to let it go. Now, these obnoxious friends of Kent's were discussing corpses at her dinner table. Forget the beef bourguignon that she had literally slaved over all fucking day. Forget the beautiful place setting and the flowers from Amber's garden. No, they wanted to talk about how delicious humans were to crabs. She poured herself another glass of wine and stole a glance at Kent, who was watching her. She silently toasted him, and he just shook his head before winking at her.

Dinner was over the moment Patrick and Jan started discussing crabs and coffins. She and Kent cleared the table of dishes, Amber bringing her own and a few others to the kitchen where she whispered, "Thank you for not serving crab."

They both burst out laughing and decided to let everyone know the chocolate cake was vegetarian aside from the organic eggs Amber had used.

Thank goodness the cake was a hit. And before long people were making noises about leaving. Good. She wanted them out of her house. Kent had given Jack a ride there from his hotel but he asked Jack to take an Uber back so he could stay with Gingie.

Gingie heard Jack ask Amber if he could walk her home, but she pointed to Mrs. Gibson's across the street and shook her head. Gingie figured Amber had enough Jack for one night and she could not blame her. Gingie was glad she'd turned him down. His sudden obsession was more than a little creepy. He was like a puppy with his favorite toy. The fact he was gorgeous made it all the more uncomfortable.

At last, it was just her and Kent. She decided not to talk first. It might be interesting to hear what he had to say.

He came up behind her, placing his arms around her from behind. A minute later, his lips started to nuzzle her neck as his hands roamed over her body, feeling the curves through the cocktail dress she was wearing.

"I'm thinking of how I will make this up to you," he said. "A spa day? Dinner at your favorite places one night a week for a month? A weekend at the beach where I'm your love slave?"

"Bingo, I'll take the third option," she said turning enough just to let herself be kissed.

"I'm sorry that some of my friends are awful," he said.

"Some?" she asked. "I thought Jan was going to attack poor Amber. And what was that with your cousin? He kept staring at her. He's like a gorgeous stalker."

"I don't know, but that is the most animated I've seen him in a year. He really likes Amber or thinks she looks like Jane. That Jane woman almost destroyed him. But I have to agree, it was a bit creepy."

"Odd, isn't it, the resemblance?" she asked.

"Yeah, but I don't care about any of it. I just want you naked, in your bed, as fast as humanly possible. How do we make that happen?"

CHAPTER FOURTEEN

Amber shut her front door and leaned against it. She turned the lock and dropped the keys. Then, she slid to the floor, still holding the empty cake pan to her chest.

Jack.

It was really him.

Damn it.

She missed him more than she missed any other human on the planet. He knew her. He knew things about her that no other living soul knew. They had shared so much in a week. They had loved for a lifetime. All those feelings from a year ago surfaced and she missed him like she'd miss her arm if it was suddenly cut off.

How many times had she thought about that night? The night she left. It had killed a part of her. Destroyed her. She had cried on the plane. She had cried for a week, month, hell, she still cried when she thought about it. So, she didn't think about it. Not anymore. She had second-guessed her decision to leave at least half a dozen times each day since she had done what she didn't want to do. But he couldn't love the *real* her. Not if he knew who she really was. And he couldn't know that because then she'd end up in jail.

Jack.

He was here and she had sat with him and had dinner and never broken character. All she wanted to do was turn to him and say, "I miss you so much there is an ache inside of me that never stops hurting."

But did he know? Deep down was he still questioning who she was? Amber thought she got away with it but how would she know for certain?

Now she wondered if she should pack up tonight and leave? No, she had unfinished business here. She had never walked away from a season when it was in progress, but Jack created a wrinkle she had not predicted. Was she getting a second chance or a last look before her life caught up with her?

He looked so good. Well, tortured, but damn good. When she'd met him in Saint Barts, he'd been confident and strong, now he looked haunted. Had she done that to him? Well, hadn't he done the same thing to her? As scared as she was, she was also thrilled. She had touched him again. And when she'd shaken his hand, she felt the electricity all the way to her toes. Was seeing him one last time enough? Could she walk away?

What if she'd have just said, "Hi Jack. I missed you too."

Well, her world would implode. She'd be arrested. She'd spend the rest of her life wearing orange or the equally bad stripes.

Her face collapsed and she cried for the first time since she'd come to Pioneer Pike.

She didn't know how long she sat there, ten minutes, thirty, an hour? All she knew was that she wasn't going to get any sleep tonight and she was betting money that he'd return. Hoping? Then what? This had to be the worst mess she had ever been in. And she didn't know how to get out of it without a lot of pain.

Would she permanently have to take care of him? She couldn't. No way.

Through her tears she did what she did best. She let her analytical mind take over. Things that she needed went in suitcases. She wiped down the house. Every surface. They would still find her DNA, there was no way around it unless she set the house on fire. It wasn't the worst idea she had come up with. The neighbors would never let it burn. The moment the flames were visible on the street it would be over before it started.

By two a.m. the car was packed. Now, all she had to do was get inside and drive away, never look back at Pioneer Pike.

But she couldn't go. Jack was here, and it had to play out. It was fate. It was karma. She could not leave. Not yet.

She wasn't thinking straight, that was for sure.

The next morning, Sunday, she gave the French press a break and went to Starbucks. She sat inside at a little table, thinking about her night before. What the hell was she supposed to do? Her passport was in her purse along with $50,000. She had three packed suitcases in her car. Should she flee? She could just walk to the bus station or take a cab to the airport. In a few hours, she'd be gone. A memory. A curiosity.

She'd never left a job undone. Could she really start now? And all the evidence... damn, all the evidence. Amber hadn't had the proper amount of time to take care of everything. She needed to go back to the house on Pioneer Pike and make sure everything was wiped down. She'd done a bit of cleanup, but she needed to do more.

After an hour, she left and ended up at the community garden. She wanted to sit on a bench and think about seeing Jack again. It was odd for her to be so indecisive, but she was a mess this morning. Using her key, she let herself inside and discovered that she wasn't alone.

Motherfucker.

"Hey there, Julia," she said, greeting her neighbor. She hadn't seen the other woman since "the flower incident" a few days earlier. It went without saying that Amber avoided Dan, but the few times they had run into her at social events, well, if looks could kill, she'd be dead. At least now he kept his distance.

"Well, hello there," Julia said, looking very happy, and seemed to hold her gaze longer than she should. Something had changed.

She was so happy. Amber was naturally suspicious.

"How have you been?" Amber offered with a smile.

Today, Julia wore tight jeans, a pretty sweater in white with a coordinating pastel scarf to ward off the spring chill.

"Good," Julia said, "And you?"

Okay, so they were going to pretend that whole ragamuffin/house cleaner conversation had never happened, that she hadn't offered to shove something up Julia's ass...good, that was probably for the best. Part of Amber wanted to flash Julia the fifty large she had in her purse. It would reinforce her earlier story and further give her away, which was a very bad idea.

But today was not a day for conflict. She was just a girl who'd seen the love of her life. She was shaken. She was confused. Murder wasn't on her mind. Although when Julia looked smug, it made Amber willing to make an exception. Maybe she found a woman worthy of her judgment.

"I'm great," she lied. "I'm sorry we had words the other day. I didn't want to start something bad."

"I forgot all about that, I've had other more pressing things on my mind."

"I'm sorry, I just wanted to visit the garden and check on things. It is pretty, isn't it?" And she might be leaving, so she might be saying goodbye to all this hard work.

Julia volunteered, "I don't know if you heard, but Dan hasn't been well. He's having a little stay in the hospital. I took him in on Friday."

She didn't know. Heck, she doubted even Gingie knew.

"I'm sorry," Amber said tentatively and wondered if Julia had taken matters into her own hands after the red meat and cigarette conversation last fall. Maybe it was taking too long for a life of decadent debauchery to catch up with him. It could end badly, but then if he recovered, Amber would have to deal with him in her own way. What he did to her in the kitchen on movie night was enough. He needed to be removed from the living population. Women didn't need to add him to their worry list of predators.

"It was scary. His heart is having some issues, but we are getting them under control for the moment. Well, his doctors have gotten him stabilized. They think I can bring him home this afternoon," she said and then smiled a smile that actually made Amber uncomfortable. Was she getting soft? "He is on a bunch of medication. It is hard to keep them straight. I think Dan will confuse them too when he comes home."

"I'm so sorry. Has he quit smoking? Cut down on the cow consumption?"

"Of course not. He hasn't quit anything, including the blowjobs that his secretary gives him every afternoon in his office. I think the little bitch visited him yesterday." Uh-oh. Dan did seem to be orally fixated and should have told his mistress not to show up. She hoped the woman didn't attempt to make Dan happy in the hospital.

"Poor, stupid woman," Amber said, for the first time in the conversation she was speaking the truth.

"Yes, she is more of a girl, twenty-one if I'm not mistaken. It reminds me of when I was young and stupid. As for the girl, he doesn't know that I know. I don't know why it matters. We both have embraced our open marriage for many years. The passion with a new lover always fades. He, of all people, should know that. It isn't always going to be good for him, not like when he was forty. There will come a time when he is past his prime and need more little blue pills to fuck the young stupids. I think we are almost there. Needless to say, I'm trying to convert him to tea over coffee."

"Tea is a good idea," Amber said. She was having a hard time keeping up. They had an open marriage? Yuck. She knew Julia had been rumored to play around, but this whole conversation was over the top. Dan had peaked years ago. The term *Dirty Old Man* was made for him, the jerk. And Julia, where to begin…

This whole conversation was so twisted. Damn it! This season was so fucked. Too many people were involved. She wasn't thinking straight. She'd lost her edge. She did not want to be talking to Julia, and hearing about the open marriage…wow this was ugly. They were ugly. Amber needed to hold it together. Julia and Dan were horrible people, so noted. At least she'd apologized. She was pleased with herself for trying.

Why did it matter?

All she had to do was go home, get to the garage, and drive away. She had everything she needed. All the people on Pioneer Pike would be in her rearview mirror. Jack would be but a sweet memory. Her emotions that kept derailing her, could be dealt with later.

Or maybe the universe was telling her to retire. Find a nice little place, like in Bend or Boring as Fuck Kansas/Texas/Alabama, wherever. If she ended up in Bend, she could buy an all-wheel drive something like a silver Subaru, learn to ski and knit her own caps and scarves. She could probably knit a marijuana leaf pattern and sell gobs of them on the internet. Yeah, sounded really fun. No, it did not…She was feeling old and completely out of control.

Maybe start researching countries that didn't extradite to the United States. That could work. Then what? Invite Jack down for a little chat and screw? Tell him all, come clean? *She was just a girl, who was a murderess, asking a boy to love her*…um…vomit! Since when did she let her emotions lead her around by the nose?

She didn't use guns or weaponry. She was an artist, and her medium was poison. Maybe it was time to get a gun and blow her own brains out. End this fucking torture of a seriously jaded life. It just got worse by the moment.

Stop it! Stop it!

"Say, I should ask you. What do you use to make tea? You are in to all that. What makes it taste good for someone who has always enjoyed his coffee and wants to make a transition?" To decaf? Or death? Amber had recipes for each. Had she missed something?

So odd. She guessed offing Dan wasn't going to come into play today. So, she'd play it straight as if Julia was wearing a wire and the transmission was going right to the homicide department who had figured out that some woman liked to off bad men. Maybe Julia ran to the cops after their last conversation. Maybe she had figured Amber out. Or maybe she'd cured cancer, why was she giving Julia so much credit?

Amber hated this conversation too, so maybe a pattern was developing.

"Well, you could add peppermint leaves or go really herbal with hibiscus, rosehips, chamomile, raspberry leaf, meadowsweet, and or marshmallow root. Would you like me to make some up for him? I'd be happy to."

"You could do that? That would be so wonderful."

Did she want it to transition Dan? Maybe relax him into a casket?

"Okay, I'll do it this afternoon." Amber wouldn't add the last of her dried foxglove. The stuff she was growing would replenish her supply, but it wouldn't be ready for a few weeks yet. This would just be a mix she liked to give to people she wanted to live.

An hour later, when she had postponed running away again, she had a mixing bowl on the drainboard in her kitchen and was adding different herbs in different proportions to make the tea taste good.

God, sometimes she felt like an idiot. This was one of those times.

At the end of the tea mixing, she moved several ingredients around in the cupboards and found what she was looking for. The hidden ingredient. She grabbed a tonka bean, illegal in the United States since 1954. She shaved it like you would shave a truffle. It would add a nice hint of vanilla depth to the tea. She shaved a little vanilla bean as well, but there was nothing like the depth of a good tonka. Of course, if too much was consumed it would have a hemorrhagic effect, so she would have to tell Julia, no more than a cup or two a day. Or she could up the tonka amount and kill two birds with one stone. Who knew? The blood thinner might end up helping Dan to recover. Plants were tricky beasts. The more you knew, the less you knew. Too bad she didn't have something that would kill an erection or neuter him like the bad, humping animal that he was. It was all too obvious, and if Amber was one thing, it wasn't obvious.

Walking down the street she enjoyed all the spring color that she observed from the sidewalk like a fucking Pollyanna. She finally ended up at the Glass's, which was the last place she wanted to be today. She'd miss Pioneer Pike. She'd miss Gingie. The woman had grown on her, and she enjoyed watching her budding relationship with Kent. Now, they were getting married. She had wanted to stay for any wedding they might have. This kind of thing, weddings, baby showers, etc. she missed them. She only seemed to go to funerals and memorial services. Well, that was her own damn fault.

She liked Libby too. The Tinder account Libby had started right before Christmas had harvested a nice corporate tax lawyer, who seemed to adore her, the kids, and Larry. Amber predicted a wedding in a year or two. Maybe Larry would make a good ring bearer. Happy endings made her a bit misty-eyed because it was something she could never have. These people had lived in one place and reaped the benefits of long friendships. She was a wanderer.

Amber didn't like Julia Glass. Okay? She could admit it. The woman was condescending and quite frankly, not a nice person. She was playing her own game, and Amber didn't like being her pet mouse in the maze.

These neighbors were, for the most part, nice people. Could she say that about any of her other seasons? No. Pioneer Pike was special.

She rang the bell of the well-appointed ranch and waited. Julia greeted her with a big smile as Amber held up the bag of tea.

"Aubry, I can't believe how fast that was! What do I owe you?" Julia asked, making Amber feel like a girl scout hocking her cookies, again.

Ah, fuck it. It wasn't like Amber was her real name anyway.

"You owe me nothing, remember? I'm loaded. Just please just buy my book when it comes out."

There would be no book, although she could write one hell of a book. Keep up the appearances, *Aubry*. Maybe next season she would be a baker, or a stripper turned baker, then she could wear lipstick again.

"I'll tell all my friends to buy your little book. You should be so proud of your accomplishments. And just think a year from now, it will be for sale, and you'll get a real job."

"I don't need a real job," Amber said. "I have one, writing my book."

"I'm sure I don't know what you mean?" Julia said and then winked.

Bite me, thought Amber. She had killed people for fucksake. She had close to $3M in the Camen Islands in numbered accounts. She didn't need this condescending bullshit. Was Julia mentally ill? Was there a brain tumor under that perfectly coifed hair that made her a bitch? Amber worried she was trusting this woman way too much. Not good, not good. She sensed danger. She'd do the neighborly thing and give her tea and then step away. Juila had more fuel to add to her fire.

"I mean just look at you, the herbs are working for you. I meant to mention it this morning. You look so fresh faced," Julia said, but Amber knew the woman didn't mean it. "And you are doing it your way. Forget labels and fashion, you are making your own statement."

Bitch.

"Well, thank you, that is very kind of you," Amber said. Truth: she didn't use any of the herbs she grew on herself; that would be dangerous because she liked the poison kind, not the medicinal, beneficial kind. She drank coffee. She despised herbal tea, especially anything with chamomile. If she needed to relax, she popped a Xanax. Also, she knew she didn't look good. She looked like she probably didn't wear deodorant and didn't know what it was like to buy makeup, as in ever.

She plucked her eyebrows. Her underarms, legs, and bikini line had been lasered when lasers really hurt ten years ago before everyone wanted Brazilian hairless bodies. She'd been a damn trend setter. That was saying something, but the rest was 100% fake hippy. Julia just might be 100% crazy.

Amber knew she could look a lot better. Jane had looked good. Amber needed a makeover. Next season she really was going to look hot. This hippy thing was getting old. She missed her red lipstick. She missed her cleavage. She hated the scent of Patchouli. Left to her own devices, she'd wear Baccarat Rouge 540 like the expats in Dubai. Jane wore the Baccarat Rouge 540. She missed it. It was unisex, but she had yet to meet a man who wore it. Let's just say if she did, she wouldn't want to.

"Now, what is in this?" Julia asked cautiously, holding up the clear bag of assorted ingredients. She should be leery. Anything

Amber made was suspect. How easy it would be to crush a few Yew seeds in the tea or add dried hemlock.

"I made you the tea I normally drink so you can drink it along with Dan. It is fine. It does have a little tonka bean in it. That is an ingredient that adds a richness, a vanilla-cinnamony twist. I also added some shaved vanilla bean, so if you see some black specs that is why. You don't want to add too much tonka because it thins the blood if you use large quantities, like super aspirin. You do not have large quantities in this tea. There is just enough for a little added depth and flavor. Just don't drink six cups a day. If you like the flavor, I'll make you some without the tonka, and that you will be able to drink it in large quantities."

She didn't know why she needed to explain about the tonka so much. They sold it on Amazon. Maybe it was just because she knew the dark side and couldn't help herself.

"Hmm...tonka beans."

"They use them on baking shows in Britain. That is how I first heard about them."

"Fascinating. It is so good that you have learned all these things," Julia said condescendingly.

Amber stepped off the curb, feigned a headache that required her to go home and lay down. Amber was now making it up as she went along. Not only should she reconsider her thoughts on killing women, she should also reconsider her thoughts on only using poison. If she had a gun, Julia Glass would be dead, and the world should throw a parade in her honor.

Was she depressed? Maybe she was. Did she want to settle down? Fat chance. But seeing Jack last night had really done a number on her. Her thoughts were all over the place. The week she'd spent with him might have been the best of her life. Okay, it *was* the best of her life. It broke her heart and a few other things to walk away from him. She wished she'd never gone to Saint Barts. Maybe if she'd never killed Bill, her boss, in the first place...wait...maybe if she'd never gone to a vegan dinner at

Paul's she'd have done something much different with her life. Maybe she'd be homeless. Maybe she'd be married and have a dog named Larry. Maybe she'd be dead herself. Fate was a tricky thing. She needed to stop thinking about it. This is what it was. She was who she was.

She walked up her driveway and looked down as she found her keys in her jean jacket pocket. Maybe she should take the rest of the day and call it a rejuvenation day. She had pretty much decided she wasn't leaving. Watch a movie, open a bottle of Prosecco, get DoorDash takeout with dessert. Put polish on her nails. Something she could later claim was organic. Yeah, that sounded good. Have girly time. Maybe she could buy some lipstick and have it sent to one of her post office boxes.

But a relaxing afternoon wasn't meant to be.

She stepped into the entryway and froze. There was someone sitting on her front step. Well, not anyone. Jack.

"Hello Jane," he said.

This was the moment that Amber became aware of the heart in her chest, worried it might explode. She should have left Pioneer Pike last night when she ran into Jack at Gingie's. This was her worst nightmare. *Deny. Deny. Deny.* Get him out of here and then run. In the meantime, keep up with the charade.

"Jack," she said. "Why are you here? And my name is Amber. Remember? I'm her doppelganger, not her. Should I call Kent? Do you need some help? Are you okay?"

"I think," he said, standing to his impressive six feet, "that you should cut the crap. Your heart-shaped freckle, you know the one on the top of your left breast, the one that fascinated me, the one I always used to kiss...well, two people who look exactly alike don't have that identical freckle."

How the hell had he seen that? Well, that really cut to the chase. Her cover was blown. No doubt about it. Now what? Damn her adorable heart shaped freckle!

"I saw it when you bent over to grab my plate last night. I

wanted to reach out and touch it, but I didn't. I thought I showed amazing restraint."

Okay, say something.

"I was running from an abusive boyfriend," she said, allowing herself a tear or two. "You can't tell anyone. He will find me. It is a life or death situation. No one knows." The tears were real. She was upset. Hell, she was terrified. "Damn it, Jack, I need you to keep this to yourself."

Jack had the audacity to laugh. Fuck. She had to make him believe, otherwise she would have to kill him. Not good, not good.

"It isn't funny," she said. "I'm scared to death. Why do you think I left Saint Barts so suddenly. He knew I was there. I didn't want him to hurt you. I've been on the run ever since. I don't mean to tell you, I'm scared. If you can discover my secret, so can he."

"Jane, or whatever your name is," he said shaking his head. "There is an old joke that seems appropriate in this moment. A woman at a rest stop picks up a hitchhiker. When they are driving away, he says, 'You really shouldn't pick up hitchhikers. For all you know, I could be a serial killer.' The driver replies with a laugh, 'Come on, what are the odds there would be two serial killers in the same car?' What are the odds that we would find each other again, *Jane?*"

What was he saying? Was he a killer too? His cousin was Officer Kent. What the hell was going on?

She hated that panicky feeling boiling up inside; it made her do very bad things at very inopportune times. Like kill people.

"I think you'd better come inside because I don't understand any of this," she said. Yes, inside, and away from prying eyes. Brilliant.

"I'd love for you to explain it. And I'd love to find how much of what happened in Saint Barts was real."

At the door, her hand on the door handle she turned to him

and said, "My feelings were real. They might have been the realist they have ever been. And please, I need you to call me Amber."

"I get it, Amber, but you will always be Jane to me."

"Jane is dead," she said.

CHAPTER FIFTEEN

There were no scenarios for this situation because it was never supposed to happen. Amber never, ever thought she'd see Jack again. She was going to have to make it up as she went along. And Amber thought she had worked out everything, every possible circumstance in her mind. Cause/effect. Hypothesis. If/Then. *If* a neighbor discovered her, *then* she would use one of her other identities and run like hell.

At no point did she think she would be face to face with Jack again. Last night and this morning had been a waste of time. She could be in Seattle, hell Vancouver B.C. by now, but no, she was exactly where she had been in Butt Fuck Eugene, Oregon. She had officially lost her edge, and it might cost her the rest of her life. Then she remembered how she looked in orange or stripes and wanted to cry.

"Would you like a drink?" she asked Jack as he followed her inside.

"Only if it is sealed and you take a sip of it first," he said.

He thought she would poison him? She would never hurt Jack. It hurt her that he thought she'd do something to him. Hell, she loved him. She'd never harm him. She couldn't hurt a hair on his head.

"Jack, how can you think that of me?"

"Easily. Now look, I don't think you'd shoot me, but after last night, I'm pretty sure you know a thing or two about poison. I think that is your weapon of choice. So, I'd rather be a little cautious. Call me paranoid, but I like living. And you will notice I don't have any guns or knives on me."

"Look, you need to believe me, I'd never poison you. I'd never hurt you. I can't," she said, her voice cracking with emotion as she looked away.

"Strangely, that is the first thing you've said that I actually believe."

"Please, you aren't making sense. I'm running away from an abusive boyfriend. He will stop at nothing."

"You know, I've spent months trying to find you. I used to wonder why I hit so many dead ends. It always niggled at that dark part of my brain. I had a good five scenarios, but it kept narrowing down to one. At first, I dismissed it, but then I put it together. Then I remembered something you said in Saint Barts. When you heard about a scuba diver who died while we were there you felt no remorse for him. You said, 'Maybe he got what he deserved. He sounds like an ass.' It stuck out to me and then I added it to everything else I knew. In fact, I think I figured it out. You change your identity because you kill people. I just don't know how deep you are into it. Do you do it independently, or are you hired?"

"What a crazy assumption," she said.

What is happening? Why was he doing this to me?

He knows something — that's it — damn it Amber, you fucked up! Are you going to have to kill him? No, she couldn't do that…

"Believe this," she said. "I'm grateful to see you and scared to death. You might be the end of me. I'm kind of at your mercy. If he finds you and asks where I am—"

"The chances of me telling a fabricated ex-boyfriend about your whereabouts are about as believable as me turning you in. It isn't going to happen."

He crossed the distance to her, gently removed her glasses, laughed when he looked through them, tossed them to the side, and pulled her into his arms. It felt like nothing had felt since he'd held her in Saint Barts. She'd been in a state of no feeling. Numb. She looked up at him, their faces less than an inch apart. She melted into him. She let herself be vulnerable although she knew at any moment he might slap cuffs on her or the SWAT team might break the door down.

But then he kissed her, and she kissed him back. Maybe he wasn't going to turn her in. Being in his arms was like coming home. She knew how to savor it because it might be a ticking time bomb. At any moment, it could end, and she might never see him again or she might see him testifying at her trial.

She'd missed him so much. She couldn't tell her body to stop when it was getting what it so badly needed. All she wanted was to feel the way Jack had made her feel when they were together. She followed him to the nearest flat surface, which happened to be the floor of the living room.

She needed to know. "Jack," she whispered, but he shushed her and kissed a trail along her skin as she pulled at his clothing, a chambray button-down and chinos. This might be how the SWAT team found them, half dressed, but at the moment, she did not care. She wanted Jack, needed him with every cell of her being.

He was so preppy, just like in Saint Barts. He'd ironed his Bermuda shorts and linen shirts and he was in neatly pressed clothing now. He was a man who sweated the details. Her heart shaped freckle, etc. How she'd missed his perfection. And as he kissed her, air hit exposed skin as he peeled away her ragamuffin layers, making her shiver. When her wrinkled tee shirt lay in a pile near his crisp button down, he kissed the heart-shaped freckle, making her gasp.

"I see you still like me, and I still seem to have the same effect on you," he said as he unbuttoned her jeans and pushed them off her legs and continued with her organic cotton panties, which were the cream color of unbleached fabric, the mark of a true hippy. She wished in that moment that she had saved a bit of Jane's lingerie.

"I never forgot you. You...there's been no one since you," she said as his fingers slipped between her legs and expertly touched her, finding her heat and manipulating her expertly to her first orgasm, which took them both by surprise. Damn! He hadn't forgotten anything about her.

When she finished gasping, he said, "No one makes you feel this good. Only me."

"No one," she said. "But you."

"I've never felt the way I do when I'm inside of you. We are two sides of the same coin."

He paused to unhook her bra, and then he feasted on her breasts.

She was embarrassed by the organic cotton. Jane always wore silk, if she wore underwear at all, which, considering how many times they made love in the open in Saint Barts, was advantageous. He'd liked that too, the ability to have her, anywhere. She was always ready for him just like now.

Soon, he was naked too, braced above her.

"Say it," he whispered.

"I love you," she said, and he replied, "I love you too."

Then he wrapped her legs around her waist and entered her none too gently.

"God, how I missed you, how I missed this," he said. "You feel so tight, so warm. It is like coming home."

She cried out at the intrusion and then smiled as her body adjusted to him. "I missed you," she said. They could solve all their problems later.

There was a frenzy to their loving. It was fast and hard, a reclaiming more than lovemaking, but when they'd both climaxed, and were still recovering, he picked her up in his arms and carried her down the long hallway.

"Where?" he managed.

"Last door on the right," she said, her arms wrapping around his neck.

They second time they made love was slower, in the Laura Ashley bedroom with the Aunt Betty quilt tossed haphazardly to the floor, but the passion was the same. It rushed over her like warm water in a luxurious shower after a long day.

"Red," Jack said, when they had both been satisfied, as he fingered some of her hair. "I don't mind it. But I liked the blonde too. It all works because you will always be my Jane."

She was pinned beneath him, but she didn't want him to move. He was still inside her, but they had finished together, and it was only a matter of time before he would slip away. She ran her thigh along his leg to prolong the moment.

"Are you trying to start something?" he asked as he kissed her neck.

"What if I am?" she asked. "What if I don't want you to go?"

"I should tell you, now that I've found you, I won't let you out of my sight. I'm not going anywhere. We will work this out. We will get our stories straight. Because I need to do this to you every night. I want to sleep with you in my arms and wake up with you the next morning. Living without you almost killed me the old-fashioned way, with a broken heart."

She could relate.

"I don't know if I felt truly alive without you. I've been going through the motions. But a part of me died when I left Saint Barts without you," she said.

In his intimate declarations at least, he hadn't said he was going to call the police.

"You are mine in a way no one else will ever be."

"I should tell you, you're closer to the truth than you know. I'm a bad person," she said. "I've done bad things."

He kissed her and said, "Welcome to the club, sweetheart."

When he said no more, she didn't ask him to elaborate. He picked her up and took her into the shower, where he ran a lavender soap drenched washcloth over every inch of her skin in slow, loving motion. She wondered what he meant. But soon, their brief respite had the desired effect and he had recovered enough to take her again.

He pulled her to him, lifted her up, arranging her legs around his waist, pinned her to the shower dampened baby blue tile inside the shower, and rode her hard. The cool tile along her back and the hot man inside her was ecstasy.

She smiled with his first thrust and then began to moan in pleasure. God, how she missed this, how she missed him. He had an edge of feral passion that matched her own. They never made sweet love. They had mind-blowing sex. There was so much for them yet to do to each other. She'd had months to fantasize about the possibilities. She wanted to explore and re-learn each inch of him. She wanted to do it with her tongue, with warm wax from a dripping candle, with an ice cube dragging lazily over his skin like she had in Saint Barts. She just didn't know where to start.

They ordered Chinese from Door Dash, eating it in her bed.

"I didn't think today would end like this," she said as she grabbed a shrimp with her chopsticks and fed it to Jack.

"I did," he said, after eating the shrimp and kissing her. "But let me guess, your car is packed, your passport, which gives you yet another name, is someplace close, like in your purse. The only fingerprints that remain in this house are the ones you left since I arrived."

"Are you some kind of ninja mind reader?"

"No," he said, "but it is what I've had done. I haven't figured out the fake passport stuff yet, but you can teach me."

"Can I ask you a question?" she asked, thinking he was the one who had a lot to ask. She had lied, he didn't know who she was, but this was her. She had the nerve and had decided to hold back nothing including her curiosity.

"Ask," he said, his eyes dreamily content in a way they had not been the night before.

"When we were in Saint Barts, I thought you were a lawyer, a divorce lawyer."

He laughed.

"I am a divorce lawyer. I have a degree. I have passed the bar. I have a practice in Minneapolis. I have an office."

Amber shook her head and said, "Yeah, but what else are you? You told me you are a bad person like me. I don't believe it."

"I've found a few occasions to meter out justice when the courts won't."

Amber ate another shrimp and said, "For a price."

"No, I selfishly arrange my own agenda. If someone is a wasted piece of humanity, I do humanity a favor. That is priceless."

Was he a killer? No...

She turned a little, so she could see his face as she asked the next question.

"Is that why you were in Saint Barts? Were you doing humanity a favor?"

"Yes, but I finished that business the morning on the day I met you," he said his voice taking on a musical if not hypnotic quality. No wonder he was a good lawyer. She'd bet he could be good at anything he tried.

She said, "I remember a scuba diver died that day. An American doctor, I think a plastic surgeon, on his honeymoon with his new wife. They were from Wisconsin. Did you have something to do with that?"

"Well, let's look at some of the details. She was his second wife. Not to be confused with the first wife who worked two jobs to put him through medical school. His first wife was the mother of his two special needs children, who were born with debilitating cognitive issues because it turned out that they both had this gene, the father and the mother, that when combined created chaos. He didn't see his two beautiful sons because they reminded him of what a jerk he was, ditching their mother for a patient who wanted larger breasts. She was struggling like I've never seen a woman struggle. Forget child support, he wanted nothing to do with his children, even offered to sign over his parental rights if it meant he could walk away. He didn't want to be responsible for the lives he'd created."

Amber shook her head, "He wanted to start a second family. The second wife was thirty years younger, or that is what the local paper said."

"She was twenty-four, actually, and stupid man that he was, he agreed to a new life insurance policy as part of the divorce to quickly conclude the ditching of his first family. He really didn't think it through. It was the only way his ex-wife and kids would be well cared for was in case of an accident that led to his premature death. It was the only way she was going to get any money for the increasing costs of the kids' medical care."

"Is that what he had? An accident?"

"Yes, he did. But you've got to ask, was the accident that day in Saint Barts or the moment he forgot his wedding vows?"

Amber thought for a moment and nodded as she said, "Valid point."

"Point taken," he said and set the takeout box on her nightstand as he gently pulled down the sheet away from Amber's body, leaned over, and took her nipple in his mouth.

Amber's body arched. He might truly understand her darker self. And they had found each other. After a few moments of contemplation, all she could do was succumb to the pleasure he was giving her.

Gingic

She looked out the curtain, pulling it back to get a good view as she held the cellphone to her ear.

He answered on the first ring, "What are you wearing?"

"Something that you will enjoy removing."

"I'll be there in twenty minutes," Kent said.

"As much as I'm enjoying this little chat, I have to ask a serious question."

"Yes, I'm going to have sex with you tonight. You are going to feel so relaxed and satisfied you won't be able to make a fist for a week."

"Will I be able to walk?" she purred.

"Yes, but every time your thighs rub together, it will hit just the right swollen spot that I've activated with my ministrations. It will make you tingle, and you will remember me and what I did to you. Things I'm going to spend the rest of my life doing to you."

"Promises, promises," she said, looking out the window.

"You know, I think I can be there in ten minutes," he said.

"I'll be waiting," she said. And then, despite what she wanted from him, she had to ask something. "As much as I'm anticipating what you'll do to me, I have a question to ask, but I don't want it to be a buzz killer."

"Oh, all right, ask."

"Does your cousin Jack have a red sports car?"

"Jack? Yeah, that is his rental while he is in town," Kent said from the other end of the phone. "We were supposed to shoot some hoops tonight, but he begged off."

"Mystery solved. He's at Amber's. Something is going on with my neighbor and Jack," Gingie said.

"Like what?" Kent asked.

"Well, a red sports car has been parked on Pioneer Pike since about noon today. I could swear I saw Jack sitting on the porch at Amber's. And now, well, when she got home, she let him in,

177

and he has been in there all afternoon and evening. The light in her bedroom is on. DoorDash made a delivery. Do you think—"

"That you are spying? Yes."

"Get over it. This is about Jack and Amber."

"They are fucking. You're kidding."

"Um, no, not kidding," Gingie said.

"Well, he seemed a little obsessed with her last night."

"I thought so too. How did he finagle that into being in her house all afternoon? Her bedroom?"

"I have no idea. She isn't the girl that he lost. She just looks like her. Maybe she found him attractive. Maybe he is scratching her itch?"

"Is your cousin, okay? I mean, do you think we should be worried?" Gingie asked. "He isn't a serial killer or anything is he?"

"No, we should not worry. He is a highly respected attorney and a heck of a nice guy. And no, it isn't like he is a serial killer. Maybe he just said enough to hit it off with your neighbor. Maybe she is a bit hard up. You said she hasn't had a date since she moved into the neighborhood. I'm serious, maybe Jack is scratching her itches. I don't think he has gotten laid since Jane in Saint Barts. Good luck to both of them. This might be a great thing. Stop worrying."

"Well, okay then, I can't argue with someone getting a little action when it is all I want at the moment. Ten minutes is a long time. Should I start without you?" she asked. "I've got an itch I can't reach, but if you don't get here, I'm going to have to try."

"We can't have that. I'm more than happy to lend my body to scratch any of your itches. But can you tell me what you're wearing? You never did, and it is bothering me. I want to think about how to get you out of it while I drive over. But I need to know what it is to make that happen."

"I'd tell you, but I don't want you to have an accident, Officer Logan. Better drive fast, the itch isn't going away until you touch it because I really can't reach it. Oh my...You see, I just tried."

"If I wasn't an officer of the law, I'd break every speeding law to get to you."

"Now don't do that, I wouldn't want you hauled away and arrested."

"The only person getting handcuffed around here is you, you bad girl."

"Well, I think a conjugal visit could be fun. I can tell you what I'd wear for that." And she did.

CHAPTER SIXTEEN

Amber reached for Jack in the middle of the night. She didn't have to search for long, his body was wrapped around her in a tight spoon. His hand cupped her breast. His nose tickled her ear. His body was warm along her back. For a moment she felt like she was back on the beach in Saint Barts.

What was power? Knowing she could nudge him awake by simply turning toward him or kissing him. They'd be making love less than a minute later.

Happily, it was the fingers that tightened on her breast, expertly tracing circles around her nipple and accompanied by warm lips kissing a trail from neck to shoulder that signaled he was already awake and wanted her as much as she wanted him.

She reached back and cupped him intimately, then turned to find a man who was ready to make her happy.

This time was different than their usual frenzied coupling. They made slow, tender love, side to side, which left her panting. This man knew how to bring out the best in her again and again. Nothing ever changed, but her need, which only grew.

"Amber," he whispered.

"Hi Jack," she said as he squeezed her butt cheek and pulled her leg around his hip.

My god, they were like a couple of randy bunnies in heat. Yet the need, it didn't get satisfied, it asked for more.

"I can't get enough of you," he said, his voice thick and emotion filled.

"I know the feeling. What are we going to do?" she asked.

"I have to leave in two days."

"No, you promised you'd stay. You found me again," she said.

"Come with me."

"To Minnesota?"

"Yes, have you ever been there?"

"I've been to the airport," she said and paused as he kissed her, their lips devouring each other, tongues dancing, illustrating the ever-present need.

"I don't want to lose you again," he said. "It is you. You are it for me. No one else will ever have a chance. We belong together."

"I don't know if I can be without you again. It was too much," she said. "I can't forget what we did in Saint Barts. That night on the beach…"

"Was amazing. I'll never forget that night," he said, his hand landing in her hair and then pulling her close for another kiss.

"There are things I need to tell you," she said.

"I told you; I think I've guessed some of it," he said.

"I'm a horrible person," she said. "You don't know that side of me. I need to tell you everything. You need to know what you're getting into."

"I'm no saint, my beautiful," he said. "I do what I do in the name of justice, but that is a pretty way to cover up what I'm really doing. Part of me thinks I enjoy it. Hell, I do enjoy it. After that first time, I promised I'd never do it again. But I can't stop myself. It is so clean and efficient. It is done, and life goes on for those who deserve to live."

"That's my problem. I do enjoy it, too. I feel like I'm metering out justice. I feel like a god," she said with a large sigh. "I think innocent, good people are alive because of what I've done to the evil ones in their lives. But that is what I tell myself, and I know it is a lie. I'm a murderer."

"So am I, darling. We have that in common."

"Is that why we found each other?" she asked.

"Birds of a feather?" he asked in reply. "Maybe. But no one else understands." Yes, there was no way anyone could know. This, what they do, could never be part of a normal conversation. But between them, they could share things...Amber didn't need to be alone anymore.

"How could they?" she said.

"You aren't a monster, Amber, my Jane."

"A small part of me must be."

"Me too, but the part that wants to be with you isn't."

It was dark, but she could see his smile in the shadows. They were similar in all the ways that counted, the good and the evil and she'd never find another man that she'd be able to share all of this with. No, Jack was it for her.

"When you know everything that I've done you might feel differently."

"Doubtful," he said. "Tell me. Unburden your soul and see how I react. Just how many evil people have you worked with?"

It was a more pleasant way of saying killed, but she appreciated the sensitivity.

"Are you sure you want to know? If I tell you, it might change how you feel about me. I don't know if I could bear that. I can't lose this," she said, cupping him again It was crude, but it was honest.

He kissed her, rolling her onto her back, his body stretching out on top of hers. She wrapped her legs around his waist. She loved the weight of him. And then he kissed her. Murder made for very interesting foreplay.

"Nothing you will ever tell me will change this," he said. "Or how much I love you."

She cried, tears of joy as he took her again. He knew she had killed, but he was inside her, intimately, the most vulnerable he could be, the most vulnerable she could be, but there was trust. He had it for her, and she had it for him.

And when he was finished and she was remembering to come back to earth, she whispered, "Eleven."

"Really?" he said with admiration. "Men and women?"

"All men, but they were bad people or had been bad, except for the terminally ill that I helped to their next soul journey, ending their pain. Ending the pain of those who have watched them whittle away. But that doesn't make me a hero, it just makes me someone who doesn't like to see others suffer. Of those, maybe three needed their suffering to end. I'd like to focus more on those who are suffering. How about you?"

"I'm embarrassed to tell you. My number isn't that impressive."

"Tell me," she said, her hands rubbing his shoulders as he whispered in her ear, "Four over fifteen years, all males, but there were others who deserved it. I just didn't want to stand out as being their common denominator. So I held back because I like where I live. I like the life I have. I don't want to lose it."

"Protect your life. I'm nomadic, it isn't fun."

"You can be with me in my life," he said. "That way, you will never be alone again."

"Thank you," she said. "By the way, four is nothing to sneeze at especially with no suspicion around you. Maybe I can help you. Maybe we could help each other."

"You'd do that for me?" he asked as he nuzzled a tender spot on her neck. She hadn't had a hickey since she was in high school, but she didn't mind that he was marking her. She hoped he was. She liked the pleasure and the pain of his teeth on her skin. She wanted to look in the mirror and see the love bite, remembering how and when she got it.

The irony of the situation wasn't lost on her. What they were doing now, what they did for a living contradicted each other in the most horrendous way. Maybe things would have to change...

Amber realized she was getting awfully sloppy this last season. Could life be satisfying without the kill? Maybe. Anything could be satisfying with Jack at her side.

"I think we need to consider what life would look like if we shared it. I'll call you Amber or whatever name you tell me as long as you don't change it when we are making love. I'm completely addicted to you, to this."

"Thank god I'm not the only one," she said and kissed a trail down his chest to one of her favorite parts of him. He needed to know what that particular part meant to her. She lavished it with attention until he moaned and could no longer put coherent words together.

Maybe she'd get a taste of happiness after all.

CHAPTER SEVENTEEN

The next morning Amber made Jack breakfast, of an omelet filled with herbs and cheese, bagels, and coffee. They were both ravenous after the night they'd had. When they were done, she said what had been on her mind since she'd found him on her doorstep.

"We need to talk. I want to tell you everything, not just the highlights. But I want you to know me."

He kissed her and pulled her to him. Then he whispered in her ear, "I want to know every one of your secrets."

He followed her into the living room where they sat on one of the floral Laura Ashley couches, and she told him about her life, starting with OldJen, the stepfathers, the blackmail, the escape, the infamous mushroom dinner party and how it led to Dr. Kelan Smith, then to Jane and Amber. Her timeline, her verbal murder diary.

It was an unburdening of her soul. It felt good to tell him. Only once or twice did little alarm bells ring in her head, possibly she was telling him too much. But unless he was recording it or had a photographic memory, even if he did have second thoughts and might run to his cousin Kent, the police, he didn't have any evidence beyond her hearsay. She could say she was rehearing a part, testing out a book plot. She was a little bit careful, not giving him all the details, just giving him the gist.

"Wow, Dr. Kelan Smith. What should I call you?"

"Call me Amber for now."

"Will I have to learn a different name every year?"

"Yes," she said "Unless I stop. Do you want me to stop?"

"I don't want you to change, unless you want to. But I might want to help. Is there room for me?"

"Oh yes, you are the partner that was born for me," she said and leaned forward for a kiss.

"But if you join me in Minnesota, you will be Amber for potentially the rest of your life."

"Yes. I should have been Amber last season and Jane this season. I like the name better."

"As they say, what is in a name?"

She said, "I've told you enough to lock me away for ten lifetimes. Now, I want to hear about you. What got you started and why? Were you really married once?"

He nodded, took a sip of his coffee, and then there was this change in his face. A trace of sadness, a trace of rage. Amber could relate.

"I was married for seven years to my college sweetheart until she cheated on me with someone who was once my friend, and we divorced. And before you get worried, she married the guy, and they are both alive, and I hear they have kids. Good for them. I'm thankful they moved to Phoenix, I didn't want to have to see that or run into them. I have control, but that might push me over the edge if I had to see them after what they did to me, to our marriage. I don't love her anymore, but I don't like what she did. I've forgiven, but I haven't forgotten."

"Nor should you. But you didn't start taking care of business until she was long gone," Amber surmised.

"You are right. The first was Barbara's ex-husband. That had to be three years after the divorce."

"Go on," Amber encouraged.

"Barbara Chambers. It started with her. She was a kind woman who discovered her husband was a cheat. She couldn't believe it. She was devastated and then he asked for a divorce after twenty-four years of marriage. She would have done anything to save that marriage. She offered to do anything, and he turned her down, said horrible things to her that weren't true. She was a lovely woman. He was cruel.

"She had this bright smile and was so incredibly sweet, you just wanted to protect her. She was your kid sister, and her husband was this bully who needed to be stopped or at least beaten up. The need to knock him upside the head was so strong. I just couldn't believe he was throwing it all away for his spoiled little girlfriend.

"The girlfriend was an intern at his office and was barely out of college. Her name was Meaghan. The kids were in high school, so Michael thought it was time to trade Barbara in for a younger model. One thing, Meaghan didn't want kids, especially not kids who were so close to her age. I couldn't prove it, I still can't, but Barbara and the kids died in a fire while we were negotiating the divorce. They were likely dead before the fire started but it destroyed every last bit of valid evidence. An accelerant was used. I know because I saw the photos. They are the worst images I've ever had to endure. I'll never forget them.

"Michael came off as this grieving widower. His whole family was dead including the family dog. Then six months later when they couldn't prove that he'd done it, he married this woman, this little intern, who didn't like children."

"How could someone kill his own family?" she asked.

"I've asked myself that question a thousand times," he said. "He had no soul."

"So, what did you do?" she asked.

"I waited. The police kept circling him, but they didn't have enough to arrest him. I waited until fall, before the lakes froze but when it got dark early. He was predictable. On Monday through Thursday, he was always at the gym, trying to be fit for

Meaghan. The thing was, he had this new black BMW, which he'd purchased with insurance money from his wife's passing.

"He complained to the other patrons of the gym that he thought the spots in the parking lot of the gym were too crowded. He didn't like door dings, so he liked to park on one of the residential streets near the gym. I watched him do it for a couple of weeks.

"It was dark that night I decided to do it. I was wearing black. No one saw me as I waited in the shadows until he arrived with his gym bag, having returned from the last workout of his life. I should mention, I disabled the alarm and the GPS on his car while I was waiting for him."

"I've done that," Amber said. "It is a rush."

"It is, and it is simpler than I thought it would be. Well, he comes back to the car, and I kidnapped him. I put a gun to his head and made him drive to one of the thousand lakes we have in Minnesota. I still wasn't sure I'd do it. He offered to give me money. I told him I knew what he'd done to Barbara and the kids. When he admitted it as easily as you might admit to speeding, I shot him in the back of the head and pushed the car with his body in it into the lake. I no longer felt guilty.

"I walked all night to a different lake and tossed the gun in it. I have a fishing cabin a few miles away, so I hiked to it. I'd left a bag in the woods that had all I needed. They still haven't found his body. Meaghan inherited everything, which is a shame, but now Barbara and the kids got the revenge they should.

"I guess that is how it started. Every few years something happens. Good people get hurt by the people who are supposed to love them. It is heartbreaking. In Saint Barts, I just added some CO to his tank. He was paranoid, wanted to pack his own gear. He'd aired it up the night before. I stole it from where he had it stored and added some CO to the tank. He died happy, and now his first wife can afford the care for his children that he did not want to provide."

"My brand of justice is similar, but I don't pull the trigger, I just analyze the situation and make it look like an accident. Or like a medical issue that finally caught up with them," Amber said. "Odd thing is, that I meet some of these men and spend months growing the plant that will kill them. Hell, I have dried foxgloves in the trunk of my car earmarked for Dan Glass, cheater and male chauvinist supreme. I'm even growing a fresh supply in the garden that I will dry and maybe use next season."

"That cannot be easy," he said. "The planning. How you make it look like a medical thing?"

"It isn't easy, but I'm getting better at it," she said. "You just don't want the death to justify an autopsy. Most of the men I target are middle aged or older, so they have existing health issues. I just try to match what they have to what I have. This year has been different as there is a woman in this neighborhood who knows. I don't like witnesses, but I don't know how to avoid this. I can't kill an innocent person. She is a mother."

"But she poses a risk, so how do you manage it?"

"That she does. But she has a new boyfriend, and she seems very happy. I think reliving the past is no longer on her agenda. Whenever she sees me, she hugs me like I'm a long-lost sister so that gives me a bit of reassurance. And since it happened, we haven't talked about it. That was September, so a little time has passed for her to adjust to life without fear. However, there is a second woman who is awful. I wouldn't mind if she accidentally died."

Jack said, "I need you to be careful."

She smiled. "I will be."

They kissed, then he pulled her onto his lap for more entertainment.

"I have to go back to my hotel and get my stuff, change out of yesterday's clothes," he said.

It was a moment of trepidation, if she stayed at home, she'd be counting the moments until he returned. If she asked to go with him, it was as if she didn't trust him. She didn't trust anyone except Neil, and, well, she was starting to trust Jack a little. Then he gave her something else to think about, and she felt sloppy for missing it.

"You know that the moment I step out of your house, my cousin will know I spent the night with you."

"Kent and Gingie will either think I'm Jane or that neighbor Amber is easy. I don't mind being easy," she said saucily. "Unless your cousin would judge. Just how much does he know about your business?"

"Not much. He thinks of me as a fair lawyer. Heck, I helped with his divorce a few years ago. As for us, I'm handling this situation right now," Jack said, holding up his cell phone.

She watched as he selected the name "Kent" and put the call on speaker.

Amber didn't like to worry, but in that moment, she was worried.

"Hey," Kent answered. "I was just about to call you. Are we still on for the Blazer game tonight or are you otherwise occupied?"

"Wow, you are so good at observation you should be a cop."

"So that is your car on the street on Pioneer Pike?"

"I hit it off with Gingie's neighbor."

"And it isn't creepy that she reminds you of someone you once dated?"

"Have you thought that maybe Amber is the one and Jane just looks like her, but I was meant to be with Amber?"

"I'm really not following you," Kent said. "But Gingie likes Amber so don't fuck it up."

"I won't," he said, smiling at Amber. "I like her, and I think she likes me. I think she is going to be visiting me in

Minneapolis. Maybe she will fly back with me when I leave on Tuesday."

"Whoa, isn't that a bit fast?"

"You know cousin, when you told me about Gingie, how she's been married a couple of times, I didn't judge your instant attraction, did I?"

"No, I guess you didn't."

"Touché. I'm going to the hotel in a few to get my stuff. I'll be staying with Amber. No flack about a walk of shame, okay?"

"Come on, I wouldn't do that."

"Well, you've grown up. Good for you. Amber is going with me, so no catcalls, no yelling, nothing, got it?"

"Oh please...do you want to grab dinner tonight? A double date?"

"No, Amber and I want to be alone. I'll call you next week after I get home," Jack said.

"Wow," Kent said. "I really didn't think Amber was your type. And now I don't even get to say goodbye?"

"Amber is my type and absolutely wonderful. I'll try to arrange a goodbye. I'll call you tomorrow," Jack said and ended the call.

"I don't even know what to say," Amber said, smiling after he put his phone down.

He kissed her. "I'm in love with you, that isn't going to change. Now, come on, let's go get my stuff and get back here."

They dropped his rental off at the airport and took an Uber back to her house once they had been to his hotel and gotten him checked out.

The next two days were a blur of physical passion, deep conversations, and planning. Lots and lots of planning.

"Come home with me," he said on Monday. "I want you to see my place. Meet my mother."

"Is it too soon for any of that?" Amber asked. She hadn't met a mother before.

"Do you really think it is too soon, or are you saying what you think you should say?"

"No, it isn't too soon," she said. "I'll stay with you for a week, then I should get back to Pioneer Pike. You could come back with me."

"How about I come back in a couple of weeks after that? That way, I can work and make a little money," he said. "It will lend to the story that we are falling for each other. People don't need to know we already fell."

"Yes, we did," she said with the first genuine smile she could remember.

On Monday afternoon, she held his hand as they walked down Pioneer Pike to the community garden. At the gate, she used her key and ushered him inside.

"You are in for a treat," she said.

"This is a gorgeous space," he said as he looked at her garden and examined all the items she had growing. When he reached for a stalk of "Queen Anne's Lace" and was about to touch Poison Hemlock, she said, "No!" It came out a little louder than it should.

She pulled him close and whispered, "That isn't just Queen Anne's Lace, I mixed it with some Poison Hemlock. Queen Anne is a decoy. You can probably touch it without gloves, but I don't want you to risk it. It might burn you or give you a rash. People respond differently, but contact dermatitis is no joke."

He responded by kissing her, then he whispered, "You really do care."

"Of course, I do," she said, smiling at him as he pulled her to him for another deep kiss that took her breath away.

"Um...well hello, excuse me," Valerie said from the entrance of the garden.

Amber felt the blush color her cheeks and then introduced Jack to Valerie as her boyfriend.

"I didn't know you were dating anyone, but this makes me very happy. Hello Jack. You have our Amber glowing."

"I like to think so. I live in Minnesota, so I won't get to see Amber as much as I'd like, but I heard about the garden and had to see it," Jack said, holding Amber's hand.

"It is so nice to meet you," Valerie said, smiling. "Hopefully, you will be in town or come back for our next party in three weeks. It is my turn, and I'm doing a 1980s theme party. Only popular food and beverage from the '80s. I hope you like wine coolers."

"Three weeks, I can be here," he said gazing at Amber. "And I'm partial to Bartles and Jaynes wine coolers."

"I remember those," Valerie said. "We will be mixing something similar. You can't even buy Zima anymore. I might just do Sangria. We'll have seven-layer dip, calamari, stuff like that. The 'it' food from the 1980s."

"I'm bringing a spinach dip in a bread bowl," Amber said as Jack snuggled her teasingly.

"I love spinach dip," Jack said.

"Too bad it is too early for garden spinach," Valerie said.

"Well, the stores do pretty well with it," Amber said and then they made their goodbyes to Valerie.

Amber felt giddy for one of the first times in her life. Jack was hers. They knew things about one another that no one else knew. Could she let herself be happy? Could she believe it?

That night she packed a bag for Minnesota to go with him the next day. He'd gotten them two seats together on the three-hour flight back to his hometown.

"I'm not used to packing a bag with the anticipation of returning," she said.

"I'm looking forward to showing you my life in Minnesota."

"And you aren't going to let me out of your sight."

"Well," he said. "I don't think I could bear losing you again, but I will have to go into the office."

"I understand but when you aren't working, I don't think that either of us should go anywhere alone again. I don't know if I can bear it."

He held out a pinkie. She did the same.

"Pinkie swear," she said.

He smiled and said, "Pinkie swear. Let's not fuck this up."

She nodded and said, "Agreed."

With everything so good, what could possibly go wrong?

CHAPTER EIGHTEEN

What did she expect, a torture chamber? No, Jack had a nice condo in a stylish building in Minneapolis that was a few blocks from his office. It was decorated in "single, successful man" style. Lots of black leather and navy linens. The refrigerator held lots of old take-out boxes, which needed to be thrown away. The liquor cabinet was generous. The television was big. There was a hint of his familiar sandalwood cologne in the bathroom. She loved the scent of him.

In his home office he had a file labeled: JANE sitting on top of his desk. She picked it up and read through it. He had assembled a lot of notes, but thankfully she saw that he hit a lot of dead ends. Good. She'd have to thank Neil.

"I won't be needing that anymore," he said and took the file from her hands.

"Do you have a shredder?" she asked.

"I have a better idea," he said and stopped in front of one of his fireplaces. He lit the folder on fire, and they watched it burn together.

"Thank you," she said.

"I will always do my best to protect you and your secrets."

"Thank you for that, and thank you for trying to find me. I missed you so much."

They embraced as they watched the folder burn, and she said, "I'm sorry I left the way I did in Saint Barts. I felt like I didn't have another choice. For what it is worth, I cried on the plane at the thought of losing you. I did a lot of soul searching over the next few weeks, hell, months."

"I'm sorry too, but now I understand it. It was too soon. We weren't ready then, but we feel ready now."

"I think we are. I just wanted you to know that it wasn't personal," she said. "I was trying to be all hard ass, but I really didn't want to be. I wanted to run into you. I wanted another chance."

"You didn't leave this time."

"No, I couldn't. You were right. I had the car packed. But I couldn't go. I hoped you'd come back to my house. I thought that if it was real, you would."

"I almost went to your house the night of the dinner party, but I thought that if it was meant to be, you'd be there the next day, although I watched you a bit before I made my move."

"How did you know I was coming back?"

"I was parked down the street. I watched you leave and walk to the Glass house."

"Stalker," she said and kissed him.

"We will make this work," he said.

"I never thought I'd find someone who was so like me," she said.

"Just because we have done things that are not what average people do, that doesn't mean we don't deserve to have our happiness," he said as he kissed her. "It doesn't mean that I don't deserve to spend my life with you, however that looks."

She openly gave him 95% of herself, the other 5% kept its antenna raised. She slept in the same bed with him, made love with him, was vulnerable to him, but it might take a while for that other 5% to let down its guard.

She resumed her tour of his place. This could be her life.

He watched her as she moved from room to room.

"Yes, I know it needs a woman's touch."

"It is very masculine."

He laughed.

"What?" she asked.

"I just wonder how long it will take for us to fully trust each other."

"I've come a long way," she said, "in a very short amount of time."

"If it makes you feel better, none of the tools I've used to take care of my business are here," he said. "No one will find them, but if they do, they won't tie back to me."

"And if it makes you feel better, all of my little plant friends are back in Oregon."

He kissed her, that was part of it, they always had to be touching. It was a need, an obsession.

"Sorry, that makes me jumpy," he said.

"I understand. It will be that way for a bit, I think. And for what it is worth, please never serve me orange marmalade. I never want to see it again."

"I promise. It is too soon, but I'm going to ask you. Do you want a house? Children?" he asked.

"I never thought of myself as a mother. I never thought anyone would want me to be the mother of their children."

"Well, I would."

He was rewarded with a kiss that led to their clothing falling to the floor. The separation of the last year and a half needed to be made up for. Amber found that the floor was much more comfortable than she had imagined, but maybe it was because she was lost in the sensation of Jack. He rolled her so that she was on top of him, his hands massaging her breasts as she set the pace.

Sitting upright with him deeply rooted inside her, she ran her hands through her hair and shut her eyes as if she were a beautiful mermaid riding waves in the ocean.

That was how they climaxed, with her riding him and his body pushing deeply inside her.

Later, they lay together as the lights of the city cast a glow on their skin. He'd pulled pillows from the sofa, thrown a cashmere blanket on top of them. They didn't speak, just listened to the soft music that he'd turned on. Her head was on his shoulder, his hand stroked her hair.

"Should I go back to blonde?" she asked, thinking about next steps after she left Oregon.

"I like either the red or the blonde, but I miss your red lipstick. When I came home from Saint Barts, I found smears of it on various items of my clothing. Giorgio Armani number 400."

"You had it analyzed?" she asked incredulously.

"Yes, and you can think of how it was for me, taking in my underwear to a lab and asking them to identify the red lipstick smear inside of it."

She started laughing. There had been a few occasions over that week in Saint Barts that they had been out somewhere, and the mood struck them. They'd find a deserted spot and make love. Well, sometimes she just wanted to see how crazy she could drive him. She always made sure she left lipstick on him. She wanted him to go back to his room to shower and change for dinner and see how much she had marked him. It worked.

"Maybe tomorrow I can find a store that sells Giorgio Armani 400 in Minneapolis. Or I could try a different shade."

"Please wear the Armani. I have a special, sentimental space in my heart for it."

She nodded, "I do too."

Gingie

"What is wrong with you?" Gingie asked. Kent was holding her, they were naked and, in her bed, but he was far, far away. What had looked like a promising move toward mind blowing sex was fizzling toward a fight.

"I'm sorry. I just, I don't know..."

These were the worst words a man could ever utter.

Gingie went rigid.

"What don't you know?" Gingie asked, pulling away from Kent.

"Gingie, it isn't about you or us. I'm thinking about Jack and how Amber is with him in Minneapolis. It is odd. Maybe she is Jane. Do you think that is possible? Change her hair color, take off her glasses, change her wardrobe. Maybe she is running from something. It might surprise you to know how many people have done things they want to run away from."

"No, I don't think she is Jane," she said, letting out the breath that she had been holding in her lungs.

"Well, what do you really know about her?"

Gingie sat up. She leaned against the pillows at her back and looked at Kent, who looked a bit like a dejected animal.

"I brought this up to you, and you blew me off the other day," she said.

"You got me thinking, that is all," he said.

"And now I'm convinced I was being paranoid. She is a friend. Her parents are dead, as is the aunt who raised her, but she has a couple of cousins left in Montana. Her aunt, the Aunt Betty we hear about, she left her money. Something tells me it was a lot. Enough that she really doesn't need to work. She said this book is a bit of following her dream. She is a free spirit. She was in the Peace Corps for a few years in Africa. I think that is what brought out the hippie in her. Okay, what else do you want to know about her? The checks always clear for rent, and she is a good neighbor."

"I just don't see her with Jack. He is uptight. He irons his sheets for shit sake. He has always been wound tight. He's a lawyer. He is the guy who sees things in black and white. Amber is like magenta to his world. What does he see in Amber?"

"Maybe they have very satisfying crazy monkey sex?" Gingie asked.

"He was at her house for a long time. What are the odds that she is Jane? I mean, it could've happened."

Gingie shook her head. "Why can't you just believe they fell for each other?"

"I don't know. It bothers me."

"Let it go Kent, seriously, you are looking for fire where there isn't even any smoke."

"What do you really know about her?"

"I know she is getting laid, and I'm jealous."

Kent seemed to pull out of his fog. He looked down at the lush woman who wanted him and said, "Are you trying to tell me something?"

"Um yes, are you listening? I want you. Stop talking and take me. Extra credit for crazy monkey sex."

"I'm sorry."

"You should be sorry. Here I am a naked woman who wants to be touched, is ready, willing and able and you are talking such nonsense I don't even know what to say."

"You know, I couldn't help but notice how pretty your lawn looks."

"My lawn?" she asked, not understanding.

"In the completely fenced backyard."

"Are you trying to ask me if I'd like to fuck on the lawn in my backyard?"

"Yeah," he said, a small smile forming on his lips. "It is the end of spring, but more like the first warm day of summer. Maybe it is time we had some crazy monkey sex in the backyard. Give us each some grass stains in interesting places."

"What if one of the neighbors just happens to be looking out their window and sees us? Or is out watering the garden and hears us?"

"Could that happen?"

"Yes," she said touching a finger to her lips. "We could be discovered."

"Then you'll just have to be quiet. Do you think you can do that?"

"You know what you do to me. I make no guarantees," she said.

He touched her breast through the sheet. "Good. I like you a bit wild especially when I'm along for the ride."

"Aw, fuck it. Race you outside," she said, throwing back her sheet and jumping out of the bed.

CHAPTER NINETEEN

Another benefit of living close to where he worked was that Jack could come home for lunch. Amber figured that he wanted to make sure she didn't disappear. Trust wasn't easy between them so soon after such longing, but they both wanted it. Nevertheless, some moments, it felt like a beautiful dream.

When Jack came home for lunch, she greeted him in an emerald silk cami and tap pantie set she had purchased that morning. And on her lips, she wore Giorgio Armani number 400. She had picked up some chicken Caesar salads from a restaurant nearby, which they ate after they'd had what Amber teased was a nooner on the leather couch in his living room.

After a quick shower, Jack redressed in his medium gray suit and kissed her on the way out.

"I think you smeared my lipstick," she said.

"I think you marked me with it," he said, and she started giggling at the memory of where she'd left lip prints.

"More shopping this afternoon?" He asked.

"I might just lay here and take a nap," she cooed. "You know, think about you and what we might do this evening."

"Better. Don't move," he said as she lay under a blanket on the couch.

"Please hurry home," she said.

"You rest up. I'll be home in four hours, and we will light a fire in the fireplace, test out the resilience of the couch."

"Sounds like a plan. Although, I might have to model a different outfit for you," she said.

"Well, that is something to think about during my quieter moments this afternoon."

"Please do think of me," she said with a smile.

"I think of you all the time," he said, kissing her again.

Over the next few days, the couch, the bed, the shower, they all held up to the physical side of Amber and Jack's rekindled romance.

Amber shopped each day. Jack having made room for her in his closet.

"Seriously, I want you to move in with me as soon as possible," he said as they shared a bottle of wine over dinner at Spoon & Stable, a restaurant close to his condo.

She knew she needed a break from the neighborhoods, and she couldn't let go of Jack again, so she was willing to try living with him.

"As soon as I finish my business in Oregon," she said. "I would like to try it for a year." She would like to try it for a lifetime, but she had to be reasonable.

"That is fair. You want to take a season off. Let me take care of you. If, at the end of the year, you aren't happy, there are a lot of neighborhoods who will always be waiting for you."

"Thank you for understanding," she said.

"It isn't that. I'm betting on us," he said.

"I like the faith you have in us."

"I do, Amber/Jane/Kelly/Kelan, my love," he said with a smile.

On Saturday, after they had been at Jack's for almost a week, they went to one of the one hundred and eighty-two Starbucks in Minnesota. It was on a side of town Amber didn't know, which was why Jack picked it. It was out of the way.

They got a coffee and some chocolate dipped Madeleines,

taking a table toward the back of the coffee shop. Jack sat with his back to the wall watching each patron arrive.

At exactly three p.m. an average looking young man with a sweet smile and thin build walked in and ordered coffee.

"I think he's here," Jack said. Amber turned around and smiled as the young man picked up his coffee and then joined Amber and Jack at the back table. Amber stood and gave Neil a huge hug. Then she introduced Jack.

Neil smiled as he sat. "I remember hearing about you," he said to Jack. "I've never seen Aunt Kel so messed up over someone as you. And, trust me, we've had a few situations."

"Yes, we have. How was your flight?" she asked.

"Good. Thank you for the ticket, the hotel, the car," he said. "It is all good."

"I'm really glad you could meet us," Amber said. "And Jack, just so you know, we like to take Neil somewhere in January or February—"

"That is sunny and warm," Jack said.

"I was thinking I could make some time in January," Neil volunteered.

"How about Fiji?" Jack asked.

Neil looked at Amber and said, "I like him."

"So do I," Amber said.

After they caught up a bit more, Amber asked the question that had prompted them to send Neil a plane ticket.

"I need to make sure my background is really solid. Amber is going to stay with me for a bit. Jack has relatives in my current neighborhood, so I need to keep Amber going."

"Possibly permanently," Jack offered, making Amber smile.

"And we need to get alternatives for Jack, if we need them," she said. She handed over an envelope of different head shots they'd spent the morning getting from out of the way quicky passport photo shops.

"You first," Neil said, lowering his voice and looking at

Amber. "I've already created a little social media for Amber as I always do. There is something on FB and Insta that looks like it has been there for a few years. You have a passport. Any creativity you've added?"

"The Peace Corps?" she said with tentative hesitation.

"I can make that work. What did you do for them?"

"I taught English in Nigeria for three years." She said and then gave him further details.

"Easy. I might even be able to get some photos of you from the school you taught at."

"You've learned a few new tricks," she said.

"I've got a few things up my sleeve," he said and took a bite of the shell-shaped cookie.

"And Jack?" she asked.

"No problem," he said.

"Tell me what you think it will cost, and I'll Venmo you," Amber said.

"How many different profiles are you looking for?"

"I have two alternates. Let's get him two as well."

"Can do," Neil said.

Amber flew back to Eugene the next day. Saying goodbye to Jack was more than a little difficult.

"I'll see you in less than two weeks. Eleven long and painful days," he said, but she started crying before they even took the airport exit. It was nice to see that she could still cry. Part of her wondered if she would eventually lose this part of her humanity, but when it came to Jack, she found that tears were easy.

"Promise me that you'll come to see me," she said.

"I love you," he said, picking up her hand, lifting it to her fingers and kissing it.

"I love you too, Jack," she said as she reached into her pocket and pulled out the $10 silver piece that she considered her good luck token. "Hold on to this. It is special to me, and give it back when you come to Eugene."

He looked at the silver coin, and said, "You told me about this. I promise, I'll take good care of it."

Then, he reached into his suit jacket and produced a black pen, a Mont Blanc that had his name engraved on it in gold lettering.

He said, "This was a gift to me when I made partner at the law firm. It is very special to me, but in a different way than you are. You hold onto it until I see you again."

This goodbye was much different than the other time they had parted. Amber, the woman who had no one really in her life, clung to Jack and prayed to whatever god who looked down on women who murdered, and asked that this work. She hadn't realized how much she needed another person in her life until he was there. She could not lose him again.

When she got back to Eugene and entered her rental for the first time, it felt cold, empty.

Maybe she should have stayed with Jack and not come back. Oh yeah, the Kent factor. They were trying to keep up appearances and not create any sort of questioning because Jack and Kent's family were close. Heck, when in Minneapolis she'd had dinner with Jack's mother and Kent's mother was there too. They appeared to like her. She didn't know how to judge their reaction because she'd never met anyone's mother.

If it all came crashing down, she'd constructed a story, which Jack thought sounded plausible. It was lame, but she thought it might work. It was there in case things got too complicated.

She didn't need to wait too long before the scrutiny began. Gingie showed up the next morning bearing cinnamon rolls from Metropol bakery, her favorite.

"Hey, what a nice surprise, come in," Amber said as Gingie stepped inside, and they made their way to the kitchen.

Amber had just boiled water for her French press and got down another mug for Gingie as it seeped.

They sat at the kitchen table and Gingie folded her arms in a mock pout.

"You and Jack?"

Amber smiled and giggled.

Gingie

Was Amber blushing? She was. Oh man, she had it bad.

"It happened very quickly," Amber said as she bit a piece of her roll.

"Okay," Gingie said, "Truth. Are you the Jane who he met in Saint Barts?"

"No, I'm not Jane. I just look a lot like her," Amber said.

"Doesn't it bother you that he is with you because you remind him of Jane and their torrid week together?"

Amber smiled a little and said, "We've had a torrid week together now, and he is no longer talking about Jane. He's talking about me."

"I think I'd hate that I reminded Kent of someone else," Gingie said. "I want to be adored for being me."

"Jane was Jack's fantasy, I'm his reality."

"You are so different from each other."

"Not really. I might look like a hippie, but before the Peace Corps, I was a lot more like Jack, all buttoned up and polished. I would sweat the small stuff. Living in a mud shack changes you, but I'm starting to remember the things I liked. I think I'm good for Jack, but I might start wearing lipstick and buying clothes that are a little more fashionable. He kind of has a fetish for red lipstick. Don't tell Kent. I don't want him to tease Jack when he comes here in ten days for a visit."

Gingie felt herself staring. How had all of this happened? Amber was this mess that lived across the street. She needed a makeover like no one else Gingie had ever met. But there was a glow to the woman that could not be denied. To be honest, she looked like she'd gotten laid, and it had gone very well for her. Repeatedly.

"Wow, when does Jack come back exactly?"

"He's coming back in time for Valerie's party. Do you think you could help me get a dress for it? Something kind of sexy? I'm also thinking of getting a pedicure. I mean, I might look a little like this Jane, and he is no longer thinking about her, but let's make sure she is really out of his mind."

"May I just ask; how did he go from being your stalker to sleeping over in like less than twenty-four hours?" Gingie asked.

"Well," Amber said with a shrug. "I was very horny, because I hadn't had sex in a long time. And he asked me nicely. It kind of took off from there. I mean, damn, Jack is a good-looking guy. I like dark haired men. And then he is all tall and stuff. We found that we are very compatible. I don't think I've been that compatible with anyone in my life. It is magical."

"Oh honey, I get it," Gingie said with a raised hand. "He looks like his cousin."

"Your fiancé," Amber said with a smile.

"Yeah, we are very compatible."

"Really?" Amber asked with a sly smile. "Who is blushing now?"

"Yeah, okay," Gingie replied, "Kent does it for me. What can I say? Halle-fucking-lujah? It's great."

They both laughed, then Amber asked, "Anything happening in the hood while I was gone?"

Gingie shrugged. "Did you hear about Dan?"

"I ran into Julia before I left, and she said he'd spent some time in the hospital. I actually made him some tea to get him off coffee. I tried to be nice considering I'd mentioned shoving something up her ass."

"That was nice of you! Especially since he is such a jerk. I hear he still isn't doing well. I think his life has finally caught up with him. I'd visit, but I don't like either one of them well enough."

"I get it," Amber said. "Maybe they were made for each other."

"Who else could stand either one of them?"

"Sounds like true love."

CHAPTER TWENTY

Jack was true to his word. They didn't just talk once a day, they talked several times a day, but still each day seemed to drag along. Night was no better. Amber reached for him, only to find an empty, cool space in her bed. How had she ever thought she was happy before?

For Amber, she never thought she'd find love. She thought it was for everyone else but her. And, right when she had decided that she would be alone with her demons in this lifetime, Jack appeared. She was so damn lucky.

As she was weeding her garden, needing a distraction, she marveled at the freshly planted gladiolas she had just added. She was counting each minute of the three days before Jack was due to come back. It had been a very long eight days since she'd left Minneapolis. A shadow fell over her before she heard the voice. Then the shape leaned close and said, "I like the look of those foxgloves."

Julia Glass. Nothing could ruin a serene moment like Julia. Well, good neighbors would at least inquire about her terrible husband despite telling her to shove something up her ass yet a few weeks ago.

"Those are actually the gladiolas starting to sprout. The foxgloves are behind them. How is Dan? How did he like the tea?" Amber asked.

She didn't like people nosing around her garden. She had

purposely hidden the foxgloves. It bothered her that Julia Glass recognized them and then called them out.

Julia stepped around her and checked out the foxgloves. "I see where they are now. Dan enjoyed the tea. I was going to ask if maybe you could make him more. I don't need it for me. I'm afraid that coffee will always be my poison, as it were."

Amber did not like the way she used the word poison.

"Has Dan's recovery brought you two closer together?" Amber asked. Why was she asking such a stupid and trivial question? First, it was none of her business, and second, they were too far gone to ever rekindle what they once had. Last season, by this time, Dan would already be pushing up the daisies. Why hadn't she already taken care of him? Was she losing her edge? Nature would take its course, but with Dan Glass it seemed to be taking its own sweet time.

"I'm not telling anyone, but his secretary suddenly started showing up at the hospital and when I brought him home, she was our most ardent visitor. Two days ago, Dan was served. She is suing him for child support. It appears my husband has fathered yet another child outside of our marriage. And here I just thought it was blowjobs. Well you can't get pregnant that way, so there had to be a little something else happening. This will be his fourth."

"Another child?" Amber asked incredulously.

"Yes, this is his second out of wedlock, next to the two little bitches he added to the world through his first wife. There is only so much embarrassment one person can take, so I asked him for a divorce, and he laughed at me. Said that our prenup ensured that I wasn't going anywhere because I didn't like shopping at Goodwill and JC Penny's. Then he asked me how I might like being a barista at Starbucks or a greeter at Walmart. Well, he got me there. I wouldn't."

Amber looked around, trying to appear discreet, and then

whispered. "So have you made any decisions about the divorce?"

"Not yet. You seem to know about plants. Which part of the foxglove is poisonous?"

"It isn't something to mess around with. I like the flowers, which are incredibly delicate. I love the color," Amber said.

"Did you know that is where digitalis comes from? The foxgloves?" Julia asked.

"Not anymore. They make synthetic digitalis, known as coumadin. It was once used as rat poison. They used to call it Witches' Glove. Dried, it is much more potent. Pretty for a bouquet, but I always wear my gloves when handling it." Why was she telling Julia all this? Ego. She wanted to shove her knowledge down the other woman's throat. "I think I mentioned I study all this for my book. Foxgloves will never go into any of my recipes."

She hoped this wasn't going to be a problem. But her spidey sense told her it was already a problem.

"Do you mind if I take a flower when they blossom? The purple will look so gorgeous in my bedroom."

"No, not at all," Amber said.

"Thank you, Aubry. You are a dear."

Shit. This was bad.

Julia stepped away, and Amber had a bad feeling. She could admit that she was a bit of a control freak. Now, she had the *rubes* going random. This was bad. She knew what Julia was planning even if Julia hadn't admitted it. She was going to do something bad to Dan using Amber's foxgloves.

Amber thought about Julia for three days as a distraction from her thoughts of Jack. Would he really come back to see her? Well, this was a test, wasn't it? She'd never dated another person who was in on her secret. Good or bad, it was something to consider.

They had used the word love. Did she really, truly love him?

Yes. How did they end each phone call? With declarations of love. Could she be happy? It was all new for her.

She parked her car in short-term parking at The Portland International Airport, having driven the two hours up to Portland so that Jack could take a direct flight and she could think about a few things.

There was a season to finish out and then she would drive to Minneapolis, trading in her car along the way, and then she would be with Jack. That was the plan anyway. He said that was what he wanted. What if he changed his mind these last eleven days when he'd been away from her? Well, one fucking drama at a time.

Would she really be able to keep the Amber identity going? Part of that was up to Neil and how much he could build her a convincing background. Damn, she wished she'd used Amber last time and Jane this time. She really disliked the name Amber. And Jane, well, she was sexy. Even the clothes she'd worn in Saint Barts, they were sexy. Amber's wardrobe was frumpy.

The relationship with Kent could create an issue with all her best laid plans. So, despite her better judgment, the Amber profile, or at least the name, was going to stay. But once in Minneapolis, Amber was going to get a mega makeover. The red hair would be gone, as would the glasses. She was going back to blonde. Her natural color was a mousy brown. She hadn't changed it until Dr. Kelan Smith needed to vanish. Amber was about to start wearing makeup and clothes that didn't come from Goodwill. The shopping back in Minneapolis had already begun. Jack had invited her to put things in his closet, and she had.

Jack's luggage would come in at carousel seven in baggage claim, where they had agreed to meet. She waited there for him, and a half hour after his plane landed, there he was. It was hard not to run to him, but the smile on her face hurt because it was so broad. He picked her off the ground, spun her around and kissed her.

It was real, it was what she had dared to dream of. He knew her, he knew what she could do, but he loved her anyway.

"Hello darling," she said in greeting as he held her tight. "How was your flight?"

"It was good, but I had an idea. I've been thinking. I don't want to spend the next two hours driving back to Eugene."

"What do you want to do?" she asked, but she had a feeling she already knew.

He whispered in her ear, "Let's check into a hotel for a couple of hours, get this reunion started, then drive to Eugene."

"We have room 575 reserved at the airport Embassy Suites," she replied. "It is less than a mile from here, and lunch should be waiting when we get to the room."

"You always surprise me," he said.

"And I always will," she said. "Good surprises only."

The drive was short, but the reunion was long.

"These last few days without you were almost worse than looking for you," he said, panting, as he rolled off her body and looked at the ceiling after their frenzied coupling.

"Those eleven days almost killed me," she said when she could get breath back in her lungs. "Waiting for you to come back and do this to me." She glanced over at him and smiled. Their bodies fit together perfectly. She had never had a better, more adroit lover. It wasn't luck, it was destiny. She was starting to accept that.

Putting her head on his shoulder, she asked, "Why is it so good between us?"

"It is honest. We know each other better than anyone knows either one of us."

"I think you're right," she said.

"We are peas in a pod, hook and eye, yin and yang, tab and slat," he said as his palm covered the mound of her breast, kneading it gently. Then he glanced down at his erect penis. "Well, we can test that last one."

"I think we already have," she said with a smile. "It's a perfect fit. That is not to say I don't think you shouldn't make sure."

He lifted her ankle and began kissing his way down her leg, "I think I would like to test my tab and slat theory."

"You have turned my world upside down. If you were anyone else, I would tell you to fear for your life. But you aren't anyone else."

"I'd say the same thing," he said. "I kill, and I'll do it again. There is a part of me that enjoys it, the rush."

"I like the rush, too," she said.

"Leopards don't change their spots," he said.

"No," she said, "but even Leopards find a mate."

"We are a mated pair. If we do this, we do it all the way."

"What do you mean?" she asked. "Kill together?"

"I've been thinking about it. There is safety in numbers. We can help each other, but that isn't all. I want everything. The house, the kids, the dog. And ten years from now, I want you to pick me up at the airport and drive me to a hotel, because you want me to fuck your brains out."

She smiled a little. Had she ever thought this was possible? No. "That goes without saying. I will always want you to fuck me. But kids? Dog? House? I never believed that was possible. I thought I'd be alone for the rest of my life, and I had to be okay with that."

"That isn't the way it is going to be. Believe in us," he said as he slipped into her, sighed, and said, "See? Perfect fit."

Four hours later, they pulled onto Pioneer Pike, after having left their hotel two hours earlier. They were immediately assaulted by flashing strobe lights in blue, red, and white.

There was an ambulance in front of Glass's house.

"Oh shit," Amber muttered.

"Is this your work?" Jack asked.

"No, I had thought about it, but I haven't done a thing yet. My guess, I think Julia went rogue."

"I hope she was careful," he said.

"Me too," she said. "*Rubes!* Damn it! They forget little details and then make it bad for the rest of us."

They parked the Volvo and immediately walked, hand in hand, to where a crowd of the usual suspects waited. Gingie did a double take when she noticed Amber was with Jack and gave a big smile. Valerie, Jim, Shelby, Clint and Libby stood with a good-looking man, the lawyer, Keith. Libby made the introductions, and they both shook Keith's hand. Amber asked Gingie, "What happened?"

"Hey Jack, welcome back," Gingie said smiling brightly. "She missed you."

"Thank you. I missed her," he said with a nod. "So what happened?"

Gingie stepped to the side and talked to them quietly. "I'm sure you heard that Dan was having heart issues. Well, I think something happened. I called Kent, and he is on his way over."

Speaking of the devil, Kent pulled up in his squad car and waved to them in greeting as he made his way into Julia and Dan's house.

A few minutes later, he came to where Gingie, Amber, and Jack waited.

"Hey Jack," he said and gave his cousin a hug. "I'm sorry to see you under these circumstances."

"What happened?" Amber asked.

"It looks like Dan had a fatal heart attack in the back yard about a half hour ago. I know he had heart issues. Julia was with him. He just collapsed, and that was it. She saw the whole thing, poor lady."

They all said the appropriate things, and then Amber and Jack broke away from the group and walked back to her house.

Once inside, Jack shut the front door and locked it before looking at Amber who was pacing in frustration and had balled her fists.

"Do you know what she did?" she complained. "That stupid, stupid woman."

"She killed him?" Jack asked.

"I bet she used my foxgloves. I bet if we go to my garden, some of it will be missing. That isn't the way this was supposed to go down. She is such an amateur. I raise things in the garden that I dry, then they are used two to three years in the future. It safeguards against a crack forensics team who takes samples from the community garden because they wonder where a poison might have come from. Even if they take samples, my foxgloves that are currently growing will not have the same DNA as the foxgloves used in the murder because I used a plant from several years earlier and the remnants are gone. Because I know how to clean up after myself," she vented as she paced.

"You are a professional and had nothing to do with this."

"What if there is an autopsy and they find my foxgloves? They can tell the DNA of plants. My foxgloves vs. some other person's foxglove. They will know it came from my garden. They will look into me and newsflash, I really don't have much of a past. I should have built a better one, but I didn't think I'd need it. Thanks, Julia!"

"You didn't give them to him. You aren't stupid. Think about this. Get ahead of it. You could beat them to the punch and tell the police about the missing foxgloves if they are missing."

"I could still be implicated. What if she tells the police about our conversations? You know the one where we talked about his beef consumption and upping his life insurance at the funeral of another neighbor! Oh my god, this is such a mess!"

"You were kidding and had a hypothetical conversation because she discussed his cheating?" he said sympathetically.

"What if your cousin decides to look into my past? I should

email Neil, get him on this, let him know I need a really, really good paper trail ASAP. Shit, what a mess! Or we could leave. Run. I've got access to $3 million in the Caymans. We can do a lot with that."

"I don't have a passport in any other name but my own," he said. "Not yet anyway."

She realized he was right and placed a hand to the side of her face. "Oh shit, you're right."

"Let's be cool. You don't know anything yet. Just relax. We aren't going to ruin the future we have planned because one stupid woman offs her husband. We have come too far. You got any booze in this house? I think we need a drink."

They ended up drinking tequila in the form of shots at the kitchen table. Lots of bad things came from drinking tequila especially when they did shots with salt and lime wedges. They were each on their fifth when Amber felt compelled to speak spitting out a lime wedge.

She really felt like crying. She rarely cried, but just when her personal life was starting to look up, there was chaos in the form of Julia Glass.

"She should have done it gradually. Maybe put it in salad or food. A blossom today, two tomorrow, and so on, until he was dead. You don't want it to be fast, that can trigger an autopsy."

"A slow death. Interesting. Good to know. See, I'm learning from you."

"You want a slow bleed. Foxglove was once rat poison. After she'd thinned out his blood, she could have pushed him down a stairway, tossed some of his meds so it looked like he messed them up or confused the dosage. I would not have killed him the way I bet she did. She probably grabbed a stalk of foxglove and put all the blossoms in the tea I made. Idiot. She needs to cover her tracks. We need to look at my garden."

"Tomorrow morning is soon enough. It is going to be okay,"

he said. "We were together, you have no history of visiting them or disliking the husband," he said.

"Well…"

"Well, what?" Jack asked.

"In February, he propositioned me. He grabbed me, but not gently and not like on the arm or hand. Like I wanted him to touch me, the pig."

"Oh shit," Jack said. "Where did he grab you?"

"I was bent over, loading the dishwasher and he grabbed my crotch from behind."

"I think I'm glad he is dead," Jack said with a slight hint of jealousy.

"After he grabbed me, I slashed his hand with a Henkel knife. I told his wife he did it to himself that his hand slipped on the cutting board. He lied to her about a bunch of stuff, so I hope he lied about the knife too. Anyway, he needed like fifteen stitches. He deserved it, the pig."

Jack stood and held out his hand. "Come on, you need a distraction, and I want to play with your crotch, but you are going to like what I do to it."

She smiled, "I always do."

"And tomorrow, we will look at the garden and make some decisions."

"Maybe we can go to the library, and I can reach out to Neil."

"That too."

After they used each other a couple of times, Amber felt satisfied, but she couldn't sleep. Jack was curled next to her, his hand, as usual, on her breast, his mouth close to her ear as he spooned her protectively. She liked the feeling of him against her, his warmth, the steady flow of his breathing. There was also something about skin-to-skin that was fabulous.

She had a lot to think about, and it was time to do just that.

Right before they fell asleep, Jack produced the silver coin she had given him for safekeeping, and she held out the pen that had been on her nightstand.

"I kept this with me all the time," he said.

"I slept with your pen on the pillow next to me."

"Sounds like love," he said as he pulled her close.

"Yes, it does," she said, snuggling against him.

CHAPTER TWENTY-ONE
Gingie

Gingie lay awake long after Kent had gone to sleep. He'd wanted to make love, and she had gone along with it, but she wasn't as into it as usual, and he'd noticed. Afterward, he'd asked, "A penny for your thoughts?"

"This neighborhood feels cursed. Is it weird that two bad husbands die in the same neighborhood nine months apart?" she asked.

"It happens," Kent said. "Now, I have to admit that it is rare, but things happen in random clusters. We will go a month without a missing person and then have three in a week. Why? Are you suspecting foul play?"

"If Libby offed her husband and got away with it, good for her. He was a bastard. I like her new lawyer boyfriend, he's cute. I didn't like Dan Glass much better than Libby's husband, but this is just swimming in my mind. Bad husbands ending up dead."

"Do you have any proof that Libby or Julia had something to do with their husbands' deaths?"

"No, I'd tell you. I'm just thinking out loud."

"They both had pretty serious pre-existing conditions."

"I know."

"Maybe try not to think about it?"

"I don't know how you can sleep. You saw them both," she said. "You saw the bodies."

"Maybe that is why I can sleep. I saw them both on site,

talked to their wives, felt good about it. These things just happen."

"Well, should we try for a double-date while your cousin is in town?" she asked.

"Now, that is interesting. If you'd told me that my cousin would be gaga over your flower muffin neighbor, I'd have said that you are crazy. I'm starting to think more about it."

"Why are you thinking so much about them? They seem like a good couple," Gingie said. "She really likes him. I guess she wasn't always a flower muffin. Africa and the Peace Corps did that to her. We actually got her a cute little cocktail dress for Valerie and Jim's party tomorrow night."

"Jack seems to really like her. Heck, my mother met her. She hasn't even met you yet."

"Now, whose fault is that?" Gingie asked.

"She will love you. We are flying to see her in a month, so relax."

"Easy for you to say. My parents are dead, so we don't know if they'd have liked you, but they would have."

"I'm sorry, I'd have loved to meet them. But, back to Jack and Amber. What are they going to do? They can't keep flying back and forth. I mean, he has a law practice in Minnesota. She is writing a book. She could go anywhere," he said.

"Don't say that. I'll miss her," Gingie said.

"We would go visit," Kent said, giving her a squeeze. "We will have to anyway. My mother likes to see me. Maybe we can stay with them when we visit in a month."

"Great," she said with no enthusiasm at all. "I want the privacy of a hotel. I haven't had sex in the great state of Minnesota."

"Okay, we will get a hotel."

"Good, now I just wish I could fall asleep."

"Is there anything I can do to help you sleep?" He asked as his fingers danced over her skin. It did feel good. She loved him.

Maybe she could shut her brain off and let Kent play her body like his favorite instrument.

Amber

She woke up to an empty bed and the smell of coffee and bacon. Okay, not a bad way to get up. She brushed her teeth and then took a quick shower before tossing on a robe and making her way to the kitchen.

Jack was singing as he cooked. He stopped when he saw her, crossed the kitchen and picked her up. He then pinned her against the wall and kissed her.

"I missed this," she said between kisses. "I can't wait until this season is over. Minneapolis will be a new adventure."

He smiled and kissed her so deeply that she was no longer thinking about breakfast. And by the hard feel of him against her, the way his penis seemed to seek her out through the open slit where the two edges of his silk robe came together, he wasn't that hungry either.

"Do you want breakfast, a coffee, or a morning fuck?" he asked.

"I have a little hangover from last night, but it isn't something a good fuck wouldn't cure," she said and smiled. That was all it took. He carried her back to the bedroom after he turned off the stove, then they were back in bed devouring each other.

Amber hadn't had a lot of healthy relationships in her past, especially with men. Jack was the best sex she'd ever had because she wanted him, she loved him, as much as someone who poisons people could love. Did she use him? As much as he used her.

They raced to the finish. The sex was raw but oddly satisfying. She didn't mind the quickness. She was a little hungry for breakfast after all.

As she bit into a piece of toast with concord jelly on it, she said, "I've been thinking about the problem in the neighborhood."

"The problem from last night?" he asked as he sipped his coffee.

"Exactly," she said. "I want to be proactive and prepared."

"Let's hear it," he said.

An hour later, they were in the Volvo, driving to Roseburg. They stopped at the community garden on the way so Amber could check on her plants.

She and Jack were alone in the space when she whispered, "*Bitch.*" Six of her foxgloves tall stems of buds which would almost be blossoming were gone. They hadn't been gently picked for a bouquet. They'd been harvested.

Seventy miles to the south of Eugene, they took the Roseburg exit and headed in the direction of a winery.

"What are you in the mood for?" Jack asked.

"Today, I'm thinking champagne and prosecco," she said. "We'll grab another bottle to bring to Valerie tonight."

They spend the next three hours wine tasting. Jack bought several bottles of wine at each winery using his credit card.

They got back in the car. Amber grabbed hold of his shirt front and pulled him close for a deep kiss.

"What was that for?" he asked with a smile as his hand touched her breast through the fabric of her maxi dress.

The need to make love to him was again strong, but they had work to do.

"I think paper trails are kinda sexy."

"I learned from the best," he said with a smile.

They kissed a few more times before Amber went back to her seat, checked out her lip gloss in the mirror and drove to a large grocery store.

They bought French bread, cheese, fruit, specifically a large bag of apricots, and two bottles of green Odwalla superfood.

They found a little park that had picnic benches in the shade.

They ate their lunch, drinking the bottled water they had brought from home. Each had several apricots for their dessert.

"Save the pit," Amber said under her breath as she dropped her pit back into the bag of pits.

"You are so sexy to me," he said.

"Maybe when we get home, before I start working, we can take a little nap."

"Only if we don't sleep."

"Sleep isn't on the agenda."

He smiled and held up an apricot pit. "Is this really dangerous?"

She smiled, "If you harvest enough of them and then ingest them, yes."

"How?" he asked. "I'm sorry, but I find this fascinating."

"Inside of the stone fruit is a substance called amygdalin. It isn't all bad. It is used in cancer drugs. But if that isn't what you are using amygdalin for and it gets into your tummy, your body, specifically your enzymes react to it, creating cyanide. Eat enough, you die."

"How many?" he asked, slowly stroking the skin of her hand.

"More than two could make you very sick," she said.

"There have to be thirty in this bag."

"I know," she said and kissed his fingertips.

Ninety minutes later, they were laughing in her bed.

"At some point, this need, this insatiable need will cool off, right?" she asked after they had sex for the second time that day.

"I don't know because I've never needed or wanted a woman like I want you."

"Maybe it is just that I'm a new toy and you want to play me," she said, "But I have to admit, I like my joystick quite a bit too." She reached down and stroked him. He knew her, he knew every little dark corner of her soul and he was still here. "May I ask you a question?"

"I don't think we have secrets," he said, picking up her hand and sucking her fingers. "We appear to be the same person."

"I agree, but I don't think I could shoot anyone. I mean, I poison, that is kind of my medium, but it isn't like I force it down their throat. I present it, and they take it. I don't do anything more than hand it to them."

"And for your goals, that works. Not for mine. I'm usually with the shitstick, and it is a death match. I know what they are capable of. Yes, I bring a gun to better my odds, but there is still a moment or two of vulnerability when I don't know what they are bringing to the show. They might think they can take me."

"That scares me," she said snuggling closer.

"I'm good at it, don't worry."

"Does the gore bother you?"

"If I have to get up close and personal. I try to do it at night, and once it is done, I don't look back. But that shitstick in Saint Barts, I just fiddled with his tank. You could consider that poisoning."

"I know, when I think about it, I kind of get hot."

"Good," he said as he ran his fingers sensually down her leg. "I liked the neatness, the anticipation that death was waiting for him. Do you feel that way?"

"Yes," she said, "I actually get nervous waiting to hear if what I did was successful."

"Has it ever failed?" he asked.

"A few ended up in the hospital, but the two that did, died eventually. I don't like them to suffer unless they are a Grade A Asshole, then I kind of want them too."

"I get that," he said and then smiled.

"What?" she asked, "Why the smile?"

"You look a little tense."

"I am a little tense," she said with a half-smile. "Can you relax me?"

230

"I'll try," he said as he moved down her body, put one of her knees over each shoulder and then feasted on her, intimately.

For a woman for whom sex was not just for pleasure, but a weapon, she was softening to the idea that love had indeed found her.

Later, in the kitchen, she donned gloves, a mask and laid out a protective covering on the drainboard. Jack watched from a distance and each time she glanced at him, he smiled.

"Do you have enough time?" he asked looking at his watch.

"Yes, we don't need to be at the party for an hour and a half. All I have to do is shower and slip into my dress."

"I'll help you," he said.

"It does have a difficult zipper, but for now, watch and learn," she said having separated the apricot from its seeds. She discarded the fruit in a special garbage bag she had prepared just for this purpose. Before her lay twenty-seven apricot seeds.

Using a special kind of nutcracker, she broke them all open, scraping out any of the contents. Then she separated the inner seed from the outer shell. In the end, she had barely enough to fill a small coffee grinder. This was a new machine and would only be used once and then discarded.

The inner seeds were ground into a fine, oily powder.

"At this point, it would taste very bitter," she said.

She added white sugar to the mix and then shook one of the two bottles of Odwalla that they had purchased at the grocery in Roseburg. Then she cracked open the bottle and added a few capfuls to the apricot powder and the sugar to create a slurry.

"Please light the candle," she said to Jack, who immediately lit a milky white candle that matched the plastic bottle and placed it near her.

Taking a large gauge syringe, she picked up the other unopened Odwalla superfood bottle and turned it on its end. She shook it vigorously and then extracted a syringe full of the superfood by piercing the bottom of the bottle. She did this twice and discarded the liquid in the sink. Then she sucked up some of the slurry and inserted it into the same hole she'd used for extraction.

Picking up the lit candle, she dropped a few drops of wax over the hole in the bottom of the bottle.

Then she wiped the bottle down and gave it a little shake. The seal at the bottom held.

She put the tainted bottle in a large Ziplock bag and took it to the garage where an auxiliary refrigerator waited. The poisoned Odwalla went into the fridge.

Back in the kitchen everything went into garbage bags. They had three that were only partially filled, but that was okay with Amber, and it spoke directly to her detail-oriented self.

"Let's go get a shower and get ready for the party," she said and watched as Jack's face broke into a smile.

The garbage bags went on top of newspapers spread in the trunk of her car. They would drop off the bags in dumpsters from Junction City north of Eugene to Pleasant Hill south of the city later tonight.

Jack zipped her into the dress she had gotten with Gingie.

"Damn," he said when she turned to give him a frontal view.

The black cocktail dress hugged her curves and showed off a bit of cleavage.

Jack leaned forward and slipped his hand into the front of her dress, where he fondled each breast in turn. She threw her head back and then smiled at him. "Are you going to do that to me later?"

"Later, I'm going to pound you until you scream in pleasure."

"Promises. Promises," she said as she pulled him closer for a hard kiss.

They were fashionably late to the party, Amber carrying spinach dip, and Jack carrying two bottles of wine. This was their first social event as a couple, aside from meeting Jack's mother and aunt. She hoped her neighbors wouldn't be too shocked.

Introductions were made and she watched how people tried to figure it out. Amber was a bit of a hippie, Jack was a good-looking attorney, but tonight they could see the potential in Amber and the relationship. She looked different. She looked sexy.

They retired to a quiet spot in the living room and were soon joined by Gingie and Kent.

Gingie smiled and hugged them both when she saw them. "How do you like Amber's dress?"

Jack smiled and looked at Amber as he said, "I think I will enjoy helping her out of it much more than I liked getting her into it."

"Jack don't say those things in front of witnesses," Amber said with a smile followed by a wink.

"Glad to have you back in the hood for a few days," Kent said eyeing his cousin who was still smiling at Amber. "You are looking better, not so...is haunted the right word? Amber must be good for you."

"I am better, because she is great to be around," Jack said, "Thank you."

"It is remarkable," Kent said.

"It is Amber, she brought me back," Jack said.

"Has anyone heard from Julia?" Amber asked, trying to change the direction of the conversation.

"There is talk of a memorial on Wednesday," Gingie said. "But it could be complicated."

Kent seemed to look uncomfortable and said, "Gingie, please."

"Complicated?" Jack asked.

"Well, they won't need a body for the memorial," Gingie said.

"What do you mean?" Amber asked.

"I think someone has had too much to drink already," Kent said. "The sangria is really good."

"You might as well tell them," Gingie said as she took a deep drag on her sangria. "It isn't going to be a secret for much longer."

"Fine. Come here," Kent said leading them to an even more desolated space in the house.

"What is it?" Amber asked.

"We did an autopsy because, well, Julia's story was causing a bunch of red flags."

"What did you find?" Amber asked.

"Foxglove blossoms that had been possibly dehydrated and hidden in his food. The toxicology for his digitalis was five hundred percent what it should have been."

"Well, I guess that solves the mystery," Jack said.

"What mystery?" Kent asked.

Amber looked upset and then said, "Someone stole a bunch of my foxgloves from the community garden. I've been wondering who would do such a thing. Oh my God, I cannot believe they were used for Dan. I hope they weren't. I don't think I'll ever be able to look at a foxglove again. I just thought they were so pretty in bouquets. I shouldn't have planted them, damn it."

"Honey," Jack said, "You didn't know they would be used this way."

"Are there still some of the foxgloves there?" Kent asked.

"Yes, only maybe five were picked. I have about thirty more."

Kent looked at them all and said, "Excuse me, I have to make a call."

On Sunday morning, Amber, holding Jack's hand, led Kent and several other officers to her garden where she was able to show the missing foxgloves.

"What gets me is that she could have driven to the beach or

gone to a garden store. Why did she steal from me?" Amber asked.

Kent just shook his head. "We don't know anything yet. But, if these were the source, it was easy."

"From the number of workers in the neighborhood she has tried to seduce, I've come to the conclusion that she is lazy," Gingie said. "She won't even go out of the neighborhood for sex."

"I want you to know, she asked me for some tea, which I mixed for her. I don't know enough about foxglove, but if she put the blossoms in the tea, would that have shown up?" Amber asked.

Kent said, "He had actual blossoms in his digestive system, but not enough to have such high numbers of digitalis. Laced tea would explain a lot. Tell me how you made it."

Kent took out his recorder and recorded her recipe, which included the orange peel, hibiscus, and meadowsweet. He nodded, and she wondered if he believed her. She didn't need him thinking that she and Julia had done it together. After all, Julia had stolen plants from her garden.

They ended up at the police station where Amber made a formal statement and then signed it. She always wondered if she'd end up at the police station, she just never thought she'd be helping the police. She was asked to show her identification. The Amber persona held up, thanks to Neil and his flawless work.

CHAPTER TWENTY-TWO

"Just how upset are you?" Jack asked as they lay in each other's arms Sunday night. He'd distracted her for a time, but she was still thinking.

"I don't know. It has been a bad season. The worst I've ever had. If Julia hadn't taken matters into her own hands, I would have. As it is, Julia could say anything or try to say we were in it together. It is a mess."

"It won't come to that. And, despite what you made yesterday, you didn't have to use it," Jack said. "And you saved Libby this season, so that worked. You need to see this as a positive year. Change your perspective."

"You are probably right. It just might take me a while to accept it. I have to see the victory where it hides this season. I just miss baiting the trap. And then seeing the results."

"How would you have done the Odwalla thing?"

"I'd have put the special bottle in my big purse, gone to the memorial service with the gathering at her house later. Then I would have volunteered to help in the kitchen, adding my special Odwalla to what I'm sure is a healthy supply in her fridge."

Once they knew the police were looking into Julia, they had gotten rid of everything last night, the apricots, all her tools. All the Odwalla was poured out, then the bottles were washed, and the bottles made it into a dumpster.

"I think your cousin is going to arrest her, which is fine by me as long as they don't arrest me," she said.

"Let's say the worst thing happened, and they did arrest you. Well, guess what? You have a very good lawyer at your beck and call. You wouldn't get arrested on my watch."

"That actually brings me a lot of comfort. Wish you could get me out of the Iowa situation, then I could be myself again."

"All in good time, darling. Which is my way of saying that I'll work on it."

"Speaking of working on things, would you be upset if I let you get me pregnant?" It was something she'd been thinking about for several weeks. She had decided she wanted a baby. The need had always been there, but she tamped it down thinking that no man would ever want her to be the mother of their child. Being with Jack made the need bloom fresh again.

Jack was kissing the tender flesh of her inner thigh when he stopped and looked up at her.

"I would be fine with the idea if you'd marry me first. Will you marry me Kelly/Kelan/Jane/Amber?"

Smiling, she whispered, "Yes."

He smiled brightly and said, "Then I guess we'd better practice making you pregnant."

"I might already be. I went off my birth control pills after I got home from Minneapolis."

Not surprised, he said, "Well, in that case, I'd better put up or shut up."

He kissed her thigh, then her lips, and got up from the bed and put his briefcase on a nearby chair. She couldn't stop looking at his body. He was perfect. Each muscle was defined. She liked the way his back tapered into his butt. She couldn't wait for him to come back to the bed so that she could touch him and watch as he trembled. More to the point, she liked to watch that butt flex as he drove into her. She was lost. A goner. She'd never get enough.

He pulled something from his briefcase and then rejoined her on the bed. He held a beat-up red leather box with gold trim in his hand. *Cartier.*

"This was my grandmother's. I was planning on asking you to marry me during this visit. I just have to ask you not to wear it until we get to Minnesota. It was Kent's grandmother's too, but when she died two years ago, she left it to me. I was her favorite. Kent is the perfect grandson, but I'm the naughty one. Gingie has one of her diamonds too, but it is the smaller one."

"I like you naughty," she said.

"That's the way I like you, too."

He joined her on the bed and opened the case to reveal a beautiful square cut diamond ring.

"Wow," she said and then met his eyes. "This calls for a celebration." She pushed him back into the pillows, straddled him, and said, "I never thought this would happen, but I'm sure as fuck glad it did." Then she lowered her mouth and feasted on him.

They fell asleep with Amber feeling loose and almost liquid. Multiple orgasms had a way of doing that. She was getting married to Jack. She could hardly believe it.

They had made plans that were a little different than just staying with him for a year. When she got to Minnesota, they would go house hunting.

"My mother always has said that women were like cats. They needed to claim their own territory and then mark it," he said.

"Your mother is a wise woman," Amber said. "But are you asking me to bite and scratch you?"

"Not that it wouldn't be fun, but I kind of like you just the way you are," he said.

She laughed, "I could be pregnant."

"Well, we had better keep trying just to make sure," he said.

"Yes, do what you think is best," she said kissing him. "Our children will be exceptional."

"How many do you want?" he asked.

"I'd like to have two and see from there. Is that good for you?"

"Yeah, I don't have to carry them or birth them, but I'll be a good dad to them."

"I see that about you," she said with a little smile. "What if I want to work?"

"What would you like to do?" he asked.

"If I keep the Amber persona, I might have to write a book. I don't want Kent and Gingie to be suspicious. What do you think I should do?"

"I think you should teach me about your poison garden, and we should travel, really help rid the world of unworthy assholes."

"Should we wait on the baby?"

"No, it adds to our credibility. How many killers travel with diapers and strollers?"

"You've got a point. And here I thought that was behind us," Amber said.

"Oh baby, we are just getting started."

Amber smiled, "Nothing would make me happier."

They spend the next day harvesting her poison garden. The fox gloves and the poison hemlock were carefully picked. The tulip bulbs, lily of the valley, ranunculus, and crocus bulbs were harvested. Early poppies and sunflowers were picked and made into a bright bouquet they left for Gingie on the way out of town, when they said goodbye.

Gingie

"But I thought you were staying through the summer," Gingie said.

"I want her to spend the summer with me," Jack interjected with a very different smile than he'd displayed the first time she'd seen him. The sadness was gone from his face. He really loved Amber.

Amber smiled and blushed. "How can I say no to this face?" she asked.

"I don't think you can," Gingie said, "But damn I'm going to miss you."

The women gave a very tight hug.

"We'll be back for the wedding," Amber said.

"You'd better come back."

"And you can come visit us," Amber said.

"We are buying our tickets today."

Gingie felt more than heard Kent appear behind her.

He pulled his cousin close, and they did that odd back patting thing that men did to each other when they wanted to feel like they were offering comfort but were still men.

Then Jack said, "Thank you, Gingie. If you hadn't had a dinner for us, I'd have never met Amber. I don't know when I've been more thankful."

"I'm the one who is thankful," Amber said and let Jack encircle him in her arms.

Julia was arrested the next afternoon for the murder of her husband.

EPILOGUE

Officer Kent used his username and password to access the records for the U.S. Customs and Border Patrol for the previous year, specifically two days in January the year before.

He had traced every airplane that left Saint Barts on the evening and early the next morning during the time that Jane had left Jack. Currently he was looking at arrivals to Atlanta. He'd already looked at New York, Miami, Dallas, and every other major airport that had flights from Saint Barts. He looked at every female's passport photo that had been scanned into Atlanta matching the passenger manifest from the inbound planes from Saint Barts on that one day. He had been looking at airline manifests and passport photos each day for the last few weeks ever since Jack had come for a visit. He owed it to his cousin. If he could find Jane, they might unravel the mystery.

Today, he got lucky. After another hour of searching, he stopped. He was looking at the passport for Rebecca DeWinter. It was Amber. He hit the print button on his computer and compared her photo to that of the side of Jane's face and a photo he had snapped on the sly of Amber at one of the neighborhood parties.

On his desk, he had a photo of a striking blonde woman who looked sexy and smart. She had a little twinkle in her eye that almost made it feel like she knew you were looking at her.

She could be a model and wasn't shy about the bright red lipstick she wore for the passport photo.

He held it next to his photo of a hippie with no makeup, big glasses, and red hair, Amber.

It did not take a genius to figure out that they were the same person. There was so much wrong here, from the phony passport to finding out who this woman really was. He had a duty to report it. But his cousin was happy, the happiest he'd ever seen him. It was love. Kent was fucked.

He looked at the framed photo of Gingie on his desk, and then looked at the photo of his family from their last family reunion where he stood next to his best friend and cousin, Jack.

Looking down at the photos of Amber/Jane/Rebecca, Kent sighed. Jack was happy, heck he was in love.

What had he said? Oh yes, he remembered because it summed up Kent's relationship as well.

"Is it too soon?" Kent remembered asking. *"I mean, I know you aren't teenagers, but it feels fast."*

Jack shook his head. *"Your soulmate is the stranger you don't recognize. I didn't expect it, but it is real. I love her, Kent. And I'm pretty sure she loves me too. We've been looking for each other for a long time."*

Kent knew how he could never lose Gingie. Even the thought was so unconceivable that it almost made him tear up. He loved her.

Kent gathered up his notes and the photos he'd printed. He walked with the pile to the supply room. Slowly, he fed every shred of paper and hint of note, including the photos he had of Amber/Jane/Rebecca, into the industrial shredder.

"The hottest love has the coldest end," he whispered, and watched everything disintegrate as he decided that there were a few things he needed to forget, like the last hour.

The End.

ACKNOWLEDGMENTS

Thank you to Leslie and Suzie, my first readers, encouragers, and sounding boards.

To my Beta readers, Thank you for helping to catch little things that would otherwise embarrass me!

ABOUT THE AUTHOR

Mary Oldham is an award winning author, and three-time Golden Heart Finalist with the Romance Writers of America in the areas of Contemporary Romance and Romantic Suspense. She is a 2023 Maggie Finalist with the Georgia Romance Writers for her book, CRUSH. Mary lives in Portland, Oregon when she is not sitting on her deck and looking at the Pacific in Yachats, Oregon, the Gem of the Oregon Coast.

Also By
Mary Oldham

Don't miss any of Mary Oldham's other books, available in Print or Digital at Amazon or Barnes and Noble:

Stand Alone Titles

CRUSH, May 2022, a Maggie Finalist with the Georgia Romance Writers

The Silver Linings Series

The Silver Linings Wedding Dress Auction, October 2021

Sisters Before Misters

The Hotel Baron's Series

A Paris Affair, November 2021

A Summer Affair, December 2021

A Roman Affair, April 2022

The Aphrodite Sisters Series

Sage's Redemption, Book 1, October 2022

Toni's Secret, Book 2, November 2022

Roxie's Circus, Book 3, December 2022

Kimberly 's Reckoning, Book 4, March 2023

Audiobooks

The Silver Linings Wedding Dress Auction, Available April 2022

Narrated by Gildart Jackson

Mary loves to hear from her readers! You can email her to sign up for her newsletter at www.maryoldham.com.

Printed in Great Britain
by Amazon